O Pioneers!

WILLA CATHER

O Pioneers!

EDITED BY

SUSAN J. ROSOWSKI AND

CHARLES W. MIGNON

WITH KATHLEEN DANKER

HISTORICAL ESSAY

& EXPLANATORY NOTES

BY DAVID STOUCK

University of Nebraska Press

Lincoln and London

1992

COMMITTEE ON
SCHOLARLY EDITIONS

AN APPROVED EDITION

MODERN LANGUAGE
ASSOCIATION OF AMERICA

The Committee on Scholarly Editions emblem
means that one of a panel of textual experts
serving the Committee has reviewed the text and textual
apparatus of the printer's copy by thorough and
scrupulous sampling, and has approved them for sound
and consistent editorial principles employed and
maximum accuracy attained. The accuracy of the text
has been guarded by careful and repeated
proofreading according to standards
set by the Committee.

Copyright © 1992 by the University of Nebraska Press
All rights reserved

Manufactured in the United States of America

Second printing: 1994

Library of Congress Cataloging-in-Publication Data
Cather, Willa, 1873-1947.
O pioneers! / Willa Cather : edited by Susan J. Rosowski
with Charles W. Mignon and Kathleen Danker;
historical essay and explanatory notes by David Stouck.
p. cm. – (The Willa Cather scholarly edition)
ISBN 0-8032-1457-X
I. Rosowski, Susan J. II. Mignon, Charles, W.
III. Danker, Kathleen A. IV. Title. V. Series.
PS3505.A8702 1992 813'.52-dc20
91-31149 CIP

CONTENTS

Preface

THE objective of the Willa Cather Scholarly Edition is to provide to readers — present and future — various kinds of information relevant to Willa Cather's writing, obtained and presented by the highest scholarly standards: a critical text faithful to her intention as she prepared it for the first edition, a historical essay providing relevant biographical and historical facts, explanatory notes identifying allusions and references, a textual commentary tracing the work through its lifetime and describing Cather's involvement with it, and a record of revisions in the text's various editions. This edition is distinctive in the comprehensiveness of its apparatus, especially in its inclusion of extensive explanatory information that illuminates the fiction of a writer who drew so extensively upon actual experience, as well as the full textual information we have come to expect in a modern critical edition. It thus connects activities that are too often separate — literary scholarship and textual editing.

Editing Cather's writing means recognizing that Cather was as fiercely protective of her novels as she was of her private life. She suppressed much of her early writing and dismissed serial publication of later work, discarded manuscripts and proofs, destroyed letters, and included in her will a stipulation against publication of her private papers. Yet the record remains surprisingly full. Manuscripts, typescripts, and proofs of some texts survive with corrections and revisions in Cather's hand; serial publications provide final "draft" versions of texts; correspondence with her editors and publishers helps clarify her intention for a work, and publishers' records detail each book's public life; correspondence with friends and acquaintances provides an intimate view of her writing; published interviews with and speeches by Cather provide a running public commentary on her career; and through their memoirs, recollections, and letters, Cather's contemporaries provide their own commentary on circumstances surrounding her writing.

In assembling pieces of the editorial puzzle, we have been guided by principles and procedures articulated by the Committee on Scholarly Editions of the Modern Language Association. Assembling and comparing texts demonstrated the basic tenet of the textual editor — that only painstaking collations reveal what is actually there. Scholars had assumed, for example, that with the exception of a single correction in spelling, *O Pioneers!* passed unchanged from the 1913 first edition to the 1937 Autograph Edition. Collations revealed nearly a hundred word changes, thus providing information not only necessary to establish a critical text and to interpret how Cather composed, but also basic to interpreting how her ideas about art changed as she matured.

Cather's revisions and corrections on typescripts and page proofs demonstrate that she brought to her own writing her extensive experience as an editor. Word changes demonstrate her practices in revising; other changes demonstrate that she gave extraordinarily close scrutiny to such matters as capitalization, punctuation, paragraphing, hyphenation, and spacing. Knowledgeable about production, Cather had intentions for her books that extended to their design and manufacture. For example, she specified typography, illustrations, page format, paper stock, ink color, covers, wrappers, and advertising copy.

To an exceptional degree, then, Cather gave to her work the close textual attention that modern editing practices respect, while in other ways she challenged her editors to expand the definition of "corruption" and "authoritative" beyond the text, to include the book's whole format and material existence. Believing that a book's physical form influenced its relationship with a reader, she selected type, paper, and format that invited the reader response she sought. The heavy texture and cream color of paper used for *O Pioneers!* and *My Ántonia*, for example, created a sense of warmth and invited a childlike play of imagination, as did these books' large dark type and wide margins. By the same principle, she expressly rejected the anthology format of assembling texts of numerous novels within the covers of one volume, with tight margins, thin paper, and condensed print.

Given Cather's explicitly stated intentions for her works, printing and publishing decisions that disregard her wishes represent their own form of corruption, and an authoritative edition of Cather must go beyond the sequence of words and punctuation to include other matters: page format, paper stock, typeface, and other features of design. The volumes in the Cather Edition respect those intentions insofar as possible within a series format that includes a comprehensive scholarly apparatus. For example, the Cather Edition has adopted the format of six by nine inches, which Cather approved in Bruce Rogers's elegant work on the 1937 Houghton Mifflin Autograph Edition, to accommodate the various elements of design. While lacking something of the intimacy of the original page, this size permits the use of large, generously leaded type and ample margins — points of style upon which the author was so insistent. In the choice of paper, we have deferred to Cather's declared preference for a warm, cream antique stock.

Today's technology makes it difficult to emulate the qualities of hot-metal typesetting and letterpress printing. In comparison, modern phototypesetting printed by offset lithography tends to look anemic and lacks the tactile quality of type impressed into the page. The version of the Caslon typeface employed in the original edition of *O Pioneers!*, were it available for phototypesetting, would hardly survive the transition. Instead, we have chosen Linotype Janson Text, a modern rendering of the type used by Rogers. The subtle adjustments of stroke weight in this reworking do much to retain the integrity of earlier metal versions. Therefore, without trying to replicate the design of single works, we seek to represent Cather's general preferences in a design that encompasses many volumes.

In each volume in the Cather Edition, the author's specific intentions for design and printing are set forth in textual commentaries. These essays also describe the history of the texts, identify those that are authoritative, explain the selection of copy-texts or basic texts, justify emendations of the copy-text, and describe patterns of variants. The textual apparatus in each volume — lists of variants, emendations, explanations of emendations, and end-of-line hyphenations — completes the textual story.

Historical essays provide essential information about the genesis, form, and transmission of each book, as well as supply its biographical, historical, and intellectual contexts. Illustrations supplement these essays with photographs, maps, and facsimiles of manuscript, typescript, or typeset pages. Finally, because Cather in her writing drew so extensively upon personal experience and historical detail, explanatory notes are an especially important part of the Cather Edition. By providing a comprehensive identification of her references to flora and fauna, to regional customs and manners, to the classics and the Bible, to popular writing, music, and other arts — as well as relevant cartography and census material — these notes provide a starting place for scholarship and criticism on subjects long slighted or ignored.

Within this overall standard format, differences occur that are informative in their own right. The straightforward textual history of *O Pioneers!* and *My Ántonia* contrasts with the more complicated textual challenges of *A Lost Lady* and *Death Comes for the Archbishop*; the allusive personal history of the Nebraska novels, so densely woven that *My Ántonia* seems drawn not merely upon Anna Pavelka but all of Webster County, contrasts with the more public allusions of novels set elsewhere. The Cather Edition reflects the individuality of each work while providing a standard of reference for critical study.

O PIONEERS!

BY

WILLA SIBERT CATHER

"Those fields, colored by various grain!"
Mickiewicz

To the memory of SARAH ORNE JEWETT
in whose beautiful and delicate work
there is the perfection
that endures

Prairie Spring

Evening and the flat land,
Rich and sombre and always silent;
The miles of fresh-plowed soil,
Heavy and black, full of strength and harshness;
The growing wheat, the growing weeds,
The toiling horses, the tired men;
The long empty roads,
Sullen fires of sunset, fading,
The eternal, unresponsive sky.
Against all this, Youth,
Flaming like the wild roses,
Singing like the larks over the plowed fields,
Flashing like a star out of the twilight;
Youth with its insupportable sweetness,
Its fierce necessity,
Its sharp desire,
Singing and singing,
Out of the lips of silence,
Out of the earthy dusk.

Contents

PART I

The Wild Land

O Pioneers!

PART I

The Wild Land

I

ONE January day, thirty years ago, the little town of Hanover, anchored on a windy Nebraska tableland, was trying not to be blown away. A mist of fine snowflakes was curling and eddying about the cluster of low drab buildings huddled on the gray prairie, under a gray sky. The dwelling-houses were set about haphazard on the tough prairie sod; some of them looked as if they had been moved in overnight, and others as if they were straying off by themselves, headed straight for the open plain. None of them had any appearance of permanence, and the howling wind blew under them as well as over them. The main street was a deeply rutted road, now frozen hard, which ran from the squat red railway station and the grain "elevator" at the north end of the town to the lumber yard and the horse pond at the south end. On either side of this road straggled two uneven rows of wooden buildings; the general merchandise stores, the two banks, the drug store, the feed store, the saloon, the post-office. The board sidewalks were gray with trampled snow, but at two o'clock in the afternoon the shopkeepers, having come back from dinner, were keeping well behind their frosty windows. The children were all in school, and there was nobody abroad in the streets but a few rough-looking countrymen in coarse overcoats, with their long caps pulled down to their noses. Some of them had brought their wives to town, and now and then a red or a plaid shawl flashed out of one store into the shelter of another. At the hitch-bars along the street a few heavy work-horses, harnessed to farm wagons, shivered under their blankets. About the station everything was quiet, for there would not be another train in until night.

On the sidewalk in front of one of the stores sat a little Swede boy, crying bitterly. He was about five years old. His black cloth coat was much too big for him and made him look like a little old man. His shrunken brown flannel dress had been washed many times and left a long stretch of stocking between the hem of his skirt and the tops of his clumsy, copper-toed shoes. His cap was pulled down over his ears; his nose and his chubby cheeks were chapped and red with cold. He cried quietly, and the few people who hurried by did not notice him. He was afraid to stop any one, afraid to go into the store and ask for help, so he sat wringing his long sleeves and looking up a telegraph pole beside him, whimpering, "My kitten, oh, my kitten! Her will fweeze!" At the top of the pole crouched a shivering gray kitten, mewing faintly and clinging desperately to the wood with her claws. The boy had been left at the store while his sister went to the doctor's office, and in her absence a dog had chased his kitten up the pole. The little creature had never been so high before, and she was too frightened to move. Her master was sunk in despair. He was a little country boy, and this village was to him a very strange and perplexing place, where people wore fine clothes and had hard hearts. He always felt shy and awkward here, and wanted to hide behind things for fear some one might laugh at him. Just now, he was too unhappy to care who laughed. At last he seemed to see a ray of hope: his sister was coming, and he got up and ran toward her in his heavy shoes.

His sister was a tall, strong girl, and she walked rapidly and resolutely, as if she knew exactly where she was going and what she was going to do next. She wore a man's long ulster (not as if it were an affliction, but as if it were very comfortable and belonged to her; carried it like a young soldier), and a round plush cap, tied down with a thick veil. She had a serious, thoughtful face, and her clear, deep blue eyes were fixed intently on the distance, without seeming to see anything, as if she were in trouble. She did not notice the little boy until he pulled her by the coat. Then she stopped short and stooped down to wipe his wet face.

"Why, Emil! I told you to stay in the store and not to come out. What is the matter with you?"

"My kitten, sister, my kitten! A man put her out, and a dog chased her up there." His forefinger, projecting from the sleeve of his coat, pointed up to the wretched little creature on the pole.

"Oh, Emil! Did n't I tell you she'd get us into trouble of some kind, if you brought her? What made you tease me so? But there, I ought to have known better myself." She went to the foot of the pole and held out her arms, crying, "Kitty, kitty, kitty," but the kitten only mewed and faintly waved its tail. Alexandra turned away decidedly. "No, she won't come down. Somebody will have to go up after her. I saw the Linstrums' wagon in town. I'll go and see if I can find Carl. Maybe he can do something. Only you must stop crying, or I won't go a step. Where's your comforter? Did you leave it in the store? Never mind. Hold still, till I put this on you."

She unwound the brown veil from her head and tied

14

it about his throat. A shabby little traveling man, who was just then coming out of the store on his way to the saloon, stopped and gazed stupidly at the shining mass of hair she bared when she took off her veil; two thick braids, pinned about her head in the German way, with a fringe of reddish-yellow curls blowing out from under her cap. He took his cigar out of his mouth and held the wet end between the fingers of his woolen glove. "My God, girl, what a head of hair!" he exclaimed, quite innocently and foolishly. She stabbed him with a glance of Amazonian fierceness and drew in her lower lip— most unnecessary severity. It gave the little clothing drummer such a start that he actually let his cigar fall to the sidewalk and went off weakly in the teeth of the wind to the saloon. His hand was still unsteady when he took his glass from the bartender. His feeble flirtatious instincts had been crushed before, but never so mercilessly. He felt cheap and ill-used, as if some one had taken advantage of him. When a drummer had been knocking about in little drab towns and crawling across the wintry country in dirty smoking-cars, was he to be blamed if, when he chanced upon a fine human creature, he suddenly wished himself more of a man?

While the little drummer was drinking to recover his nerve, Alexandra hurried to the drug store as the most likely place to find Carl Linstrum. There he was, turning over a portfolio of chromo "studies" which the druggist sold to the Hanover women who did china-painting. Alexandra explained her predicament, and the boy followed her to the corner, where Emil still sat by the pole.

"I'll have to go up after her, Alexandra. I think at the depot they have some spikes I can strap on my feet. Wait a minute." Carl thrust his hands into his pockets, lowered his head, and darted up the street against the north wind. He was a tall boy of fifteen, slight and narrow-chested. When he came back with the spikes, Alexandra asked him what he had done with his overcoat.

"I left it in the drug store. I could n't climb in it, anyhow. Catch me if I fall, Emil," he called back as he began his ascent. Alexandra watched him anxiously; the cold was bitter enough on the ground. The kitten would not budge an inch. Carl had to go to the very top of the pole, and then had some difficulty in tearing her from her hold. When he reached the ground, he handed the cat to her tearful little master. "Now go into the store with her, Emil, and get warm." He opened the door for the child. "Wait a minute, Alexandra. Why can't I drive for you as far as our place? It's getting colder every minute. Have you seen the doctor?"

16

"Yes. He is coming over to-morrow. But he says father can't get better; can't get well." The girl's lip trembled. She looked fixedly up the bleak street as if she were gathering her strength to face something, as if she were trying with all her might to grasp a situation which, no matter how painful, must be met and dealt with somehow. The wind flapped the skirts of her heavy coat about her.

Carl did not say anything, but she felt his sympathy. He, too, was lonely. He was a thin, frail boy, with brooding dark eyes, very quiet in all his movements. There was a delicate pallor in his thin face, and his mouth was too sensitive for a boy's. The lips had already a little curl of bitterness and skepticism. The two friends stood for a few moments on the windy street corner, not speaking a word, as two travelers, who have lost their way, sometimes stand and admit their perplexity in silence. When Carl turned away he said, "I'll see to your team." Alexandra went into the store to have her purchases packed in the egg-boxes, and to get warm before she set out on her long cold drive.

When she looked for Emil, she found him sitting on a step of the staircase that led up to the clothing and carpet department. He was playing with a little Bohemian girl, Marie Tovesky, who was tying her handkerchief over the kitten's head for a bonnet. Marie was a stranger in the country, having come from Omaha with her mother to visit her uncle, Joe Tovesky. She was a dark child, with brown curly hair, like a brunette doll's, a coaxing little red mouth, and round, yellow-brown eyes. Every one noticed her eyes; the brown iris had golden glints that made them look like gold-stone, or, in softer lights, like that Colorado mineral called tiger-eye.

The country children thereabouts wore their dresses to their shoe-tops, but this city child was dressed in what was then called the "Kate Greenaway" manner, and her red cashmere frock, gathered full from the yoke, came almost to the floor. This, with her poke bonnet, gave her the look of a quaint little woman. She had a white fur tippet about her neck and made no fussy objections when Emil fingered it admiringly. Alexandra had not the heart to take him away from so pretty a playfellow, and she let them tease the kitten together until Joe Tovesky came in noisily and picked up his little niece, setting her on his shoulder for every one to see. His children were all boys, and he adored this little creature. His cronies formed a circle about him, admiring and teasing the little girl, who took their jokes with great good nature. They were all delighted with her, for they seldom saw so pretty and carefully nurtured a child. They told her that she must choose one of them for a sweetheart, and each began pressing his suit and offering her bribes; candy, and little pigs, and spotted calves. She looked archly into the big, brown, mustached faces, smelling of spirits and tobacco, then she ran her tiny forefinger delicately over Joe's bristly chin and said, "Here is my sweetheart."

The Bohemians roared with laughter, and Marie's uncle hugged her until she cried, "Please don't, Uncle Joe! You hurt me." Each of Joe's friends gave her a bag of candy, and she kissed them all around, though she did not like country candy very well. Perhaps that was why she bethought herself of Emil. "Let me down, Uncle Joe," she said, "I want to give some of my candy to that nice little boy I found." She walked graciously over to Emil, followed by her lusty admirers, who formed a new circle and teased the little boy until he hid his face in his sister's skirts, and she had to scold him for being such a baby.

The farm people were making preparations to start for home. The women were checking over their groceries and pinning their big red shawls about their heads. The men were buying tobacco and candy with what money they had left, were showing each other new boots and gloves and blue flannel shirts. Three big Bohemians were drinking raw alcohol, tinctured with oil of cinnamon. This was said to fortify one effectually against the cold, and they smacked their lips after each pull at the flask. Their volubility drowned every other noise in the place, and the overheated store sounded of their spirited language as it reeked of pipe smoke, damp woolens, and kerosene.

Carl came in, wearing his overcoat and carrying a wooden box with a brass handle. "Come," he said, "I've fed and watered your team, and the wagon is ready." He carried Emil out and tucked him down in the straw in the wagonbox. The heat had made the little boy sleepy, but he still clung to his kitten.

"You were awful good to climb so high and get my kitten, Carl. When I get big I'll climb and get little boys' kittens for them," he murmured drowsily. Before the horses were over the first hill, Emil and his cat were both fast asleep.

Although it was only four o'clock, the winter day was fading. The road led southwest, toward the streak of pale, watery light that glimmered in the leaden sky. The light fell upon the two sad young faces that were turned mutely toward it: upon the eyes of the girl, who seemed to be looking with such anguished perplexity into the future; upon the sombre eyes of the boy, who seemed already to be looking into the past. The little town behind them had vanished as if it had never been, had fallen behind the swell of the prairie, and the stern frozen country received them into its bosom. The homesteads were few and far apart; here and there a windmill gaunt against the sky, a sod house crouching in a hollow. But the great fact was the land itself, which seemed to overwhelm the little beginnings of human society that struggled in its sombre wastes. It was from facing this vast hardness that the boy's mouth had become so bitter; because he felt that men were too weak to make any mark here, that the land wanted to be let alone, to preserve its own fierce strength, its peculiar, savage kind of beauty, its uninterrupted mournfulness.

The wagon jolted along over the frozen road. The two friends had less to say to each other than usual, as if the cold had somehow penetrated to their hearts.

"Did Lou and Oscar go to the Blue to cut wood today?" Carl asked.

"Yes. I'm almost sorry I let them go, it's turned so cold. But mother frets if the wood gets low." She stopped and put her hand to her forehead, brushing back her hair. "I don't know what is to become of us, Carl, if father has to die. I don't dare to think about it. I wish we could all go with him and let the grass grow back over everything."

Carl made no reply. Just ahead of them was the Norwegian graveyard, where the grass had, indeed, grown back over everything, shaggy and red, hiding even the wire fence. Carl realized that he was not a very helpful companion, but there was nothing he could say.

"Of course," Alexandra went on, steadying her voice a little, "the boys are strong and work hard, but we've always depended so on father that I don't see how we can go ahead. I almost feel as if there were nothing to go ahead for."

"Does your father know?"

"Yes, I think he does. He lies and counts on his fingers all day. I think he is trying to count up what he is leaving for us. It's a comfort to him that my chickens are laying right on through the cold weather and bringing in a little money. I wish we could keep his mind off such things, but I don't have much time to be with him now."

"I wonder if he'd like to have me bring my magic lantern over some evening?"

Alexandra turned her face toward him. "Oh, Carl! Have you got it?"

"Yes. It's back there in the straw. Did n't you notice the box I was carrying? I tried it all morning in the drug-store cellar, and it worked ever so well, makes fine big pictures."

"What are they about?"

"Oh, hunting pictures in Germany, and Robinson Crusoe and funny pictures about cannibals. I'm going to paint some slides for it on glass, out of the Hans Andersen book."

Alexandra seemed actually cheered. There is often a good deal of the child left in people who have had to grow up too soon. "Do bring it over, Carl. I can hardly wait to see it, and I'm sure it will please father. Are the pictures colored? Then I know he'll like them. He likes the calendars I get him in town. I wish I could get more. You must leave me here, must n't you? It's been nice to have company."

Carl stopped the horses and looked dubiously up at the black sky. "It's pretty dark. Of course the horses will take you home, but I think I'd better light your lantern, in case you should need it."

He gave her the reins and climbed back into the wagon-box, where he crouched down and made a tent of his overcoat. After a dozen trials he succeeded in lighting the lantern, which he placed in front of Alexandra, half covering it with a blanket so that the light would not shine in her eyes. "Now, wait until I find my box. Yes, here it is. Good-night, Alexandra. Try not to worry." Carl sprang to the ground and ran off across the fields toward the Linstrum homestead. "Hoo, hoo-o-o-o!" he called back as he disappeared over a ridge and dropped into a sand gully. The wind answered him like an echo, "Hoo, hoo-o-o-o-o-o!" Alexandra drove off alone. The rattle of her wagon was lost in the howling of the wind, but her lantern, held firmly between her feet, made a moving point of light along the highway, going deeper and deeper into the dark country.

II

O N one of the ridges of that wintry waste stood the low log house in which John Bergson was dying. The Bergson homestead was easier to find than many another, because it overlooked Norway Creek, a shallow, muddy stream that sometimes flowed, and sometimes stood still, at the bottom of a winding ravine with steep, shelving sides overgrown with brush and cottonwoods and dwarf ash. This creek gave a sort of identity to the farms that bordered upon it. Of all the bewildering things about a new country, the absence of human landmarks is one of the most depressing and disheartening. The houses on the Divide were small and were usually tucked away in low places; you did not see them until you came directly upon them. Most of them were built of the sod itself, and were only the unescapable ground in another form. The roads were but faint tracks in the grass, and the fields were scarcely noticeable. The record of the plow was insignificant, like the feeble scratches on stone left by prehistoric races, so indeterminate that they may, after all, be only the markings of glaciers, and not a record of human strivings.

In eleven long years John Bergson had made but little impression upon the wild land he had come to tame. It was still a wild thing that had its ugly moods; and no one knew when they were likely to come, or why. Mischance hung over it. Its Genius was unfriendly to man. The sick man was feeling this as he lay looking out of the window, after the doctor had left him, on the day following Alexandra's trip to town. There it lay outside his door, the same land, the same lead-colored miles. He knew every ridge and draw and gully between him and the horizon. To the south, his plowed fields; to the east, the sod stables, the cattle corral, the pond, — and then the grass.

Bergson went over in his mind the things that had held him back. One winter his cattle had perished in a blizzard. The next summer one of his plow horses broke its leg in a prairie-dog hole and had to be shot. Another summer he lost his hogs from cholera, and a valuable stallion died from a rattlesnake bite. Time and again his crops had failed. He had lost two children, boys, that came between Lou and Emil, and there had been the cost of sickness and death. Now, when he had at last struggled out of debt, he was going to die himself. He was only forty-six, and had, of course, counted upon more time.

The Wild Land

Bergson had spent his first five years on the Divide getting into debt, and the last six getting out. He had paid off his mortgages and had ended pretty much where he began, with the land. He owned exactly six hundred and forty acres of what stretched outside his door; his own original homestead and timber claim, making three hundred and twenty acres, and the half-section adjoining, the homestead of a younger brother who had given up the fight, gone back to Chicago to work in a fancy bakery and distinguish himself in a Swedish athletic club. So far John had not attempted to cultivate the second half-section, but used it for pasture land, and one of his sons rode herd there in open weather.

John Bergson had the Old-World belief that land, in itself, is desirable. But this land was an enigma. It was like a horse that no one knows how to break to harness, that runs wild and kicks things to pieces. He had an idea that no one understood how to farm it properly, and this he often discussed with Alexandra. Their neighbors, certainly, knew even less about farming than he did. Many of them had never worked on a farm until they took up their homesteads. They had been *handwerkers* at home; tailors, locksmiths, joiners, cigarmakers, etc. Bergson himself had worked in a shipyard.

For weeks, John Bergson had been thinking about these things. His bed stood in the sitting-room, next to the kitchen. Through the day, while the baking and washing and ironing were going on, the father lay and looked up at the roof beams that he himself had hewn, or out at the cattle in the corral. He counted the cattle over and over. It diverted him to speculate as to how much weight each of the steers would probably put on by spring. He often called his daughter in to talk to her about this. Before Alexandra was twelve years old she had begun to be a help to him, and as she grew older he had come to depend more and more upon her resourcefulness and good judgment. His boys were willing enough to work, but when he talked with them they usually irritated him. It was Alexandra who read the papers and followed the markets, and who learned by the mistakes of their neighbors. It was Alexandra who could always tell about what it had cost to fatten each steer, and who could guess the weight of a hog before it went on the scales closer than John Bergson himself. Lou and Oscar were industrious, but he could never teach them to use their heads about their work.

Alexandra, her father often said to himself, was like her grandfather; which was his way of saying that she was intelligent. John Bergson's father had been a ship-

builder, a man of considerable force and of some fortune. Late in life he married a second time, a Stockholm
woman of questionable character, much younger than
he, who goaded him into every sort of extravagance. On
the shipbuilder's part, this marriage was an infatuation,
the despairing folly of a powerful man who cannot bear
to grow old. In a few years his unprincipled wife warped
the probity of a lifetime. He speculated, lost his own
fortune and funds entrusted to him by poor seafaring
men, and died disgraced, leaving his children nothing.
But when all was said, he had come up from the sea
himself, had built up a proud little business with no
capital but his own skill and foresight, and had proved
himself a man. In his daughter, John Bergson recognized the strength of will, and the simple direct way of
thinking things out, that had characterized his father in
his better days. He would much rather, of course, have
seen this likeness in one of his sons, but it was not a
question of choice. As he lay there day after day he had
to accept the situation as it was, and to be thankful that
there was one among his children to whom he could
entrust the future of his family and the possibilities of
his hard-won land.

The winter twilight was fading. The sick man heard
his wife strike a match in the kitchen, and the light of

a lamp glimmered through the cracks of the door. It seemed like a light shining far away. He turned painfully in his bed and looked at his white hands, with all the work gone out of them. He was ready to give up, he felt. He did not know how it had come about, but he was quite willing to go deep under his fields and rest, where the plow could not find him. He was tired of making mistakes. He was content to leave the tangle to other hands; he thought of his Alexandra's strong ones.

"*Dotter*," he called feebly, "*dotter!*" He heard her quick step and saw her tall figure appear in the doorway, with the light of the lamp behind her. He felt her youth and strength, how easily she moved and stooped and lifted. But he would not have had it again if he could, not he! He knew the end too well to wish to begin again. He knew where it all went to, what it all became.

His daughter came and lifted him up on his pillows. She called him by an old Swedish name that she used to call him when she was little and took his dinner to him in the shipyard.

"Tell the boys to come here, daughter. I want to speak to them."

"They are feeding the horses, father. They have just come back from the Blue. Shall I call them?"

He sighed. "No, no. Wait until they come in. Alexandra, you will have to do the best you can for your brothers. Everything will come on you."

"I will do all I can, father."

"Don't let them get discouraged and go off like Uncle Otto. I want them to keep the land."

"We will, father. We will never lose the land."

There was a sound of heavy feet in the kitchen. Alexandra went to the door and beckoned to her brothers, two strapping boys of seventeen and nineteen. They came in and stood at the foot of the bed. Their father looked at them searchingly, though it was too dark to see their faces; they were just the same boys, he told himself, he had not been mistaken in them. The square head and heavy shoulders belonged to Oscar, the elder. The younger boy was quicker, but vacillating.

"Boys," said the father wearily, "I want you to keep the land together and to be guided by your sister. I have talked to her since I have been sick, and she knows all my wishes. I want no quarrels among my children, and so long as there is one house there must be one head. Alexandra is the oldest, and she knows my wishes. She will do the best she can. If she makes mistakes, she will not make so many as I have made. When you marry, and want a house of your own, the land will be divided fairly, according to the courts. But for the next few years you will have it hard, and you must all keep together. Alexandra will manage the best she can."

Oscar, who was usually the last to speak, replied because he was the older, "Yes, father. It would be so anyway, without your speaking. We will all work the place together."

"And you will be guided by your sister, boys, and be good brothers to her, and good sons to your mother? That is good. And Alexandra must not work in the fields any more. There is no necessity now. Hire a man when you need help. She can make much more with her eggs and butter than the wages of a man. It was one of my mistakes that I did not find that out sooner. Try to break a little more land every year; sod corn is good for fodder. Keep turning the land, and always put up more hay than you need. Don't grudge your mother a little time for plowing her garden and setting out fruit trees, even if it comes in a busy season. She has been a good mother to you, and she has always missed the old country."

When they went back to the kitchen the boys sat down silently at the table. Throughout the meal they looked down at their plates and did not lift their red eyes. They did not eat much, although they had been working in the cold all day, and there was a rabbit stewed in gravy for supper, and prune pies.

The Wild Land

John Bergson had married beneath him, but he had married a good housewife. Mrs. Bergson was a fair-skinned, corpulent woman, heavy and placid like her son, Oscar, but there was something comfortable about her; perhaps it was her own love of comfort. For eleven years she had worthily striven to maintain some semblance of household order amid conditions that made order very difficult. Habit was very strong with Mrs. Bergson, and her unremitting efforts to repeat the routine of her old life among new surroundings had done a great deal to keep the family from disintegrating morally and getting careless in their ways. The Bergsons had a log house, for instance, only because Mrs. Bergson would not live in a sod house. She missed the fish diet of her own country, and twice every summer she sent the boys to the river, twenty miles to the southward, to fish for channel cat. When the children were little she used to load them all into the wagon, the baby in its crib, and go fishing herself.

Alexandra often said that if her mother were cast upon a desert island, she would thank God for her deliverance, make a garden, and find something to preserve. Preserving was almost a mania with Mrs. Bergson. Stout as she was, she roamed the scrubby banks of Norway Creek looking for fox grapes and

goose plums, like a wild creature in search of prey. She
made a yellow jam of the insipid ground-cherries that
grew on the prairie, flavoring it with lemon peel; and
she made a sticky dark conserve of garden tomatoes.
She had experimented even with the rank buffalo-pea,
and she could not see a fine bronze cluster of them
without shaking her head and murmuring, "What a
pity!" When there was nothing more to preserve, she
began to pickle. The amount of sugar she used in these
processes was sometimes a serious drain upon the family resources. She was a good mother, but she was glad
when her children were old enough not to be in her
way in the kitchen. She had never quite forgiven John
Bergson for bringing her to the end of the earth; but,
now that she was there, she wanted to be let alone to
reconstruct her old life in so far as that was possible. She
could still take some comfort in the world if she had
bacon in the cave, glass jars on the shelves, and sheets in
the press. She disapproved of all her neighbors because
of their slovenly housekeeping, and the women thought
her very proud. Once when Mrs. Bergson, on her way
to Norway Creek, stopped to see old Mrs. Lee, the
old woman hid in the haymow "for fear Mis' Bergson
would catch her barefoot."

III

ONE Sunday afternoon in July, six months after John Bergson's death, Carl was sitting in the doorway of the Linstrum kitchen, dreaming over an illustrated paper, when he heard the rattle of a wagon along the hill road. Looking up he recognized the Bergsons' team, with two seats in the wagon, which meant they were off for a pleasure excursion. Oscar and Lou, on the front seat, wore their cloth hats and coats, never worn except on Sundays, and Emil, on the second seat with Alexandra, sat proudly in his new trousers, made from a pair of his father's, and a pink-striped shirt, with a wide ruffled collar. Oscar stopped the horses and waved to Carl, who caught up his hat and ran through the melon patch to join them.

"Want to go with us?" Lou called. "We're going to Crazy Ivar's to buy a hammock."

"Sure." Carl ran up panting, and clambering over the wheel sat down beside Emil. "I've always wanted to see Ivar's pond. They say it's the biggest in all the country. Are n't you afraid to go to Ivar's in that new shirt, Emil? He might want it and take it right off your back."

Emil grinned. "I'd be awful scared to go," he admitted, "if you big boys were n't along to take care of me. Did you ever hear him howl, Carl? People say sometimes he runs about the country howling at night because he is afraid the Lord will destroy him. Mother thinks he must have done something awful wicked."

Lou looked back and winked at Carl. "What would you do, Emil, if you was out on the prairie by yourself and seen him coming?"

Emil stared. "Maybe I could hide in a badger-hole," he suggested doubtfully.

"But suppose there was n't any badger-hole," Lou persisted. "Would you run?"

"No, I'd be too scared to run," Emil admitted mournfully, twisting his fingers. "I guess I'd sit right down on the ground and say my prayers."

The big boys laughed, and Oscar brandished his whip over the broad backs of the horses.

"He would n't hurt you, Emil," said Carl persuasively. "He came to doctor our mare when she ate green corn and swelled up most as big as the water-tank. He petted her just like you do your cats. I could n't understand much he said, for he don't talk any English, but he kept patting her and groaning as if he had the pain himself, and saying, 'There now, sister, that's easier, that's better!'"

Lou and Oscar laughed, and Emil giggled delightedly and looked up at his sister.

"I don't think he knows anything at all about doctor-
ing," said Oscar scornfully. "They say when horses have
distemper he takes the medicine himself, and then prays
over the horses."

Alexandra spoke up. "That's what the Crows said, but
he cured their horses, all the same. Some days his mind
is cloudy, like. But if you can get him on a clear day,
you can learn a great deal from him. He understands
animals. Did n't I see him take the horn off the Berquists' cow when she had torn it loose and went crazy?
She was tearing all over the place, knocking herself
against things. And at last she ran out on the roof of the
old dugout and her legs went through and there she
stuck, bellowing. Ivar came running with his white bag,
and the moment he got to her she was quiet and let him
saw her horn off and daub the place with tar."

Emil had been watching his sister, his face reflecting
the sufferings of the cow. "And then did n't it hurt her
any more?" he asked.

Alexandra patted him. "No, not any more. And in
two days they could use her milk again."

The road to Ivar's homestead was a very poor one.
He had settled in the rough country across the county

line, where no one lived but some Russians, — half a dozen families who dwelt together in one long house, divided off like barracks. Ivar had explained his choice by saying that the fewer neighbors he had, the fewer temptations. Nevertheless, when one considered that his chief business was horse-doctoring, it seemed rather short-sighted of him to live in the most inaccessible place he could find. The Bergson wagon lurched along over the rough hummocks and grass banks, followed the bottom of winding draws, or skirted the margin of wide lagoons, where the golden coreopsis grew up out of the clear water and the wild ducks rose with a whirr of wings.

Lou looked after them helplessly. "I wish I'd brought my gun, anyway, Alexandra," he said fretfully. "I could have hidden it under the straw in the bottom of the wagon."

"Then we'd have had to lie to Ivar. Besides, they say he can smell dead birds. And if he knew, we would n't get anything out of him, not even a hammock. I want to talk to him, and he won't talk sense if he's angry. It makes him foolish."

Lou sniffed. "Whoever heard of him talking sense, anyhow! I'd rather have ducks for supper than Crazy Ivar's tongue."

Emil was alarmed. "Oh, but, Lou, you don't want to make him mad! He might howl!"

They all laughed again, and Oscar urged the horses up the crumbling side of a clay bank. They had left the lagoons and the red grass behind them. In Crazy Ivar's country the grass was short and gray, the draws deeper than they were in the Bergsons' neighborhood, and the land was all broken up into hillocks and clay ridges. The wild flowers disappeared, and only in the bottom of the draws and gullies grew a few of the very toughest and hardiest: shoestring, and ironweed, and snow-on-the-mountain.

"Look, look, Emil, there's Ivar's big pond!" Alexandra pointed to a shining sheet of water that lay at the bottom of a shallow draw. At one end of the pond was an earthen dam, planted with green willow bushes, and above it a door and a single window were set into the hillside. You would not have seen them at all but for the reflection of the sunlight upon the four panes of window-glass. And that was all you saw. Not a shed, not a corral, not a well, not even a path broken in the curly grass. But for the piece of rusty stovepipe sticking up through the sod, you could have walked over the roof of Ivar's dwelling without dreaming that you were near a human habitation. Ivar had lived for three years in the clay bank, without defiling the face of nature any more than the coyote that had lived there before him had done.

When the Bergsons drove over the hill, Ivar was sitting in the doorway of his house, reading the Norwegian Bible. He was a queerly shaped old man, with a thick, powerful body set on short bow-legs. His shaggy white hair, falling in a thick mane about his ruddy cheeks, made him look older than he was. He was barefoot, but he wore a clean shirt of unbleached cotton, open at the neck. He always put on a clean shirt when Sunday morning came round, though he never went to church. He had a peculiar religion of his own and could not get on with any of the denominations. Often he did not see anybody from one week's end to another. He kept a calendar, and every morning he checked off a day, so that he was never in any doubt as to which day of the week it was. Ivar hired himself out in threshing and corn-husking time, and he doctored sick animals when he was sent for. When he was at home, he made hammocks out of twine and committed chapters of the Bible to memory.

Ivar found contentment in the solitude he had sought out for himself. He disliked the litter of human dwellings: the broken food, the bits of broken china, the old wash-boilers and tea-kettles thrown into the sunflower patch. He preferred the cleanness and tidiness of the wild sod. He always said that the badgers had cleaner houses than people, and that when he took a housekeeper her name would be Mrs. Badger. He best expressed his preference for his wild homestead by saying that his Bible seemed truer to him there. If one stood in the doorway of his cave, and looked off at the rough land, the smiling sky, the curly grass white in the hot sunlight; if one listened to the rapturous song of the lark, the drumming of the quail, the burr of the locust against that vast silence, one understood what Ivar meant.

On this Sunday afternoon his face shone with happiness. He closed the book on his knee, keeping the place with his horny finger, and repeated softly: —

He sendeth the springs into the valleys, which run
    among the hills;
They give drink to every beast of the field; the wild
    asses quench their thirst.
The trees of the Lord are full of sap; the cedars of
    Lebanon which he hath planted;
Where the birds make their nests: as for the stork, the
    fir trees are her house.
The high hills are a refuge for the wild goats; and the
    rocks for the conies.

Before he opened his Bible again, Ivar heard the Bergsons' wagon approaching, and he sprang up and ran toward it.

"No guns, no guns!" he shouted, waving his arms distractedly.

"No, Ivar, no guns," Alexandra called reassuringly.

He dropped his arms and went up to the wagon, smiling amiably and looking at them out of his pale blue eyes.

"We want to buy a hammock, if you have one," Alexandra explained, "and my little brother, here, wants to see your big pond, where so many birds come."

Ivar smiled foolishly, and began rubbing the horses' noses and feeling about their mouths behind the bits. "Not many birds just now. A few ducks this morning; and some snipe come to drink. But there was a crane last week. She spent one night and came back the next evening. I don't know why. It is not her season, of course. Many of them go over in the fall. Then the pond is full of strange voices every night."

Alexandra translated for Carl, who looked thoughtful. "Ask him, Alexandra, if it is true that a sea gull came here once. I have heard so."

She had some difficulty in making the old man understand.

He looked puzzled at first, then smote his hands together as he remembered. "Oh, yes, yes! A big white bird with long wings and pink feet. My! what a voice she had! She came in the afternoon and kept flying about the pond and screaming until dark. She was in trouble of some sort, but I could not understand her. She was going over to the other ocean, maybe, and did not know how far it was. She was afraid of never getting there. She was more mournful than our birds here; she cried in the night. She saw the light from my window and darted up to it. Maybe she thought my house was a boat, she was such a wild thing. Next morning, when the sun rose, I went out to take her food, but she flew up into the sky and went on her way." Ivar ran his fingers through his thick hair. "I have many strange birds stop with me here. They come from very far away and are great company. I hope you boys never shoot wild birds?"

Lou and Oscar grinned, and Ivar shook his bushy head. "Yes, I know boys are thoughtless. But these wild things are God's birds. He watches over them and counts them, as we do our cattle; Christ says so in the New Testament."

"Now, Ivar," Lou asked, "may we water our horses at your pond and give them some feed? It's a bad road to your place."

"Yes, yes, it is." The old man scrambled about and began to loose the tugs. "A bad road, eh, girls? And the bay with a colt at home!"

Oscar brushed the old man aside. "We'll take care of the horses, Ivar. You'll be finding some disease on them. Alexandra wants to see your hammocks."

Ivar led Alexandra and Emil to his little cave house. He had but one room, neatly plastered and white-washed, and there was a wooden floor. There was a kitchen stove, a table covered with oilcloth, two chairs, a clock, a calendar, a few books on the window-shelf; nothing more. But the place was as clean as a cupboard.

"But where do you sleep, Ivar?" Emil asked, looking about.

Ivar unslung a hammock from a hook on the wall; in it was rolled a buffalo robe. "There, my son. A hammock is a good bed, and in winter I wrap up in this skin. Where I go to work, the beds are not half so easy as this."

By this time Emil had lost all his timidity. He thought a cave a very superior kind of house. There was something pleasantly unusual about it and about Ivar. "Do the birds know you will be kind to them, Ivar? Is that why so many come?" he asked.

Ivar sat down on the floor and tucked his feet under

44

him. "See, little brother, they have come from a long way, and they are very tired. From up there where they are flying, our country looks dark and flat. They must have water to drink and to bathe in before they can go on with their journey. They look this way and that, and far below them they see something shining, like a piece of glass set in the dark earth. That is my pond. They come to it and are not disturbed. Maybe I sprinkle a little corn. They tell the other birds, and next year more come this way. They have their roads up there, as we have down here."

Emil rubbed his knees thoughtfully. "And is that true, Ivar, about the head ducks falling back when they are tired, and the hind ones taking their place?"

"Yes. The point of the wedge gets the worst of it; they cut the wind. They can only stand it there a little while — half an hour, maybe. Then they fall back and the wedge splits a little, while the rear ones come up the middle to the front. Then it closes up and they fly on, with a new edge. They are always changing like that, up in the air. Never any confusion; just like soldiers who have been drilled."

Alexandra had selected her hammock by the time the boys came up from the pond. They would not come in, but sat in the shade of the bank outside while Alexandra and Ivar talked about the birds and about his house-keeping, and why he never ate meat, fresh or salt.

Alexandra was sitting on one of the wooden chairs, her arms resting on the table. Ivar was sitting on the floor at her feet. "Ivar," she said suddenly, beginning to trace the pattern on the oilcloth with her forefinger, "I came to-day more because I wanted to talk to you than because I wanted to buy a hammock."

"Yes?" The old man scraped his bare feet on the plank floor.

"We have a big bunch of hogs, Ivar. I would n't sell in the spring, when everybody advised me to, and now so many people are losing their hogs that I am frightened. What can be done?"

Ivar's little eyes began to shine. They lost their vagueness.

"You feed them swill and such stuff? Of course! And sour milk? Oh, yes! And keep them in a stinking pen? I tell you, sister, the hogs of this country are put upon! They become unclean, like the hogs in the Bible. If you kept your chickens like that, what would happen? You have a little sorghum patch, maybe? Put a fence around it, and turn the hogs in. Build a shed to give them shade, a thatch on poles. Let the boys haul water to them in barrels, clean water, and plenty. Get them off the old stinking ground, and do not let them go back there until winter. Give them only grain and clean feed, such as you would give horses or cattle. Hogs do not like to be filthy."

The boys outside the door had been listening. Lou nudged his brother. "Come, the horses are done eating. Let's hitch up and get out of here. He'll fill her full of notions. She'll be for having the pigs sleep with us, next."

Oscar grunted and got up. Carl, who could not understand what Ivar said, saw that the two boys were displeased. They did not mind hard work, but they hated experiments and could never see the use of taking pains. Even Lou, who was more elastic than his older brother, disliked to do anything different from their neighbors. He felt that it made them conspicuous and gave people a chance to talk about them.

Once they were on the homeward road, the boys forgot their ill-humor and joked about Ivar and his birds. Alexandra did not propose any reforms in the care of the pigs, and they hoped she had forgotten Ivar's talk. They agreed that he was crazier than ever, and would never be able to prove up on his land because he worked it so little. Alexandra privately resolved that she would have a talk with Ivar about this and stir him up.

The boys persuaded Carl to stay for supper and go swimming in the pasture pond after dark.

That evening, after she had washed the supper dishes, Alexandra sat down on the kitchen doorstep, while her mother was mixing the bread. It was a still, deep-breathing summer night, full of the smell of the hay fields. Sounds of laughter and splashing came up from the pasture, and when the moon rose rapidly above the bare rim of the prairie, the pond glittered like polished metal, and she could see the flash of white bodies as the boys ran about the edge, or jumped into the water. Alexandra watched the shimmering pool dreamily, but eventually her eyes went back to the sorghum patch south of the barn, where she was planning to make her new pig corral.

IV

For the first three years after John Bergson's death, the affairs of his family prospered. Then came the hard times that brought every one on the Divide to the brink of despair; three years of drouth and failure, the last struggle of a wild soil against the encroaching plowshare. The first of these fruitless summers the Bergson boys bore courageously. The failure of the corn crop made labor cheap. Lou and Oscar hired two men and put in bigger crops than ever before. They lost everything they spent. The whole country was discouraged. Farmers who were already in debt had to give up their land. A few foreclosures demoralized the county. The settlers sat about on the wooden sidewalks in the little town and told each other that the country was never meant for men to live in; the thing to do was to get back to Iowa, to Illinois, to any place that had been proved habitable. The Bergson boys, certainly, would have been happier with their uncle Otto, in the bakery shop in Chicago. Like most of their neighbors, they were meant to follow in paths already marked out for them, not to break trails in a new country. A steady job, a few holidays, nothing to think about, and they would have been very happy. It was no fault of theirs that they had been dragged into the wilderness when they were little boys. A pioneer should have imagination, should be able to enjoy the idea of things more than the things themselves.

The second of these barren summers was passing. One September afternoon Alexandra had gone over to the garden across the draw to dig sweet potatoes — they had been thriving upon the weather that was fatal to everything else. But when Carl Linstrum came up the garden rows to find her, she was not working. She was standing lost in thought, leaning upon her pitchfork, her sunbonnet lying beside her on the ground. The dry garden patch smelled of drying vines and was strewn with yellow seed-cucumbers and pumpkins and citrons. At one end, next the rhubarb, grew feathery asparagus, with red berries. Down the middle of the garden was a row of gooseberry and currant bushes. A few tough zinnias and marigolds and a row of scarlet sage bore witness to the buckets of water that Mrs. Bergson had carried there after sundown, against the prohibition of her sons. Carl came quietly and slowly up the garden path, looking intently at Alexandra. She did not hear him. She was standing perfectly still, with that serious ease so characteristic of her. Her thick, reddish braids, twisted about her head, fairly burned in the sunlight. The air was cool enough to make the warm sun pleasant on one's back and shoulders, and so clear that the eye could follow a hawk up and up, into the blazing blue depths of the sky. Even Carl, never a very cheerful boy, and considerably darkened by these last two bitter years, loved the country on days like this, felt something strong and young and wild come out of it, that laughed at care.

"Alexandra," he said as he approached her, "I want to talk to you. Let's sit down by the gooseberry bushes." He picked up her sack of potatoes and they crossed the garden. "Boys gone to town?" he asked as he sank down on the warm, sun-baked earth. "Well, we have made up our minds at last, Alexandra. We are really going away."

She looked at him as if she were a little frightened. "Really, Carl? Is it settled?"

"Yes, father has heard from St. Louis, and they will give him back his old job in the cigar factory. He must be there by the first of November. They are taking on new men then. We will sell the place for whatever we can get, and auction the stock. We haven't enough to ship. I am going to learn engraving with a German engraver there, and then try to get work in Chicago."

Alexandra's hands dropped in her lap. Her eyes became dreamy and filled with tears.

Carl's sensitive lower lip trembled. He scratched in the soft earth beside him with a stick. "That's all I hate about it, Alexandra," he said slowly. "You've stood by us through so much and helped father out so many times, and now it seems as if we were running off and leaving you to face the worst of it. But it is n't as if we could really ever be of any help to you. We are only one more drag, one more thing you look out for and feel responsible for. Father was never meant for a farmer, you know that. And I hate it. We'd only get in deeper and deeper."

"Yes, yes, Carl, I know. You are wasting your life here. You are able to do much better things. You are nearly nineteen now, and I would n't have you stay. I've always hoped you would get away. But I can't help feeling scared when I think how I will miss you—more than you will ever know." She brushed the tears from her cheeks, not trying to hide them.

"But, Alexandra," he said sadly and wistfully, "I've never been any real help to you, beyond sometimes trying to keep the boys in a good humor."

Alexandra smiled and shook her head. "Oh, it's not that. Nothing like that. It's by understanding me, and the boys, and mother, that you've helped me. I expect that is the only way one person ever really can help another. I think you are about the only one that ever helped me. Somehow it will take more courage to bear your going than everything that has happened before."

Carl looked at the ground. "You see, we've all depended so on you," he said, "even father. He makes me laugh. When anything comes up he always says, 'I wonder what the Bergsons are going to do about that? I guess I'll go and ask her.' I'll never forget that time, when we first came here, and our horse had the colic, and I ran over to your place — your father was away, and you came home with me and showed father how to let the wind out of the horse. You were only a little girl then, but you knew ever so much more about farmwork than poor father. You remember how homesick I used to get, and what long talks we used to have coming from school? We've someway always felt alike about things."

"Yes, that's it; we've liked the same things and we've liked them together, without anybody else knowing. And we've had good times, hunting for Christmas trees and going for ducks and making our plum wine together every year. We've never either of us had any other close friend. And now —" Alexandra wiped her eyes with the corner of her apron, "and now I must remember that you are going where you will have many friends, and will find the work you were meant to do. But you'll write to me, Carl? That will mean a great deal to me here."

"I'll write as long as I live," cried the boy impetuously. "And I'll be working for you as much as for myself, Alexandra. I want to do something you'll like and be proud of. I'm a fool here, but I know I can do something!" He sat up and frowned at the red grass.

Alexandra sighed. "How discouraged the boys will be when they hear. They always come home from town discouraged, anyway. So many people are trying to leave the country, and they talk to our boys and make them low-spirited. I'm afraid they are beginning to feel hard toward me because I won't listen to any talk about going. Sometimes I feel like I'm getting tired of standing up for this country."

"I won't tell the boys yet, if you'd rather not."

"Oh, I'll tell them myself, to-night, when they come home. They'll be talking wild, anyway, and no good comes of keeping bad news. It's all harder on them than it is on me. Lou wants to get married, poor boy, and he can't until times are better. See, there goes the sun, Carl. I must be getting back. Mother will want her potatoes. It's chilly already, the moment the light goes."

Alexandra rose and looked about. A golden afterglow

throbbed in the west, but the country already looked empty and mournful. A dark moving mass came over the western hill, the Lee boy was bringing in the herd from the other half-section. Emil ran from the windmill to open the corral gate. From the log house, on the little rise across the draw, the smoke was curling. The cattle lowed and bellowed. In the sky the pale half-moon was slowly silvering. Alexandra and Carl walked together down the potato rows. "I have to keep telling myself what is going to happen," she said softly. "Since you have been here, ten years now, I have never really been lonely. But I can remember what it was like before. Now I shall have nobody but Emil. But he is my boy, and he is tender-hearted."

That night, when the boys were called to supper, they sat down moodily. They had worn their coats to town, but they ate in their striped shirts and suspenders. They were grown men now, and, as Alexandra said, for the last few years they had been growing more and more like themselves. Lou was still the slighter of the two, the quicker and more intelligent, but apt to go off at half-cock. He had a lively blue eye, a thin, fair skin (always burned red to the neckband of his shirt in summer), stiff, yellow hair that would not lie down on his head, and a bristly little yellow mustache, of which he was very proud. Oscar could not grow a mustache; his pale face was as bare as an egg, and his white eyebrows gave it an empty look. He was a man of powerful body and unusual endurance; the sort of man you could attach to a corn-sheller as you would an engine. He would turn it all day, without hurrying, without slowing down. But he was as indolent of mind as he was unsparing of his body. His love of routine amounted to a vice. He worked like an insect, always doing the same thing over in the same way, regardless of whether it was best or no. He felt that there was a sovereign virtue in mere bodily toil, and he rather liked to do things in the hardest way. If a field had once been in corn, he could n't bear to put it into wheat. He liked to begin his corn-planting at the same time every year, whether the season were backward or forward. He seemed to feel that by his own irreproachable regularity he would clear himself of blame and reprove the weather. When the wheat crop failed, he threshed the straw at a dead loss to demonstrate how little grain there was, and thus prove his case against Providence.

Lou, on the other hand, was fussy and flighty; always planned to get through two days' work in one, and often got only the least important things done. He liked to keep the place up, but he never got round to doing odd

jobs until he had to neglect more pressing work to attend to them. In the middle of the wheat harvest, when
the grain was over-ripe and every hand was needed, he
would stop to mend fences or to patch the harness; then
dash down to the field and overwork and be laid up in
bed for a week. The two boys balanced each other, and
they pulled well together. They had been good friends
since they were children. One seldom went anywhere,
even to town, without the other.

To-night, after they sat down to supper, Oscar kept
looking at Lou as if he expected him to say something,
and Lou blinked his eyes and frowned at his plate. It was
Alexandra herself who at last opened the discussion.

"The Linstrums," she said calmly, as she put another
plate of hot biscuit on the table, "are going back to St.
Louis. The old man is going to work in the cigar factory
again."

At this Lou plunged in. "You see, Alexandra, everybody who can crawl out is going away. There's no use of
us trying to stick it out, just to be stubborn. There's
something in knowing when to quit."

"Where do you want to go, Lou?"

"Any place where things will grow," said Oscar
grimly.

Lou reached for a potato. "Chris Arnson has traded
his half-section for a place down on the river."

"Who did he trade with?"

"Charley Fuller, in town."

"Fuller the real estate man? You see, Lou, that Fuller has a head on him. He's buying and trading for every bit of land he can get up here. It'll make him a rich man, some day."

"He's rich now, that's why he can take a chance."

"Why can't we? We'll live longer than he will. Some day the land itself will be worth more than all we can ever raise on it."

Lou laughed. "It could be worth that, and still not be worth much. Why, Alexandra, you don't know what you're talking about. Our place would n't bring now what it would six years ago. The fellows that settled up here just made a mistake. Now they're beginning to see this high land was n't never meant to grow nothing on, and everybody who ain't fixed to graze cattle is trying to crawl out. It's too high to farm up here. All the Americans are skinning out. That man Percy Adams, north of town, told me that he was going to let Fuller take his land and stuff for four hundred dollars and a ticket to Chicago."

"There's Fuller again!" Alexandra exclaimed. "I wish that man would take me for a partner. He's feathering his nest! If only poor people could learn a little from rich people! But all these fellows who are running off are bad farmers, like poor Mr. Linstrum. They could n't get ahead even in good years, and they all got into debt while father was getting out. I think we ought to hold on as long as we can on father's account. He was so set on keeping this land. He must have seen harder times than this, here. How was it in the early days, mother?"

Mrs. Bergson was weeping quietly. These family discussions always depressed her, and made her remember all that she had been torn away from. "I don't see why the boys are always taking on about going away," she said, wiping her eyes. "I don't want to move again; out to some raw place, maybe, where we'd be worse off than we are here, and all to do over again. I won't move! If the rest of you go, I will ask some of the neighbors to take me in, and stay and be buried by father. I'm not going to leave him by himself on the prairie, for cattle to run over." She began to cry more bitterly.

The boys looked angry. Alexandra put a soothing hand on her mother's shoulder. "There's no question of that, mother. You don't have to go if you don't want to. A third of the place belongs to you by American law, and we can't sell without your consent. We only want you to advise us. How did it use to be when you and father first came? Was it really as bad as this, or not?"

"Oh, worse! Much worse," moaned Mrs. Bergson. "Drouth, chinch-bugs, hail, everything! My garden all cut to pieces like *sauerkraut.* No grapes on the creek, no nothing. The people all lived just like coyotes."

Oscar got up and tramped out of the kitchen. Lou followed him. They felt that Alexandra had taken an unfair advantage in turning their mother loose on them. The next morning they were silent and reserved. They did not offer to take the women to church, but went down to the barn immediately after breakfast and stayed there all day. When Carl Linstrum came over in the afternoon, Alexandra winked to him and pointed toward the barn. He understood her and went down to play cards with the boys. They believed that a very wicked thing to do on Sunday, and it relieved their feelings.

Alexandra stayed in the house. On Sunday afternoon Mrs. Bergson always took a nap, and Alexandra read. During the week she read only the newspaper, but on Sunday, and in the long evenings of winter, she read a good deal; read a few things over a great many times. She knew long portions of the "Frithjof Saga" by heart, and, like most Swedes who read at all, she was fond of Longfellow's verse, — the ballads and the "Golden Legend" and "The Spanish Student." To-day she sat in the wooden rocking-chair with the Swedish Bible open on her knees, but she was not reading. She was looking thoughtfully away at the point where the upland road disappeared over the rim of the prairie. Her body was in an attitude of perfect repose, such as it was apt to take when she was thinking earnestly. Her mind was slow, truthful, steadfast. She had not the least spark of cleverness.

All afternoon the sitting-room was full of quiet and sunlight. Emil was making rabbit traps in the kitchen shed. The hens were clucking and scratching brown holes in the flower beds, and the wind was teasing the prince's feather by the door.

That evening Carl came in with the boys to supper.

"Emil," said Alexandra, when they were all seated at the table, "how would you like to go traveling? Because I am going to take a trip, and you can go with me if you want to."

The boys looked up in amazement; they were always afraid of Alexandra's schemes. Carl was interested.

"I've been thinking, boys," she went on, "that maybe I am too set against making a change. I'm going to take Brigham and the buckboard to-morrow and drive down to the river country and spend a few days looking over what they've got down there. If I find anything good, you boys can go down and make a trade."

"Nobody down there will trade for anything up here," said Oscar gloomily.

"That's just what I want to find out. Maybe they are just as discontented down there as we are up here. Things away from home often look better than they are. You know what your Hans Andersen book says, Carl, about the Swedes liking to buy Danish bread and the Danes liking to buy Swedish bread, because people always think the bread of another country is better than their own. Anyway, I've heard so much about the river farms, I won't be satisfied till I've seen for myself."

Lou fidgeted. "Look out! Don't agree to anything. Don't let them fool you."

Lou was apt to be fooled himself. He had not yet learned to keep away from the shell-game wagons that followed the circus.

After supper Lou put on a necktie and went across the fields to court Annie Lee, and Carl and Oscar sat down to a game of checkers, while Alexandra read "The Swiss Family Robinson" aloud to her mother and Emil. It was not long before the two boys at the table neglected their game to listen. They were all big children together, and they found the adventures of the family in the tree house so absorbing that they gave them their undivided attention.

V

ALEXANDRA and Emil spent five days down among the river farms, driving up and down the valley. Alexandra talked to the men about their crops and to the women about their poultry. She spent a whole day with one young farmer who had been away at school, and who was experimenting with a new kind of clover hay. She learned a great deal. As they drove along, she and Emil talked and planned. At last, on the sixth day, Alexandra turned Brigham's head northward and left the river behind.

"There's nothing in it for us down there, Emil. There are a few fine farms, but they are owned by the rich men in town, and could n't be bought. Most of the land is rough and hilly. They can always scrape along down there, but they can never do anything big. Down there they have a little certainty, but up with us there is a big chance. We must have faith in the high land, Emil. I want to hold on harder than ever, and when you're a man you'll thank me." She urged Brigham forward.

When the road began to climb the first long swells of the Divide, Alexandra hummed an old Swedish hymn, and Emil wondered why his sister looked so happy. Her face was so radiant that he felt shy about asking her. For the first time, perhaps, since that land emerged from the waters of geologic ages, a human face was set toward it with love and yearning. It seemed beautiful to her, rich and strong and glorious. Her eyes drank in the breadth of it, until her tears blinded her. Then the Genius of the Divide, the great, free spirit which breathes across it, must have bent lower than it ever bent to a human will before. The history of every country begins in the heart of a man or a woman.

Alexandra reached home in the afternoon. That evening she held a family council and told her brothers all that she had seen and heard.

"I want you boys to go down yourselves and look it over. Nothing will convince you like seeing with your own eyes. The river land was settled before this, and so they are a few years ahead of us, and have learned more about farming. The land sells for three times as much as this, but in five years we will double it. The rich men down there own all the best land, and they are buying all they can get. The thing to do is to sell our cattle and what little old corn we have, and buy the Linstrum place. Then the next thing to do is to take out two loans on our half-sections, and buy Peter Crow's place; raise every dollar we can, and buy every acre we can."

The Wild Land

"Mortgage the homestead again?" Lou cried. He sprang up and began to wind the clock furiously. "I won't slave to pay off another mortgage. I'll never do it. You'd just as soon kill us all, Alexandra, to carry out some scheme!"

Oscar rubbed his high, pale forehead. "How do you propose to pay off your mortgages?"

Alexandra looked from one to the other and bit her lip. They had never seen her so nervous. "See here," she brought out at last. "We borrow the money for six years. Well, with the money we buy a half-section from Linstrum and a half from Crow, and a quarter from Struble, maybe. That will give us upwards of fourteen hundred acres, won't it? You won't have to pay off your mortgages for six years. By that time, any of this land will be worth thirty dollars an acre — it will be worth fifty, but we'll say thirty; then you can sell a garden patch anywhere, and pay off a debt of sixteen hundred dollars. It's not the principal I'm worried about, it's the interest and taxes. We'll have to strain to meet the payments. But as sure as we are sitting here to-night, we can sit down here ten years from now independent landowners, not struggling farmers any longer. The chance that father was always looking for has come."

Lou was pacing the floor. "But how do you *know* that

65

land is going to go up enough to pay the mortgages and — ”

“And make us rich besides?” Alexandra put in firmly. “I can’t explain that, Lou. You’ll have to take my word for it. I *know*, that’s all. When you drive about over the country you can feel it coming.”

Oscar had been sitting with his head lowered, his hands hanging between his knees. “But we can’t work so much land,” he said dully, as if he were talking to himself. “We can’t even try. It would just lie there and we’d work ourselves to death.” He sighed, and laid his calloused fist on the table.

Alexandra’s eyes filled with tears. She put her hand on his shoulder. “You poor boy, you won’t have to work it. The men in town who are buying up other people’s land don’t try to farm it. They are the men to watch, in a new country. Let’s try to do like the shrewd ones, and not like these stupid fellows. I don’t want you boys always to have to work like this. I want you to be independent, and Emil to go to school.”

Lou held his head as if it were splitting. “Everybody will say we are crazy. It must be crazy, or everybody would be doing it.”

“If they were, we would n’t have much chance. No, Lou, I was talking about that with the smart young man who is raising the new kind of clover. He says the right thing is usually just what everybody don't do. Why are we better fixed than any of our neighbors? Because father had more brains. Our people were better people than these in the old country. We *ought* to do more than they do, and see further ahead. Yes, mother, I'm going to clear the table now."

Alexandra rose. The boys went to the stable to see to the stock, and they were gone a long while. When they came back Lou played on his *dragharmonika* and Oscar sat figuring at his father's secretary all evening. They said nothing more about Alexandra's project, but she felt sure now that they would consent to it. Just before bedtime Oscar went out for a pail of water. When he did not come back, Alexandra threw a shawl over her head and ran down the path to the windmill. She found him sitting there with his head in his hands, and she sat down beside him.

"Don't do anything you don't want to do, Oscar," she whispered. She waited a moment, but he did not stir. "I won't say any more about it, if you'd rather not. What makes you so discouraged?"

"I dread signing my name to them pieces of paper," he said slowly. "All the time I was a boy we had a mortgage hanging over us."

67

"Then don't sign one. I don't want you to, if you feel that way."

Oscar shook his head. "No, I can see there's a chance that way. I've thought a good while there might be. We're in so deep now, we might as well go deeper. But it's hard work pulling out of debt. Like pulling a threshing-machine out of the mud; breaks your back. Me and Lou's worked hard, and I can't see it's got us ahead much."

"Nobody knows about that as well as I do, Oscar. That's why I want to try an easier way. I don't want you to have to grub for every dollar."

"Yes, I know what you mean. Maybe it'll come out right. But signing papers is signing papers. There ain't no maybe about that." He took his pail and trudged up the path to the house.

Alexandra drew her shawl closer about her and stood leaning against the frame of the mill, looking at the stars which glittered so keenly through the frosty autumn air. She always loved to watch them, to think of their vastness and distance, and of their ordered march. It fortified her to reflect upon the great operations of nature, and when she thought of the law that lay behind them, she felt a sense of personal security. That night she had a new consciousness of the country, felt almost a new relation to it. Even her talk with the boys had not taken away the feeling that had overwhelmed her when she drove back to the Divide that afternoon. She had never known before how much the country meant to her. The chirping of the insects down in the long grass had been like the sweetest music. She had felt as if her heart were hiding down there, somewhere, with the quail and the plover and all the little wild things that crooned or buzzed in the sun. Under the long shaggy ridges, she felt the future stirring.

PART II

Neighboring Fields

PART II

Neighboring Fields

I

I⊤ is sixteen years since John Bergson died. His wife
now lies beside him, and the white shaft that marks
their graves gleams across the wheatfields. Could he
rise from beneath it, he would not know the country
under which he had been asleep. The shaggy coat of
the prairie, which they lifted to make him a bed, has
vanished forever. From the Norwegian graveyard one
looks out over a vast checker-board, marked off in
squares of wheat and corn; light and dark, dark and
light. Telephone wires hum along the white roads,
which always run at right angles. From the graveyard
gate one can count a dozen gayly painted farmhouses;
the gilded weather-vanes on the big red barns wink
at each other across the green and brown and yellow
fields. The light steel windmills tremble throughout
their frames and tug at their moorings, as they vibrate
in the wind that often blows from one week's end to

73

another across that high, active, resolute stretch of country.

The Divide is now thickly populated. The rich soil yields heavy harvests; the dry, bracing climate and the smoothness of the land make labor easy for men and beasts. There are few scenes more gratifying than a spring plowing in that country, where the furrows of a single field often lie a mile in length, and the brown earth, with such a strong, clean smell, and such a power of growth and fertility in it, yields itself eagerly to the plow; rolls away from the shear, not even dimming the brightness of the metal, with a soft, deep sigh of happiness. The wheat-cutting sometimes goes on all night as well as all day, and in good seasons there are scarcely men and horses enough to do the harvesting. The grain is so heavy that it bends toward the blade and cuts like velvet.

There is something frank and joyous and young in the open face of the country. It gives itself ungrudgingly to the moods of the season, holding nothing back. Like the plains of Lombardy, it seems to rise a little to meet the sun. The air and the earth are curiously mated and intermingled, as if the one were the breath of the other. You feel in the atmosphere the same tonic, puissant quality that is in the tilth, the same strength and reso-luteness.

Neighboring Fields

One June morning a young man stood at the gate of the Norwegian graveyard, sharpening his scythe in strokes unconsciously timed to the tune he was whistling. He wore a flannel cap and duck trousers, and the sleeves of his white flannel shirt were rolled back to the elbow. When he was satisfied with the edge of his blade, he slipped the whetstone into his hip pocket and began to swing his scythe, still whistling, but softly, out of respect to the quiet folk about him. Unconscious respect, probably, for he seemed intent upon his own thoughts, and, like the Gladiator's, they were far away. He was a splendid figure of a boy, tall and straight as a young pine tree, with a handsome head, and stormy gray eyes, deeply set under a serious brow. The space between his two front teeth, which were unusually far apart, gave him the proficiency in whistling for which he was distinguished at college. (He also played the cornet in the University band.)

When the grass required his close attention, or when he had to stoop to cut about a headstone, he paused in his lively air, — the "Jewel" song, — taking it up where he had left it when his scythe swung free again. He was not thinking about the tired pioneers over whom his blade glittered. The old wild country, the struggle in which his sister was destined to succeed while so

75

many men broke their hearts and died, he can scarcely remember. That is all among the dim things of childhood and has been forgotten in the brighter pattern life weaves to-day, in the bright facts of being captain of the track team, and holding the interstate record for the high jump, in the all-suffusing brightness of being twenty-one. Yet sometimes, in the pauses of his work, the young man frowned and looked at the ground with an intentness which suggested that even twenty-one might have its problems.

When he had been mowing the better part of an hour, he heard the rattle of a light cart on the road behind him. Supposing that it was his sister coming back from one of her farms, he kept on with his work. The cart stopped at the gate and a merry contralto voice called, "Almost through, Emil?" He dropped his scythe and went toward the fence, wiping his face and neck with his handkerchief. In the cart sat a young woman who wore driving gauntlets and a wide shade-hat, trimmed with red poppies. Her face, too, was rather like a poppy, round and brown, with rich color in her cheeks and lips, and her dancing yellow-brown eyes bubbled with gayety. The wind was flapping her big hat and teasing a curl of her chestnut-colored hair. She shook her head at the tall youth.

"What time did you get over here? That's not much of a job for an athlete. Here I've been to town and back. Alexandra lets you sleep late. Oh, I know! Lou's wife was telling me about the way she spoils you. I was going to give you a lift, if you were done." She gathered up her reins.

"But I will be, in a minute. Please wait for me, Marie," Emil coaxed. "Alexandra sent me to mow our lot, but I've done half a dozen others, you see. Just wait till I finish off the Kourdnas'. By the way, they were Bohemians. Why are n't they up in the Catholic graveyard?"

"Free-thinkers," replied the young woman laconically.

"Lots of the Bohemian boys at the University are," said Emil, taking up his scythe again. "What did you ever burn John Huss for, anyway? It's made an awful row. They still jaw about it in history classes."

"We'd do it right over again, most of us," said the young woman hotly. "Don't they ever teach you in your history classes that you'd all be heathen Turks if it had n't been for the Bohemians?"

Emil had fallen to mowing. "Oh, there's no denying you're a spunky little bunch, you Czechs," he called back over his shoulder.

Marie Shabata settled herself in her seat and watched

the rhythmical movement of the young man's long arms, swinging her foot as if in time to some air that was going through her mind. The minutes passed. Emil mowed vigorously and Marie sat sunning herself and watching the long grass fall. She sat with the ease that belongs to persons of an essentially happy nature, who can find a comfortable spot almost anywhere; who are supple, and quick in adapting themselves to circumstances. After a final swish, Emil snapped the gate and sprang into the cart, holding his scythe well out over the wheel. "There," he sighed. "I gave old man Lee a cut or so, too. Lou's wife need n't talk. I never see Lou's scythe over here."

Marie clucked to her horse. "Oh, you know Annie!" She looked at the young man's bare arms. "How brown you've got since you came home. I wish I had an athlete to mow my orchard. I get wet to my knees when I go down to pick cherries."

"You can have one, any time you want him. Better wait until after it rains." Emil squinted off at the horizon as if he were looking for clouds.

"Will you? Oh, there's a good boy!" She turned her head to him with a quick, bright smile. He felt it rather than saw it. Indeed, he had looked away with the purpose of not seeing it. "I've been up looking at

Angélique's wedding clothes," Marie went on, "and I'm
so excited I can hardly wait until Sunday. Amédée will
be a handsome bridegroom. Is anybody but you going
to stand up with him? Well, then it will be a handsome
wedding party." She made a droll face at Emil, who
flushed. "Frank," Marie continued, flicking her horse,
"is cranky at me because I loaned his saddle to Jan
Smirka, and I'm terribly afraid he won't take me to the
dance in the evening. Maybe the supper will tempt him.
All Angélique's folks are baking for it, and all Amédée's
twenty cousins. There will be barrels of beer. If once I
get Frank to the supper, I'll see that I stay for the dance.
And by the way, Emil, you must n't dance with me but
once or twice. You must dance with all the French girls.
It hurts their feelings if you don't. They think you're
proud because you've been away to school or something."

Emil sniffed. "How do you know they think that?"

"Well, you did n't dance with them much at Raoul
Marcel's party, and I could tell how they took it by the
way they looked at you — and at me."

"All right," said Emil shortly, studying the glittering
blade of his scythe.

They drove westward toward Norway Creek, and
toward a big white house that stood on a hill, several

miles across the fields. There were so many sheds and outbuildings grouped about it that the place looked not unlike a tiny village. A stranger, approaching it, could not help noticing the beauty and fruitfulness of the out-lying fields. There was something individual about the great farm, a most unusual trimness and care for detail. On either side of the road, for a mile before you reached the foot of the hill, stood tall osage orange hedges, their glossy green marking off the yellow fields. South of the hill, in a low, sheltered swale, surrounded by a mulberry hedge, was the orchard, its fruit trees knee-deep in tim-othy grass. Any one thereabouts would have told you that this was one of the richest farms on the Divide, and that the farmer was a woman, Alexandra Bergson.

If you go up the hill and enter Alexandra's big house, you will find that it is curiously unfinished and un-even in comfort. One room is papered, carpeted, over-furnished; the next is almost bare. The pleasantest rooms in the house are the kitchen — where Alexandra's three young Swedish girls chatter and cook and pickle and preserve all summer long — and the sitting-room, in which Alexandra has brought together the old homely furniture that the Bergsons used in their first log house, the family portraits, and the few things her mother brought from Sweden.

Neighboring Fields

When you go out of the house into the flower garden, there you feel again the order and fine arrangement manifest all over the great farm; in the fencing and hedging, in the windbreaks and sheds, in the symmetrical pasture ponds, planted with scrub willows to give shade to the cattle in fly-time. There is even a white row of beehives in the orchard, under the walnut trees. You feel that, properly, Alexandra's house is the big out-of-doors, and that it is in the soil that she expresses herself best.

E MIL reached home a little past noon, and when he went into the kitchen Alexandra was already seated at the head of the long table, having dinner with her men, as she always did unless there were visitors. He slipped into his empty place at his sister's right. The three pretty young Swedish girls who did Alexandra's housework were cutting pies, refilling coffee-cups, placing platters of bread and meat and potatoes upon the red tablecloth, and continually getting in each other's way between the table and the stove. To be sure they always wasted a good deal of time getting in each other's way and giggling at each other's mistakes. But, as Alexandra had pointedly told her sisters-in-law, it was to hear them giggle that she kept three young things in her kitchen; the work she could do herself, if it were necessary. These girls, with their long letters from home, their finery, and their love-affairs, afforded her a great deal of entertainment, and they were company for her when Emil was away at school.

Of the youngest girl, Signa, who has a pretty figure, mottled pink cheeks, and yellow hair, Alexandra is very fond, though she keeps a sharp eye upon her. Signa is apt to be skittish at mealtime, when the men are about, and to spill the coffee or upset the cream. It is supposed that Nelse Jensen, one of the six men at the dinner-table, is courting Signa, though he has been so careful not to commit himself that no one in the house, least of all Signa, can tell just how far the matter has progressed. Nelse watches her glumly as she waits upon the table, and in the evening he sits on a bench behind the stove with his *dragharmonika*, playing mournful airs and watching her as she goes about her work. When Alexandra asked Signa whether she thought Nelse was in earnest, the poor child hid her hands under her apron and murmured, "I don't know, ma'm. But he scolds me about everything, like as if he wanted to have me!"

At Alexandra's left sat a very old man, barefoot and wearing a long blue blouse, open at the neck. His shaggy head is scarcely whiter than it was sixteen years ago, but his little blue eyes have become pale and watery, and his ruddy face is withered, like an apple that has clung all winter to the tree. When Ivar lost his land through mismanagement a dozen years ago, Alexandra took him in, and he has been a member of her household ever since. He is too old to work in the fields, but he hitches and unhitches the work-teams and looks after the health of the stock. Sometimes of a winter evening Alexandra calls him into the sitting-room to read the Bible aloud to her, for he still reads very well. He dislikes human habitations, so Alexandra has fitted him up a room in the barn, where he is very comfortable, being near the horses and, as he says, further from temptations. No one has ever found out what his temptations are. In cold weather he sits by the kitchen fire and makes hammocks or mends harness until it is time to go to bed. Then he says his prayers at great length behind the stove, puts on his buffalo-skin coat and goes out to his room in the barn.

Alexandra herself has changed very little. Her figure is fuller, and she has more color. She seems sunnier and more vigorous than she did as a young girl. But she still has the same calmness and deliberation of manner, the same clear eyes, and she still wears her hair in two braids wound round her head. It is so curly that fiery ends escape from the braids and make her head look like one of the big double sunflowers that fringe her vegetable garden. Her face is always tanned in summer, for her sunbonnet is oftener on her arm than on her head. But where her collar falls away from her neck, or where her sleeves are pushed back from her wrist, the skin is of such smoothness and whiteness as none but Swedish women ever possess; skin with the freshness of the snow itself.

Alexandra did not talk much at the table, but she encouraged her men to talk, and she always listened attentively, even when they seemed to be talking foolishly.

To-day Barney Flinn, the big red-headed Irishman who had been with Alexandra for five years and who was actually her foreman, though he had no such title, was grumbling about the new silo she had put up that spring. It happened to be the first silo on the Divide, and Alexandra's neighbors and her men were skeptical about it. "To be sure, if the thing don't work, we'll have plenty of feed without it, indeed," Barney conceded.

Nelse Jensen, Signa's gloomy suitor, had his word. "Lou, he says he would n't have no silo on his place if you'd give it to him. He says the feed outen it gives the stock the bloat. He heard of somebody lost four head of horses, feedin' 'em that stuff."

Alexandra looked down the table from one to another. "Well, the only way we can find out is to try. Lou and I have different notions about feeding stock, and that's a good thing. It's bad if all the members of a family think alike. They never get anywhere. Lou can learn by my mistakes and I can learn by his. Is n't that fair, Barney?"

The Irishman laughed. He had no love for Lou, who was always uppish with him and who said that Alexandra paid her hands too much. "I've no thought but to give the thing an honest try, mum. 'T would be only right, after puttin' so much expense into it. Maybe Emil will come out an' have a look at it wid me." He pushed back his chair, took his hat from the nail, and marched out with Emil, who, with his university ideas, was supposed to have instigated the silo. The other hands followed them, all except old Ivar. He had been depressed throughout the meal and had paid no heed to the talk of the men, even when they mentioned cornstalk bloat, upon which he was sure to have opinions.

"Did you want to speak to me, Ivar?" Alexandra asked as she rose from the table. "Come into the sitting-room."

The old man followed Alexandra, but when she motioned him to a chair he shook his head. She took up her workbasket and waited for him to speak. He stood looking at the carpet, his bushy head bowed, his hands clasped in front of him. Ivar's bandy legs seemed to have grown shorter with years, and they were completely misfitted to his broad, thick body and heavy shoulders.

"Well, Ivar, what is it?" Alexandra asked after she had waited longer than usual.

Ivar had never learned to speak English and his Norwegian was quaint and grave, like the speech of the more old-fashioned people. He always addressed Alexandra in terms of the deepest respect, hoping to set a good example to the kitchen girls, whom he thought too familiar in their manners.

"Mistress," he began faintly, without raising his eyes, "the folk have been looking coldly at me of late. You know there has been talk."

"Talk about what, Ivar?"

"About sending me away; to the asylum."

Alexandra put down her sewing-basket. "Nobody has come to me with such talk," she said decidedly. "Why need you listen? You know I would never consent to such a thing."

Ivar lifted his shaggy head and looked at her out of his little eyes. "They say that you cannot prevent it if the folk complain of me, if your brothers complain to the authorities. They say that your brothers are afraid — God forbid! — that I may do you some injury when my spells are on me. Mistress, how can any one think that? — that I could bite the hand that fed me!" The tears trickled down on the old man's beard.

Alexandra frowned. "Ivar, I wonder at you, that you should come bothering me with such nonsense. I am still running my own house, and other people have nothing to do with either you or me. So long as I am suited with you, there is nothing to be said."

Ivar pulled a red handkerchief out of the breast of his blouse and wiped his eyes and beard. "But I should not wish you to keep me if, as they say, it is against your interests, and if it is hard for you to get hands because I am here."

Alexandra made an impatient gesture, but the old man put out his hand and went on earnestly: —

"Listen, mistress, it is right that you should take these things into account. You know that my spells come from God, and that I would not harm any living creature. You believe that every one should worship God in the way revealed to him. But that is not the way of this country. The way here is for all to do alike. I am despised because I do not wear shoes, because I do not cut my hair, and because I have visions. At home, in the old country, there were many like me, who had been touched by God, or who had seen things in the graveyard at night and were different afterward. We thought nothing of it, and let them alone. But here, if a man is different in his feet or in his head, they put him in the asylum. Look at Peter Kralik; when he was a boy, drinking out of a creek, he swallowed a snake, and always after that he could eat only such food as the creature liked, for when he ate anything else, it became enraged and gnawed him. When he felt it whipping about in him, he drank alcohol to stupefy it and get some ease for himself. He could work as good as any man, and his head was clear, but they locked him up for being different in his stomach. That is the way; they have built the asylum for people who are different, and they will not even let us live in the holes with the badgers. Only your great prosperity has protected me so far. If you had had ill-fortune, they would have taken me to Hastings long ago."

As Ivar talked, his gloom lifted. Alexandra had found that she could often break his fasts and long penances by talking to him and letting him pour out the thoughts that troubled him. Sympathy always cleared his mind, and ridicule was poison to him.

"There is a great deal in what you say, Ivar. Like as not they will be wanting to take me to Hastings because I have built a silo; and then I may take you with me. But at present I need you here. Only don't come to me again telling me what people say. Let people go on talking as they like, and we will go on living as we think best. You have been with me now for twelve years, and I have gone to you for advice oftener than I have ever gone to any one. That ought to satisfy you."

Ivar bowed humbly. "Yes, mistress, I shall not trouble you with their talk again. And as for my feet, I have observed your wishes all these years, though you have never questioned me; washing them every night, even in winter."

Alexandra laughed. "Oh, never mind about your feet, Ivar. We can remember when half our neighbors went barefoot in summer. I expect old Mrs. Lee would love to slip her shoes off now sometimes, if she dared. I'm glad I'm not Lou's mother-in-law."

Ivar looked about mysteriously and lowered his voice almost to a whisper. "You know what they have over at Lou's house? A great white tub, like the stone water-troughs in the old country, to wash themselves in. When you sent me over with the strawberries, they were all in town but the old woman Lee and the baby. She took me in and showed me the thing, and she told me it was impossible to wash yourself clean in it, because, in so much water, you could not make a strong suds. So when they fill it up and send her in there, she pretends, and makes a splashing noise. Then, when they are all asleep, she washes herself in a little wooden tub she keeps under her bed."

Alexandra shook with laughter. "Poor old Mrs. Lee! They won't let her wear nightcaps, either. Never mind;

when she comes to visit me, she can do all the old things in the old way, and have as much beer as she wants. We'll start an asylum for old-time people, Ivar."

Ivar folded his big handkerchief carefully and thrust it back into his blouse. "This is always the way, mistress. I come to you sorrowing, and you send me away with a light heart. And will you be so good as to tell the Irishman that he is not to work the brown gelding until the sore on its shoulder is healed?"

"That I will. Now go and put Emil's mare to the cart. I am going to drive up to the north quarter to meet the man from town who is to buy my alfalfa hay."

III

ALEXANDRA was to hear more of Ivar's case, however. On Sunday her married brothers came to dinner. She had asked them for that day because Emil, who hated family parties, would be absent, dancing at Amédée Chevalier's wedding, up in the French country. The table was set for company in the dining-room, where highly varnished wood and colored glass and useless pieces of china were conspicuous enough to satisfy the standards of the new prosperity. Alexandra had put herself into the hands of the Hanover furniture dealer, and he had conscientiously done his best to make her dining-room look like his display window. She said frankly that she knew nothing about such things, and she was willing to be governed by the general conviction that the more useless and utterly unusable objects were, the greater their virtue as ornament. That seemed reasonable enough. Since she liked plain things herself, it was all the more necessary to have jars and punchbowls and candlesticks in the company rooms for people who did appreciate them. Her guests liked to see about them these reassuring emblems of prosperity.

Neighboring Fields

The family party was complete except for Emil, and Oscar's wife who, in the country phrase, "was not going anywhere just now." Oscar sat at the foot of the table and his four tow-headed little boys, aged from twelve to five, were ranged at one side. Neither Oscar nor Lou has changed much; they have simply, as Alexandra said of them long ago, grown to be more and more like themselves. Lou now looks the older of the two; his face is thin and shrewd and wrinkled about the eyes, while Oscar's is thick and dull. For all his dullness, however, Oscar makes more money than his brother, which adds to Lou's sharpness and uneasiness and tempts him to make a show. The trouble with Lou is that he is tricky, and his neighbors have found out that, as Ivar says, he has not a fox's face for nothing. Politics being the natural field for such talents, he neglects his farm to attend conventions and to run for county offices.

Lou's wife, formerly Annie Lee, has grown to look curiously like her husband. Her face has become longer, sharper, more aggressive. She wears her yellow hair in a high pompadour, and is bedecked with rings and chains and "beauty pins." Her tight, high-heeled shoes give her an awkward walk, and she is always more or less preoccupied with her clothes. As she sat at the table, she kept telling her youngest daughter to "be careful now, and not drop anything on mother."

The conversation at the table was all in English. Oscar's wife, from the malaria district of Missouri, was ashamed of marrying a foreigner, and his boys do not understand a word of Swedish. Annie and Lou sometimes speak Swedish at home, but Annie is almost as much afraid of being "caught" at it as ever her mother was of being caught barefoot. Oscar still has a thick accent, but Lou speaks like anybody from Iowa.

"When I was in Hastings to attend the convention," he was saying, "I saw the superintendent of the asylum, and I was telling him about Ivar's symptoms. He says Ivar's case is one of the most dangerous kind, and it's a wonder he has n't done something violent before this."

Alexandra laughed good-humoredly. "Oh, nonsense, Lou! The doctors would have us all crazy if they could. Ivar's queer, certainly, but he has more sense than half the hands I hire."

Lou flew at his fried chicken. "Oh, I guess the doctor knows his business, Alexandra. He was very much surprised when I told him how you'd put up with Ivar. He says he's likely to set fire to the barn any night, or to take after you and the girls with an axe."

Little Signa, who was waiting on the table, giggled and fled to the kitchen. Alexandra's eyes twinkled. "That was too much for Signa, Lou. We all know that

Ivar's perfectly harmless. The girls would as soon expect me to chase them with an axe."

Lou flushed and signaled to his wife. "All the same, the neighbors will be having a say about it before long. He may burn anybody's barn. It's only necessary for one property-owner in the township to make complaint, and he'll be taken up by force. You'd better send him yourself and not have any hard feelings."

Alexandra helped one of her little nephews to gravy. "Well, Lou, if any of the neighbors try that, I'll have myself appointed Ivar's guardian and take the case to court, that's all. I am perfectly satisfied with him."

"Pass the preserves, Lou," said Annie in a warning tone. She had reasons for not wishing her husband to cross Alexandra too openly. "But don't you sort of hate to have people see him around here, Alexandra?" she went on with persuasive smoothness. "He *is* a disgraceful object, and you're fixed up so nice now. It sort of makes people distant with you, when they never know when they'll hear him scratching about. My girls are afraid as death of him, are n't you, Milly, dear?"

Milly was fifteen, fat and jolly and pompadoured, with a creamy complexion, square white teeth, and a short upper lip. She looked like her grandmother Bergson, and had her comfortable and comfort-loving nature. She grinned at her aunt, with whom she was a great deal more at ease than she was with her mother. Alexandra winked a reply.

"Milly need n't be afraid of Ivar. She's an especial favorite of his. In my opinion Ivar has just as much right to his own way of dressing and thinking as we have. But I'll see that he does n't bother other people. I'll keep him at home, so don't trouble any more about him, Lou. I've been wanting to ask you about your new bath-tub. How does it work?"

Annie came to the fore to give Lou time to recover himself. "Oh, it works something grand! I can't keep him out of it. He washes himself all over three times a week now, and uses all the hot water. I think it's weaken-ing to stay in as long as he does. You ought to have one, Alexandra."

"I'm thinking of it. I might have one put in the barn for Ivar, if it will ease people's minds. But before I get a bathtub, I'm going to get a piano for Milly."

Oscar, at the end of the table, looked up from his plate. "What does Milly want of a pianny? What's the matter with her organ? She can make some use of that, and play in church."

Annie looked flustered. She had begged Alexandra not to say anything about this plan before Oscar, who was apt to be jealous of what his sister did for Lou's children. Alexandra did not get on with Oscar's wife at all. "Milly can play in church just the same, and she'll still play on the organ. But practising on it so much spoils her touch. Her teacher says so," Annie brought out with spirit.

Oscar rolled his eyes. "Well, Milly must have got on pretty good if she's got past the organ. I know plenty of grown folks that ain't," he said bluntly.

Annie threw up her chin. "She has got on good, and she's going to play for her commencement when she graduates in town next year."

"Yes," said Alexandra firmly, "I think Milly deserves a piano. All the girls around here have been taking lessons for years, but Milly is the only one of them who can ever play anything when you ask her. I'll tell you when I first thought I would like to give you a piano, Milly, and that was when you learned that book of old Swedish songs that your grandfather used to sing. He had a sweet tenor voice, and when he was a young man he loved to sing. I can remember hearing him singing with the sailors down in the shipyard, when I was no bigger than Stella here," pointing to Annie's younger daughter.

Milly and Stella both looked through the door into

the sitting-room, where a crayon portrait of John Bergson hung on the wall. Alexandra had had it made from a little photograph, taken for his friends just before he left Sweden; a slender man of thirty-five, with soft hair curling about his high forehead, a drooping mustache, and wondering, sad eyes that looked forward into the distance, as if they already beheld the New World.

After dinner Lou and Oscar went to the orchard to pick cherries — they had neither of them had the patience to grow an orchard of their own — and Annie went down to gossip with Alexandra's kitchen girls while they washed the dishes. She could always find out more about Alexandra's domestic economy from the prattling maids than from Alexandra herself, and what she discovered she used to her own advantage with Lou. On the Divide, farmers' daughters no longer went out into service, so Alexandra got her girls from Sweden, by paying their fare over. They stayed with her until they married, and were replaced by sisters or cousins from the old country.

Alexandra took her three nieces into the flower garden. She was fond of the little girls, especially of Milly, who came to spend a week with her aunt now and then, and read aloud to her from the old books about the house, or listened to stories about the early days on the Divide. While they were walking among the flower beds, a buggy drove up the hill and stopped in front of the gate. A man got out and stood talking to the driver. The little girls were delighted at the advent of a stranger, some one from very far away, they knew by his clothes, his gloves, and the sharp, pointed cut of his dark beard. The girls fell behind their aunt and peeped out at him from among the castor beans. The stranger came up to the gate and stood holding his hat in his hand, smiling, while Alexandra advanced slowly to meet him. As she approached he spoke in a low, pleasant voice.

"Don't you know me, Alexandra? I would have known you, anywhere."

Alexandra shaded her eyes with her hand. Suddenly she took a quick step forward. "Can it be!" she exclaimed with feeling; "can it be that it is Carl Linstrum? Why, Carl, it is!" She threw out both her hands and caught his across the gate. "Sadie, Milly, run tell your father and Uncle Oscar that our old friend Carl Linstrum is here. Be quick! Why, Carl, how did it happen? I can't believe this!" Alexandra shook the tears from her eyes and laughed.

The stranger nodded to his driver, dropped his suitcase inside the fence, and opened the gate. "Then you are glad to see me, and you can put me up overnight? I could n't go through this country without stopping off to have a look at you. How little you have changed! Do you know, I was sure it would be like that. You simply could n't be different. How fine you are!" He stepped back and looked at her admiringly.

Alexandra blushed and laughed again. "But you yourself, Carl — with that beard — how could I have known you? You went away a little boy." She reached for his suitcase and when he intercepted her she threw up her hands. "You see, I give myself away. I have only women come to visit me, and I do not know how to behave. Where is your trunk?"

"It's in Hanover. I can stay only a few days. I am on my way to the coast."

They started up the path. "A few days? After all these years!" Alexandra shook her finger at him. "See this, you have walked into a trap. You do not get away so easy." She put her hand affectionately on his shoulder. "You owe me a visit for the sake of old times. Why must you go to the coast at all?"

"Oh, I must! I am a fortune hunter. From Seattle I go on to Alaska."

"Alaska?" She looked at him in astonishment. "Are you going to paint the Indians?"

"Paint?" the young man frowned. "Oh! I'm not a painter, Alexandra. I'm an engraver. I have nothing to do with painting."

"But on my parlor wall I have the paintings — "

He interrupted nervously. "Oh, water-color sketches — done for amusement. I sent them to remind you of me, not because they were good. What a wonderful place you have made of this, Alexandra." He turned and looked back at the wide, map-like prospect of field and hedge and pasture. "I would never have believed it could be done. I'm disappointed in my own eye, in my imagination."

At this moment Lou and Oscar came up the hill from the orchard. They did not quicken their pace when they saw Carl; indeed, they did not openly look in his direction. They advanced distrustfully, and as if they wished the distance were longer.

Alexandra beckoned to them. "They think I am trying to fool them. Come, boys, it's Carl Linstrum, our old Carl!"

Lou gave the visitor a quick, sidelong glance and thrust out his hand. "Glad to see you." Oscar followed with "How d' do." Carl could not tell whether their offishness came from unfriendliness or from embarrassment. He and Alexandra led the way to the porch.

"Carl," Alexandra explained, "is on his way to Seattle. He is going to Alaska."

Oscar studied the visitor's yellow shoes. "Got business there?" he asked.

Carl laughed. "Yes, very pressing business. I'm going there to get rich. Engraving's a very interesting profession, but a man never makes any money at it. So I'm going to try the gold-fields."

Alexandra felt that this was a tactful speech, and Lou looked up with some interest. "Ever done anything in that line before?"

"No, but I'm going to join a friend of mine who went out from New York and has done well. He has offered to break me in."

"Turrible cold winters, there, I hear," remarked Oscar. "I thought people went up there in the spring."

"They do. But my friend is going to spend the winter in Seattle and I am to stay with him there and learn something about prospecting before we start north next year."

Lou looked skeptical. "Let's see, how long have you been away from here?"

"Sixteen years. You ought to remember that, Lou, for you were married just after we went away."

"Going to stay with us some time?" Oscar asked.

"A few days, if Alexandra can keep me."

"I expect you'll be wanting to see your old place," Lou observed more cordially. "You won't hardly know it. But there's a few chunks of your old sod house left. Alexandra would n't never let Frank Shabata plough over it."

Annie Lee, who, ever since the visitor was announced, had been touching up her hair and settling her lace and wishing she had worn another dress, now emerged with her three daughters and introduced them. She was greatly impressed by Carl's urban appearance, and in her excitement talked very loud and threw her head about. "And you ain't married yet? At your age, now! Think of that! You'll have to wait for Milly. Yes, we've got a boy, too. The youngest. He's at home with his grandma. You must come over to see mother and hear Milly play. She's the musician of the family. She does pyrography, too. That's burnt wood, you know. You would n't believe what she can do with her poker. Yes, she goes to school in town, and she is the youngest in her class by two years."

Milly looked uncomfortable and Carl took her hand again. He liked her creamy skin and happy, innocent eyes, and he could see that her mother's way of talking distressed her. "I'm sure she's a clever little girl," he

murmured, looking at her thoughtfully. "Let me see —
Ah, it's your mother that she looks like, Alexandra. Mrs.
Bergson must have looked just like this when she was a
little girl. Does Milly run about over the country as you
and Alexandra used to, Annie?"

Milly's mother protested. "Oh, my, no! Things has
changed since we was girls. Milly has it very different.
We are going to rent the place and move into town as
soon as the girls are old enough to go out into company.
A good many are doing that here now. Lou is going into
business."

Lou grinned. "That's what she says. You better go get
your things on. Ivar's hitching up," he added, turning to
Annie.

Young farmers seldom address their wives by name.
It is always "you," or "she."

Having got his wife out of the way, Lou sat down on
the step and began to whittle. "Well, what do folks
in New York think of William Jennings Bryan?" Lou
began to bluster, as he always did when he talked politics. "We gave Wall Street a scare in ninety-six, all right,
and we're fixing another to hand them. Silver was n't
the only issue," he nodded mysteriously. "There's a
good many things got to be changed. The West is going
to make itself heard."

Carl laughed. "But, surely, it did do that, if nothing else."

Lou's thin face reddened up to the roots of his bristly hair. "Oh, we've only begun. We're waking up to a sense of our responsibilities, out here, and we ain't afraid, neither. You fellows back there must be a tame lot. If you had any nerve you'd get together and march down to Wall Street and blow it up. Dynamite it, I mean," with a threatening nod.

He was so much in earnest that Carl scarcely knew how to answer him. "That would be a waste of powder. The same business would go on in another street. The street does n't matter. But what have you fellows out here got to kick about? You have the only safe place there is. Morgan himself could n't touch you. One only has to drive through this country to see that you're all as rich as barons."

"We have a good deal more to say than we had when we were poor," said Lou threateningly. "We're getting on to a whole lot of things."

As Ivar drove a double carriage up to the gate, Annie came out in a hat that looked like the model of a battle-ship. Carl rose and took her down to the carriage, while Lou lingered for a word with his sister.

"What do you suppose he's come for?" he asked, jerking his head toward the gate.

"Why, to pay us a visit. I've been begging him to for years."

Oscar looked at Alexandra. "He did n't let you know he was coming?"

"No. Why should he? I told him to come at any time."

Lou shrugged his shoulders. "He does n't seem to have done much for himself. Wandering around this way!"

Oscar spoke solemnly, as from the depths of a cavern. "He never was much account."

Alexandra left them and hurried down to the gate where Annie was rattling on to Carl about her new dining-room furniture. "You must bring Mr. Linstrum over real soon, only be sure to telephone me first," she called back, as Carl helped her into the carriage. Old Ivar, his white head bare, stood holding the horses. Lou came down the path and climbed into the front seat, took up the reins, and drove off without saying anything further to any one. Oscar picked up his youngest boy and trudged off down the road, the other three trotting after him. Carl, holding the gate open for Alexandra, began to laugh. "Up and coming on the Divide, eh, Alexandra?" he cried gayly.

IV

CARL had changed, Alexandra felt, much less than one might have expected. He had not become a trim, self-satisfied city man. There was still something homely and wayward and definitely personal about him. Even his clothes, his Norfolk coat and his very high collars, were a little unconventional. He seemed to shrink into himself as he used to do; to hold himself away from things, as if he were afraid of being hurt. In short, he was more self-conscious than a man of thirty-five is expected to be. He looked older than his years and not very strong. His black hair, which still hung in a triangle over his pale forehead, was thin at the crown, and there were fine, relentless lines about his eyes. His back, with its high, sharp shoulders, looked like the back of an overworked German professor off on his holiday. His face was intelligent, sensitive, unhappy.

That evening after supper, Carl and Alexandra were sitting by the clump of castor beans in the middle of the flower garden. The gravel paths glittered in the moonlight, and below them the fields lay white and still.

"Do you know, Alexandra," he was saying, "I've been

107

thinking how strangely things work out. I've been away engraving other men's pictures, and you've stayed at home and made your own." He pointed with his cigar toward the sleeping landscape. "How in the world have you done it? How have your neighbors done it?"

"We had n't any of us much to do with it, Carl. The land did it. It had its little joke. It pretended to be poor because nobody knew how to work it right; and then, all at once, it worked itself. It woke up out of its sleep and stretched itself, and it was so big, so rich, that we suddenly found we were rich, just from sitting still. As for me, you remember when I began to buy land. For years after that I was always squeezing and borrowing until I was ashamed to show my face in the banks. And then, all at once, men began to come to me offering to lend me money — and I did n't need it! Then I went ahead and built this house. I really built it for Emil. I want you to see Emil, Carl. He is so different from the rest of us!"

"How different?"

"Oh, you'll see! I'm sure it was to have sons like Emil, and to give them a chance, that father left the old country. It's curious, too; on the outside Emil is just like an American boy, — he graduated from the State University in June, you know, — but underneath he is more Swedish than any of us. Sometimes he is so like father that he frightens me; he is so violent in his feelings like that."

"Is he going to farm here with you?"

"He shall do whatever he wants to," Alexandra declared warmly. "He is going to have a chance, a whole chance; that's what I've worked for. Sometimes he talks about studying law, and sometimes, just lately, he's been talking about going out into the sand hills and taking up more land. He has his sad times, like father. But I hope he won't do that. We have land enough, at last!" Alexandra laughed.

"How about Lou and Oscar? They've done well, have n't they?"

"Yes, very well; but they are different, and now that they have farms of their own I do not see so much of them. We divided the land equally when Lou married. They have their own way of doing things, and they do not altogether like my way, I am afraid. Perhaps they think me too independent. But I have had to think for myself a good many years and am not likely to change. On the whole, though, we take as much comfort in each other as most brothers and sisters do. And I am very fond of Lou's oldest daughter."

"I think I liked the old Lou and Oscar better, and they probably feel the same about me. I even, if you can keep a secret," — Carl leaned forward and touched her arm, smiling, — "I even think I liked the old country better. This is all very splendid in its way, but there was something about this country when it was a wild old beast that has haunted me all these years. Now, when I come back to all this milk and honey, I feel like the old German song, '*Wo bist du, wo bist du, mein geliebtest Land?*' — Do you ever feel like that, I wonder?"

"Yes, sometimes, when I think about father and mother and those who are gone; so many of our old neighbors." Alexandra paused and looked up thoughtfully at the stars. "We can remember the graveyard when it was wild prairie, Carl, and now — "

"And now the old story has begun to write itself over there," said Carl softly. "Is n't it queer: there are only two or three human stories, and they go on repeating themselves as fiercely as if they had never happened before; like the larks in this country, that have been singing the same five notes over for thousands of years."

"Oh, yes! The young people, they live so hard. And yet I sometimes envy them. There is my little neighbor, now; the people who bought your old place. I would n't have sold it to any one else, but I was always fond of that girl. You must remember her, little Marie Tovesky, from Omaha, who used to visit here? When she was eighteen she ran away from the convent school and got married, crazy child! She came out here a bride, with her father and husband. He had nothing, and the old man was willing to buy them a place and set them up. Your farm took her fancy, and I was glad to have her so near me. I've never been sorry, either. I even try to get along with Frank on her account."

"Is Frank her husband?"

"Yes. He's one of these wild fellows. Most Bohemians are good-natured, but Frank thinks we don't appreciate him here, I guess. He's jealous about everything, his farm and his horses and his pretty wife. Everybody likes her, just the same as when she was little. Sometimes I go up to the Catholic church with Emil, and it's funny to see Marie standing there laughing and shaking hands with people, looking so excited and gay, with Frank sulking behind her as if he could eat everybody alive. Frank's not a bad neighbor, but to get on with him you've got to make a fuss over him and act as if you thought he was a very important person all the time, and different from other people. I find it hard to keep that up from one year's end to another."

"I should n't think you'd be very successful at that kind of thing, Alexandra." Carl seemed to find the idea amusing.

"Well," said Alexandra firmly, "I do the best I can, on Marie's account. She has it hard enough, anyway. She's too young and pretty for this sort of life. We're all ever so much older and slower. But she's the kind that won't be downed easily. She'll work all day and go to a Bohemian wedding and dance all night, and drive the hay wagon for a cross man next morning. I could stay by a job, but I never had the go in me that she has, when I was going my best. I'll have to take you over to see her to-morrow."

Carl dropped the end of his cigar softly among the castor beans and sighed. "Yes, I suppose I must see the old place. I'm cowardly about things that remind me of myself. It took courage to come at all, Alexandra. I would n't have, if I had n't wanted to see you very, very much."

Alexandra looked at him with her calm, deliberate eyes. "Why do you dread things like that, Carl?" she asked earnestly. "Why are you dissatisfied with yourself?"

Her visitor winced. "How direct you are, Alexandra! Just like you used to be. Do I give myself away so quickly? Well, you see, for one thing, there's nothing to look forward to in my profession. Wood-engraving is the only thing I care about, and that had gone out before I began. Everything's cheap metal work nowadays, touching up miserable photographs, forcing up poor drawings, and spoiling good ones. I'm absolutely sick of it all." Carl frowned. "Alexandra, all the way out from New York I've been planning how I could deceive you and make you think me a very enviable fellow, and here I am telling you the truth the first night. I waste a lot of time pretending to people, and the joke of it is, I don't think I ever deceive any one. There are too many of my kind; people know us on sight."

Carl paused. Alexandra pushed her hair back from her brow with a puzzled, thoughtful gesture. "You see," he went on calmly, "measured by your standards here, I'm a failure. I couldn't buy even one of your cornfields. I've enjoyed a great many things, but I've got nothing to show for it all."

"But you show for it yourself, Carl. I'd rather have had your freedom than my land."

Carl shook his head mournfully. "Freedom so often means that one isn't needed anywhere. Here you are an individual, you have a background of your own, you would be missed. But off there in the cities there are thousands of rolling stones like me. We are all alike; we have no ties, we know nobody, we own nothing. When one of us dies, they scarcely know where to bury him. Our landlady and the delicatessen man are our mourners, and we leave nothing behind us but a frock-coat and a fiddle, or an easel, or a typewriter, or whatever tool we got our living by. All we have ever managed to do is to pay our rent, the exorbitant rent that one has to pay for a few square feet of space near the heart of things. We have no house, no place, no people of our own. We live in the streets, in the parks, in the theatres. We sit in restaurants and concert halls and look about at the hundreds of our own kind and shudder."

Alexandra was silent. She sat looking at the silver spot the moon made on the surface of the pond down in the pasture. He knew that she understood what he meant. At last she said slowly, "And yet I would rather have Emil grow up like that than like his two brothers. We pay a high rent, too, though we pay differently. We grow hard and heavy here. We don't move lightly and easily as you do, and our minds get stiff. If the world were no wider than my cornfields, if there were not something beside this, I would n't feel that it was much worth while to work. No, I would rather have Emil like you than like them. I felt that as soon as you came."

"I wonder why you feel like that?" Carl mused.

"I don't know. Perhaps I am like Carrie Jensen, the

sister of one of my hired men. She had never been out of the cornfields, and a few years ago she got despondent and said life was just the same thing over and over, and she did n't see the use of it. After she had tried to kill herself once or twice, her folks got worried and sent her over to Iowa to visit some relations. Ever since she's come back she's been perfectly cheerful, and she says she's contented to live and work in a world that's so big and interesting. She said that anything as big as the bridges over the Platte and the Missouri reconciled her. And it's what goes on in the world that reconciles me."

V

ALEXANDRA did not find time to go to her neighbor's the next day, nor the next. It was a busy season on the farm, with the corn-plowing going on, and even Emil was in the field with a team and cultivator. Carl went about over the farms with Alexandra in the morning, and in the afternoon and evening they found a great deal to talk about. Emil, for all his track practice, did not stand up under farmwork very well, and by night he was too tired to talk or even to practise on his cornet.

On Wednesday morning Carl got up before it was light, and stole downstairs and out of the kitchen door just as old Ivar was making his morning ablutions at the pump. Carl nodded to him and hurried up the draw, past the garden, and into the pasture where the milking cows used to be kept.

The dawn in the east looked like the light from some great fire that was burning under the edge of the world. The color was reflected in the globules of dew that sheathed the short gray pasture grass. Carl walked rapidly until he came to the crest of the second hill, where the Bergson pasture joined the one that had belonged to his father. There he sat down and waited for the sun to rise. It was just there that he and Alexandra used to do their milking together, he on his side of the fence, she on hers. He could remember exactly how she looked when she came over the close-cropped grass, her skirts pinned up, her head bare, a bright tin pail in either hand, and the milky light of the early morning all about her. Even as a boy he used to feel, when he saw her coming with her free step, her upright head and calm shoulders, that she looked as if she had walked straight out of the morning itself. Since then, when he had happened to see the sun come up in the country or on the water, he had often remembered the young Swedish girl and her milking pails.

Carl sat musing until the sun leaped above the prairie, and in the grass about him all the small creatures of day began to tune their tiny instruments. Birds and insects without number began to chirp, to twitter, to snap and whistle, to make all manner of fresh shrill noises. The pasture was flooded with light; every clump of ironweed and snow-on-the-mountain threw a long shadow, and the golden light seemed to be rippling through the curly grass like the tide racing in.

He crossed the fence into the pasture that was now

the Shabatas' and continued his walk toward the pond. He had not gone far, however, when he discovered that he was not the only person abroad. In the draw below, his gun in his hands, was Emil, advancing cautiously, with a young woman beside him. They were moving softly, keeping close together, and Carl knew that they expected to find ducks on the pond. At the moment when they came in sight of the bright spot of water, he heard a whirr of wings and the ducks shot up into the air. There was a sharp crack from the gun, and five of the birds fell to the ground. Emil and his companion laughed delightedly, and Emil ran to pick them up. When he came back, dangling the ducks by their feet, Marie held her apron and he dropped them into it. As she stood looking down at them, her face changed. She took up one of the birds, a rumpled ball of feathers with the blood dripping slowly from its mouth, and looked at the live color that still burned on its plumage.

As she let it fall, she cried in distress, "Oh, Emil, why did you?"

"I like that!" the boy exclaimed indignantly. "Why, Marie, you asked me to come yourself."

"Yes, yes, I know," she said tearfully, "but I did n't think. I hate to see them when they are first shot. They were having such a good time, and we've spoiled it all for them."

Emil gave a rather sore laugh. "I should say we had! I'm not going hunting with you any more. You're as bad as Ivar. Here, let me take them." He snatched the ducks out of her apron.

"Don't be cross, Emil. Only — Ivar's right about wild things. They're too happy to kill. You can tell just how they felt when they flew up. They were scared, but they did n't really think anything could hurt them. No, we won't do that any more."

"All right," Emil assented. "I'm sorry I made you feel bad." As he looked down into her tearful eyes, there was a curious, sharp young bitterness in his own.

Carl watched them as they moved slowly down the draw. They had not seen him at all. He had not overheard much of their dialogue, but he felt the import of it. It made him, somehow, unreasonably mournful to find two young things abroad in the pasture in the early morning. He decided that he needed his breakfast.

VI

A T dinner that day Alexandra said she thought they must really manage to go over to the Shabatas' that afternoon. "It's not often I let three days go by without seeing Marie. She will think I have forsaken her, now that my old friend has come back."

After the men had gone back to work, Alexandra put on a white dress and her sun-hat, and she and Carl set forth across the fields. "You see we have kept up the old path, Carl. It has been so nice for me to feel that there was a friend at the other end of it again."

Carl smiled a little ruefully. "All the same, I hope it has n't been *quite* the same."

Alexandra looked at him with surprise. "Why, no, of course not. Not the same. She could not very well take your place, if that's what you mean. I'm friendly with all my neighbors, I hope. But Marie is really a companion, some one I can talk to quite frankly. You would n't want me to be more lonely than I have been, would you?"

Carl laughed and pushed back the triangular lock of hair with the edge of his hat. "Of course I don't. I ought to be thankful that this path has n't been worn by —

well, by friends with more pressing errands than your little Bohemian is likely to have." He paused to give Alexandra his hand as she stepped over the stile. "Are you the least bit disappointed in our coming together again?" he asked abruptly. "Is it the way you hoped it would be?"

Alexandra smiled at this. "Only better. When I've thought about your coming, I've sometimes been a little afraid of it. You have lived where things move so fast, and everything is slow here; the people slowest of all. Our lives are like the years, all made up of weather and crops and cows. How you hated cows!" She shook her head and laughed to herself.

"I did n't when we milked together. I walked up to the pasture corners this morning. I wonder whether I shall ever be able to tell you all that I was thinking about up there. It's a strange thing, Alexandra; I find it easy to be frank with you about everything under the sun except — yourself!"

"You are afraid of hurting my feelings, perhaps." Alexandra looked at him thoughtfully.

"No, I'm afraid of giving you a shock. You've seen yourself for so long in the dull minds of the people about you, that if I were to tell you how you seem to me, it would startle you. But you must see that you astonish me. You must feel when people admire you."

Alexandra blushed and laughed with some confusion. "I felt that you were pleased with me, if you mean that."

"And you've felt when other people were pleased with you?" he insisted.

"Well, sometimes. The men in town, at the banks and the county offices, seem glad to see me. I think, myself, it is more pleasant to do business with people who are clean and healthy-looking," she admitted blandly.

Carl gave a little chuckle as he opened the Shabatas' gate for her. "Oh, do you?" he asked dryly.

There was no sign of life about the Shabatas' house except a big yellow cat, sunning itself on the kitchen doorstep.

Alexandra took the path that led to the orchard. "She often sits there and sews. I did n't telephone her we were coming, because I did n't want her to go to work and bake cake and freeze ice-cream. She'll always make a party if you give her the least excuse. Do you recognize the apple trees, Carl?"

Linstrum looked about him. "I wish I had a dollar for every bucket of water I've carried for those trees. Poor father, he was an easy man, but he was perfectly merciless when it came to watering the orchard."

"That's one thing I like about Germans; they make

an orchard grow if they can't make anything else. I'm so glad these trees belong to some one who takes comfort in them. When I rented this place, the tenants never kept the orchard up, and Emil and I used to come over and take care of it ourselves. It needs mowing now. There she is, down in the corner. Maria-a-a!" she called.

A recumbent figure started up from the grass and came running toward them through the flickering screen of light and shade.

"Look at her! Is n't she like a little brown rabbit?" Alexandra laughed.

Marie ran up panting and threw her arms about Alexandra. "Oh, I had begun to think you were not coming at all, maybe. I knew you were so busy. Yes, Emil told me about Mr. Linstrum being here. Won't you come up to the house?"

"Why not sit down there in your corner? Carl wants to see the orchard. He kept all these trees alive for years, watering them with his own back."

Marie turned to Carl. "Then I'm thankful to you, Mr. Linstrum. We'd never have bought the place if it had n't been for this orchard, and then I would n't have had Alexandra, either." She gave Alexandra's arm a little squeeze as she walked beside her. "How nice your dress smells, Alexandra; you put rosemary leaves in your chest, like I told you."

She led them to the northwest corner of the orchard, sheltered on one side by a thick mulberry hedge and bordered on the other by a wheatfield, just beginning to yellow. In this corner the ground dipped a little, and the bluegrass, which the weeds had driven out in the upper part of the orchard, grew thick and luxuriant. Wild roses were flaming in the tufts of bunchgrass along the fence. Under a white mulberry tree there was an old wagon-seat. Beside it lay a book and a work-basket.

"You must have the seat, Alexandra. The grass would stain your dress," the hostess insisted. She dropped down on the ground at Alexandra's side and tucked her feet under her. Carl sat at a little distance from the two women, his back to the wheatfield, and watched them. Alexandra took off her shade-hat and threw it on the ground. Marie picked it up and played with the white ribbons, twisting them about her brown fingers as she talked. They made a pretty picture in the strong sunlight, the leafy pattern surrounding them like a net; the Swedish woman so white and gold, kindly and amused, but armored in calm, and the alert brown one, her full lips parted, points of yellow light dancing in her eyes as she laughed and chattered. Carl had never forgotten little Marie Tovesky's eyes, and he was glad to have an opportunity to study them. The brown iris, he found, was curiously slashed with yellow, the color of sunflower honey, or of old amber. In each eye one of these streaks must have been larger than the others, for the effect was that of two dancing points of light, two little yellow bubbles, such as rise in a glass of champagne. Sometimes they seemed like the sparks from a forge. She seemed so easily excited, to kindle with a fierce little flame if one but breathed upon her. "What a waste," Carl reflected. "She ought to be doing all that for a sweetheart. How awkwardly things come about!"

It was not very long before Marie sprang up out of the grass again. "Wait a moment. I want to show you something." She ran away and disappeared behind the low-growing apple trees.

"What a charming creature," Carl murmured. "I don't wonder that her husband is jealous. But can't she walk? does she always run?"

Alexandra nodded. "Always. I don't see many people, but I don't believe there are many like her, anywhere."

Marie came back with a branch she had broken from an apricot tree, laden with pale-yellow, pink-cheeked fruit. She dropped it beside Carl. "Did you plant those, too? They are such beautiful little trees."

125

Carl fingered the blue-green leaves, porous like blotting-paper and shaped like birch leaves, hung on waxen red stems. "Yes, I think I did. Are these the circus trees, Alexandra?"

"Shall I tell her about them?" Alexandra asked. "Sit down like a good girl, Marie, and don't ruin my poor hat, and I'll tell you a story. A long time ago, when Carl and I were, say, sixteen and twelve, a circus came to Hanover and we went to town in our wagon, with Lou and Oscar, to see the parade. We had n't money enough to go to the circus. We followed the parade out to the circus grounds and hung around until the show began and the crowd went inside the tent. Then Lou was afraid we looked foolish standing outside in the pasture, so we went back to Hanover feeling very sad. There was a man in the streets selling apricots, and we had never seen any before. He had driven down from somewhere up in the French country, and he was selling them twenty-five cents a peck. We had a little money our fathers had given us for candy, and I bought two pecks and Carl bought one. They cheered us a good deal, and we saved all the seeds and planted them. Up to the time Carl went away, they had n't borne at all."

"And now he's come back to eat them," cried Marie, nodding at Carl. "That *is* a good story. I can remember you a little, Mr. Linstrum. I used to see you in Hanover sometimes, when Uncle Joe took me to town. I remember you because you were always buying pencils and tubes of paint at the drug store. Once, when my uncle left me at the store, you drew a lot of little birds and flowers for me on a piece of wrapping-paper. I kept them for a long while. I thought you were very romantic because you could draw and had such black eyes."

Carl smiled. "Yes, I remember that time. Your uncle bought you some kind of a mechanical toy, a Turkish lady sitting on an ottoman and smoking a hookah, was n't it? And she turned her head backwards and forwards."

"Oh, yes! Was n't she splendid! I knew well enough I ought not to tell Uncle Joe I wanted it, for he had just come back from the saloon and was feeling good. You remember how he laughed? She tickled him, too. But when we got home, my aunt scolded him for buying toys when she needed so many things. We wound our lady up every night, and when she began to move her head my aunt used to laugh as hard as any of us. It was a music-box, you know, and the Turkish lady played a tune while she smoked. That was how she made you feel so jolly. As I remember her, she was lovely, and had a gold crescent on her turban."

Half an hour later, as they were leaving the house, Carl and Alexandra were met in the path by a strapping fellow in overalls and a blue shirt. He was breathing hard, as if he had been running, and was muttering to himself.

Marie ran forward, and, taking him by the arm, gave him a little push toward her guests. "Frank, this is Mr. Linstrum."

Frank took off his broad straw hat and nodded to Alexandra. When he spoke to Carl, he showed a fine set of white teeth. He was burned a dull red down to his neckband, and there was a heavy three-days' stubble on his face. Even in his agitation he was handsome, but he looked a rash and violent man.

Barely saluting the callers, he turned at once to his wife and began, in an outraged tone, "I have to leave my team to drive the old woman Hiller's hogs out-a my wheat. I go to take dat old woman to de court if she ain't careful, I tell you!"

His wife spoke soothingly. "But, Frank, she has only her lame boy to help her. She does the best she can."

Alexandra looked at the excited man and offered a suggestion. "Why don't you go over there some afternoon and hog-tight her fences? You'd save time for yourself in the end."

Frank's neck stiffened. "Not-a-much, I won't. I keep my hogs home. Other peoples can do like me. See? If that Louis can mend shoes, he can mend fence."

"Maybe," said Alexandra placidly; "but I've found it sometimes pays to mend other people's fences. Good-bye, Marie. Come to see me soon."

Alexandra walked firmly down the path and Carl followed her.

Frank went into the house and threw himself on the sofa, his face to the wall, his clenched fist on his hip. Marie, having seen her guests off, came in and put her hand coaxingly on his shoulder.

"Poor Frank! You've run until you've made your head ache, now have n't you? Let me make you some coffee."

"What else am I to do?" he cried hotly in Bohemian. "Am I to let any old woman's hogs root up my wheat? Is that what I work myself to death for?"

"Don't worry about it, Frank. I'll speak to Mrs. Hiller again. But, really, she almost cried last time they got out, she was so sorry."

Frank bounced over on his other side. "That's it; you always side with them against me. They all know it. Anybody here feels free to borrow the mower and break it, or turn their hogs in on me. They know you won't care!"

Marie hurried away to make his coffee. When she came back, he was fast asleep. She sat down and looked at him for a long while, very thoughtfully. When the kitchen clock struck six she went out to get supper, closing the door gently behind her. She was always sorry for Frank when he worked himself into one of these rages, and she was sorry to have him rough and quarrelsome with his neighbors. She was perfectly aware that the neighbors had a good deal to put up with, and that they bore with Frank for her sake.

VII

MARIE'S father, Albert Tovesky, was one of the
more intelligent Bohemians who came West in
the early seventies. He settled in Omaha and became a
leader and adviser among his people there. Marie was
his youngest child, by a second wife, and was the apple
of his eye. She was barely sixteen, and was in the gradu-
ating class of the Omaha High School, when Frank
Shabata arrived from the old country and set all the
Bohemian girls in a flutter. He was easily the buck of the
beer-gardens, and on Sunday he was a sight to see, with
his silk hat and tucked shirt and blue frock-coat, wearing gloves and carrying a little wisp of a yellow cane. He
was tall and fair, with splendid teeth and close-cropped
yellow curls, and he wore a slightly disdainful expression, proper for a young man with high connections,
whose mother had a big farm in the Elbe valley. There
was often an interesting discontent in his blue eyes, and
every Bohemian girl he met imagined herself the cause
of that unsatisfied expression. He had a way of drawing
out his cambric handkerchief slowly, by one corner,
from his breast-pocket, that was melancholy and ro-

131

mantic in the extreme. He took a little flight with each
of the more eligible Bohemian girls, but it was when he
was with little Marie Tovesky that he drew his handkerchief out most slowly, and, after he had lit a fresh
cigar, dropped the match most despairingly. Any one
could see, with half an eye, that his proud heart was
bleeding for somebody.

One Sunday, late in the summer after Marie's grad-
uation, she met Frank at a Bohemian picnic down
the river and went rowing with him all the afternoon.
When she got home that evening she went straight to
her father's room and told him that she was engaged to
Shabata. Old Tovesky was having a comfortable pipe
before he went to bed. When he heard his daughter's
announcement, he first prudently corked his beer bottle
and then leaped to his feet and had a turn of temper. He
characterized Frank Shabata by a Bohemian expression
which is the equivalent of stuffed shirt.

"Why don't he go to work like the rest of us did? His
farm in the Elbe valley, indeed! Ain't he got plenty
brothers and sisters? It's his mother's farm, and why
don't he stay at home and help her? Have n't I seen his
mother out in the morning at five o'clock with her ladle
and her big bucket on wheels, putting liquid manure
on the cabbages? Don't I know the look of old Eva

Shabata's hands? Like an old horse's hoofs they are —
and this fellow wearing gloves and rings! Engaged, indeed! You are n't fit to be out of school, and that's what's
the matter with you. I will send you off to the Sisters of
the Sacred Heart in St. Louis, and they will teach you
some sense, *I* guess!"

Accordingly, the very next week, Albert Tovesky
took his daughter, pale and tearful, down the river to
the convent. But the way to make Frank want anything
was to tell him he could n't have it. He managed to
have an interview with Marie before she went away, and
whereas he had been only half in love with her before,
he now persuaded himself that he would not stop at
anything. Marie took with her to the convent, under the
canvas lining of her trunk, the results of a laborious and
satisfying morning on Frank's part; no less than a dozen
photographs of himself, taken in a dozen different love-
lorn attitudes. There was a little round photograph for
her watch-case, photographs for her wall and dresser,
and even long narrow ones to be used as bookmarks.
More than once the handsome gentleman was torn to
pieces before the French class by an indignant nun.

Marie pined in the convent for a year, until her
eighteenth birthday was passed. Then she met Frank
Shabata in the Union Station in St. Louis and ran away

with him. Old Tovesky forgave his daughter because there was nothing else to do, and bought her a farm in the country that she had loved so well as a child. Since then her story had been a part of the history of the Divide. She and Frank had been living there for five years when Carl Linstrum came back to pay his long deferred visit to Alexandra. Frank had, on the whole, done better than one might have expected. He had flung himself at the soil with savage energy. Once a year he went to Hastings or to Omaha, on a spree. He stayed away for a week or two, and then came home and worked like a demon. He did work; if he felt sorry for himself, that was his own affair.

VIII

ON the evening of the day of Alexandra's call at the Shabatas', a heavy rain set in. Frank sat up until a late hour reading the Sunday newspapers. One of the Goulds was getting a divorce, and Frank took it as a personal affront. In printing the story of the young man's marital troubles, the knowing editor gave a sufficiently colored account of his career, stating the amount of his income and the manner in which he was supposed to spend it. Frank read English slowly, and the more he read about this divorce case, the angrier he grew. At last he threw down the page with a snort. He turned to his farm-hand who was reading the other half of the paper.

"By God! if I have that young feller in de hayfield once, I show him someting. Listen here what he do wit his money." And Frank began the catalogue of the young man's reputed extravagances.

Marie sighed. She thought it hard that the Goulds, for whom she had nothing but good will, should make her so much trouble. She hated to see the Sunday newspapers come into the house. Frank was always reading about the doings of rich people and feeling outraged. He had an inexhaustible stock of stories about their crimes and follies, how they bribed the courts and shot down their butlers with impunity whenever they chose. Frank and Lou Bergson had very similar ideas, and they were two of the political agitators of the county.

The next morning broke clear and brilliant, but Frank said the ground was too wet to plow, so he took the cart and drove over to Sainte-Agnès to spend the day at Moïse Marcel's saloon. After he was gone, Marie went out to the back porch to begin her butter-making. A brisk wind had come up and was driving puffy white clouds across the sky. The orchard was sparkling and rippling in the sun. Marie stood looking toward it wistfully, her hand on the lid of the churn, when she heard a sharp ring in the air, the merry sound of the whetstone on the scythe. That invitation decided her. She ran into the house, put on a short skirt and a pair of her husband's boots, caught up a tin pail and started for the orchard. Emil had already begun work and was mowing vigorously. When he saw her coming, he stopped and wiped his brow. His yellow canvas leggings and khaki trousers were splashed to the knees.

"Don't let me disturb you, Emil. I'm going to pick cherries. Is n't everything beautiful after the rain? Oh, but I'm glad to get this place mowed! When I heard it raining in the night, I thought maybe you would come and do it for me to-day. The wind wakened me. Did n't it blow dreadfully? Just smell the wild roses! They are always so spicy after a rain. We never had so many of them in here before. I suppose it's the wet season. Will you have to cut them, too?"

"If I cut the grass, I will," Emil said teasingly. "What's the matter with you? What makes you so flighty?"

"Am I flighty? I suppose that's the wet season, too, then. It's exciting to see everything growing so fast, — and to get the grass cut! Please leave the roses till last, if you must cut them. Oh, I don't mean all of them, I mean that low place down by my tree, where there are so many. Are n't you splashed! Look at the spider-webs all over the grass. Good-bye. I'll call you if I see a snake."

She tripped away and Emil stood looking after her. In a few moments he heard the cherries dropping smartly into the pail, and he began to swing his scythe with that long, even stroke that few American boys ever learn. Marie picked cherries and sang softly to herself, stripping one glittering branch after another, shivering when she caught a shower of rain-drops on her neck and hair. And Emil mowed his way slowly down toward the cherry trees.

That summer the rains had been so many and op-
portune that it was almost more than Shabata and his
man could do to keep up with the corn; the orchard was
a neglected wilderness. All sorts of weeds and herbs and
flowers had grown up there; splotches of wild larkspur,
pale green-and-white spikes of hoarhound, plantations
of wild cotton, tangles of foxtail and wild wheat. South
of the apricot trees, cornering on the wheatfield, was
Frank's alfalfa, where myriads of white and yellow butterflies were always fluttering above the purple blos-
soms. When Emil reached the lower corner by the
hedge, Marie was sitting under her white mulberry tree,
the pailful of cherries beside her, looking off at the gen-
tle, tireless swelling of the wheat.

"Emil," she said suddenly—he was mowing quietly
about under the tree so as not to disturb her—"what
religion did the Swedes have away back, before they
were Christians?"

Emil paused and straightened his back. "I don't
know. About like the Germans', was n't it?"

Marie went on as if she had not heard him. "The
Bohemians, you know, were tree worshipers before the
missionaries came. Father says the people in the mountains still do queer things, sometimes,—they believe
that trees bring good or bad luck."

Emil looked superior. "Do they? Well, which are the lucky trees? I'd like to know."

"I don't know all of them, but I know lindens are. The old people in the mountains plant lindens to purify the forest, and to do away with the spells that come from the old trees they say have lasted from heathen times. I'm a good Catholic, but I think I could get along with caring for trees, if I had n't anything else."

"That's a poor saying," said Emil, stooping over to wipe his hands in the wet grass.

"Why is it? If I feel that way, I feel that way. I like trees because they seem more resigned to the way they have to live than other things do. I feel as if this tree knows everything I ever think of when I sit here. When I come back to it, I never have to remind it of anything; I begin just where I left off."

Emil had nothing to say to this. He reached up among the branches and began to pick the sweet, insipid fruit,—long ivory-colored berries, tipped with faint pink, like white coral, that fall to the ground unheeded all summer through. He dropped a handful into her lap.

"Do you like Mr. Linstrum?" Marie asked suddenly.

"Yes. Don't you?"

"Oh, ever so much; only he seems kind of staid and

school-teachery. But, of course, he is older than Frank, even. I'm sure I don't want to live to be more than thirty, do you? Do you think Alexandra likes him very much?"

"I suppose so. They were old friends."

"Oh, Emil, you know what I mean!" Marie tossed her head impatiently. "Does she really care about him? When she used to tell me about him, I always wondered whether she was n't a little in love with him."

"Who, Alexandra?" Emil laughed and thrust his hands into his trousers pockets. "Alexandra's never been in love, you crazy!" He laughed again. "She would n't know how to go about it. The idea!"

Marie shrugged her shoulders. "Oh, you don't know Alexandra as well as you think you do! If you had any eyes, you would see that she is very fond of him. It would serve you all right if she walked off with Carl. I like him because he appreciates her more than you do."

Emil frowned. "What are you talking about, Marie? Alexandra's all right. She and I have always been good friends. What more do you want? I like to talk to Carl about New York and what a fellow can do there."

"Oh, Emil! Surely you are not thinking of going off there?"

"Why not? I must go somewhere, must n't I?" The

young man took up his scythe and leaned on it. "Would you rather I went off in the sand hills and lived like Ivar?"

Marie's face fell under his brooding gaze. She looked down at his wet leggings. "I'm sure Alexandra hopes you will stay on here," she murmured.

"Then Alexandra will be disappointed," the young man said roughly. "What do I want to hang around here for? Alexandra can run the farm all right, without me. I don't want to stand around and look on. I want to be doing something on my own account."

"That's so," Marie sighed. "There are so many, many things you can do. Almost anything you choose."

"And there are so many, many things I can't do." Emil echoed her tone sarcastically. "Sometimes I don't want to do anything at all, and sometimes I want to pull the four corners of the Divide together," — he threw out his arm and brought it back with a jerk, — "so, like a table-cloth. I get tired of seeing men and horses going up and down, up and down."

Marie looked up at his defiant figure and her face clouded. "I wish you were n't so restless, and did n't get so worked up over things," she said sadly.

"Thank you," he returned shortly.

She sighed despondently. "Everything I say makes

you cross, don't it? And you never used to be cross to me."

Emil took a step nearer and stood frowning down at her bent head. He stood in an attitude of self-defense, his feet well apart, his hands clenched and drawn up at his sides, so that the cords stood out on his bare arms. "I can't play with you like a little boy any more," he said slowly. "That's what you miss, Marie. You'll have to get some other little boy to play with." He stopped and took a deep breath. Then he went on in a low tone, so intense that it was almost threatening: "Sometimes you seem to understand perfectly, and then sometimes you pretend you don't. You don't help things any by pretending. It's then that I want to pull the corners of the Divide together. If you *won't* understand, you know, I could make you!"

Marie clasped her hands and started up from her seat. She had grown very pale and her eyes were shining with excitement and distress. "But, Emil, if I understand, then all our good times are over, we can never do nice things together any more. We shall have to behave like Mr. Linstrum. And, anyhow, there's nothing to understand!" She struck the ground with her little foot fiercely. "That won't last. It will go away, and things will be just as they used to. I wish you were a Catholic. The

Church helps people, indeed it does. I pray for you, but that's not the same as if you prayed yourself."

She spoke rapidly and pleadingly, looked entreatingly into his face. Emil stood defiant, gazing down at her.

"I can't pray to have the things I want," he said slowly, "and I won't pray not to have them, not if I'm damned for it."

Marie turned away, wringing her hands. "Oh, Emil, you won't try! Then all our good times are over."

"Yes; over. I never expect to have any more."

Emil gripped the hand-holds of his scythe and began to mow. Marie took up her cherries and went slowly toward the house, crying bitterly.

IX

O N Sunday afternoon, a month after Carl Linstrum's arrival, he rode with Emil up into the
French country to attend a Catholic fair. He sat for
most of the afternoon in the basement of the church,
where the fair was held, talking to Marie Shabata, or
strolled about the gravel terrace, thrown up on the hillside in front of the basement doors, where the French
boys were jumping and wrestling and throwing the
discus. Some of the boys were in their white baseball
suits; they had just come up from a Sunday practice
game down in the ball-grounds. Amédée, the newly
married, Emil's best friend, was their pitcher, renowned
among the country towns for his dash and skill. Amédée
was a little fellow, a year younger than Emil and much
more boyish in appearance; very lithe and active and
neatly made, with a clear brown and white skin, and
flashing white teeth. The Sainte-Agnès boys were to
play the Hastings nine in a fortnight, and Amédée's
lightning balls were the hope of his team. The little
Frenchman seemed to get every ounce there was in him
behind the ball as it left his hand.

Neighboring Fields

"You'd have made the battery at the University for sure, 'Médée," Emil said as they were walking from the ball-grounds back to the church on the hill. "You're pitching better than you did in the spring."

Amédée grinned. "Sure! A married man don't lose his head no more." He slapped Emil on the back as he caught step with him. "Oh, Emil, you wanna get married right off quick! It's the greatest thing ever!"

Emil laughed. "How am I going to get married without any girl?"

Amédée took his arm. "Pooh! There are plenty girls will have you. You wanna get some nice French girl, now. She treat you well; always be jolly. See," — he began checking off on his fingers, — "there is Séverine, and Alphonsine, and Joséphine, and Hectorine, and Louise, and Malvina — why, I could love any of them girls! Why don't you get after them? Are you stuck up, Emil, or is anything the matter with you? I never did know a boy twenty-two years old before that did n't have no girl. You wanna be a priest, maybe? Not-a for me!" Amédée swaggered. "I bring many good Catholics into this world, I hope, and that's a way I help the Church."

Emil looked down and patted him on the shoulder. "Now you're windy, 'Médée. You Frenchies like to brag."

But Amédée had the zeal of the newly married, and he was not to be lightly shaken off. "Honest and true, Emil, don't you want *any* girl? Maybe there's some young lady in Lincoln, now, very grand," — Amédée waved his hand languidly before his face to denote the fan of heartless beauty, — "and you lost your heart up there. Is that it?"

"Maybe," said Emil.

But Amédée saw no appropriate glow in his friend's face. "Bah!" he exclaimed in disgust. "I tell all the French girls to keep 'way from you. You gotta rock in there," thumping Emil on the ribs.

When they reached the terrace at the side of the church, Amédée, who was excited by his success on the ball-grounds, challenged Emil to a jumping-match, though he knew he would be beaten. They belted themselves up, and Raoul Marcel, the choir tenor and Father Duchesne's pet, and Jean Bordelau, held the string over which they vaulted. All the French boys stood round, cheering and humping themselves up when Emil or Amédée went over the wire, as if they were helping in the lift. Emil stopped at five-feet-five, declaring that he would spoil his appetite for supper if he jumped any more.

Angélique, Amédée's pretty bride, as blonde and fair

as her name, who had come out to watch the match, tossed her head at Emil and said: —

" 'Médée could jump much higher than you if he were as tall. And anyhow, he is much more graceful. He goes over like a bird, and you have to hump yourself all up."

"Oh, I do, do I?" Emil caught her and kissed her saucy mouth squarely, while she laughed and struggled and called, " 'Médée! 'Médée!"

"There, you see your 'Médée is n't even big enough to get you away from me. I could run away with you right now and he could only sit down and cry about it. I'll show you whether I have to hump myself!" Laughing and panting, he picked Angélique up in his arms and began running about the rectangle with her. Not until he saw Marie Shabata's tiger eyes flashing from the gloom of the basement doorway did he hand the disheveled bride over to her husband. "There, go to your graceful; I have n't the heart to take you away from him."

Angélique clung to her husband and made faces at Emil over the white shoulder of Amédée's ball-shirt. Emil was greatly amused at her air of proprietorship and at Amédée's shameless submission to it. He was delighted with his friend's good fortune. He liked to see and to think about Amédée's sunny, natural, happy love.

147

He and Amédée had ridden and wrestled and larked together since they were lads of twelve. On Sundays and holidays they were always arm in arm. It seemed strange that now he should have to hide the thing that Amédée was so proud of, that the feeling which gave one of them such happiness should bring the other such despair. It was like that when Alexandra tested her seed-corn in the spring, he mused. From two ears that had grown side by side, the grains of one shot up joyfully into the light, projecting themselves into the future, and the grains from the other lay still in the earth and rotted; and nobody knew why.

X

WHILE Emil and Carl were amusing themselves at the fair, Alexandra was at home, busy with her account-books, which had been neglected of late. She was almost through with her figures when she heard a cart drive up to the gate, and looking out of the window she saw her two older brothers. They had seemed to avoid her ever since Carl Linstrum's arrival, four weeks ago that day, and she hurried to the door to welcome them. She saw at once that they had come with some very definite purpose. They followed her stiffly into the sitting-room. Oscar sat down, but Lou walked over to the window and remained standing, his hands behind him.

"You are by yourself?" he asked, looking toward the doorway into the parlor.

"Yes. Carl and Emil went up to the Catholic fair."

For a few moments neither of the men spoke.

Then Lou came out sharply. "How soon does he intend to go away from here?"

"I don't know, Lou. Not for some time, I hope." Alexandra spoke in an even, quiet tone that often exasperated her brothers. They felt that she was trying to be superior with them.

Oscar spoke up grimly. "We thought we ought to tell you that people have begun to talk," he said meaningly.

Alexandra looked at him. "What about?"

Oscar met her eyes blankly. "About you, keeping him here so long. It looks bad for him to be hanging on to a woman this way. People think you're getting taken in."

Alexandra shut her account-book firmly. "Boys," she said seriously, "don't let's go on with this. We won't come out anywhere. I can't take advice on such a matter. I know you mean well, but you must not feel responsible for me in things of this sort. If we go on with this talk it will only make hard feeling."

Lou whipped about from the window. "You ought to think a little about your family. You're making us all ridiculous."

"How am I?"

"People are beginning to say you want to marry the fellow."

"Well, and what is ridiculous about that?"

Lou and Oscar exchanged outraged looks. "Alexandra! Can't you see he's just a tramp and he's after your money? He wants to be taken care of, he does!"

"Well, suppose I want to take care of him? Whose business is it but my own?"

"Don't you know he'd get hold of your property?"

"He'd get hold of what I wished to give him, certainly."

Oscar sat up suddenly and Lou clutched at his bristly hair.

"Give him?" Lou shouted. "Our property, our homestead?"

"I don't know about the homestead," said Alexandra quietly. "I know you and Oscar have always expected that it would be left to your children, and I'm not sure but what you're right. But I'll do exactly as I please with the rest of my land, boys."

"The rest of your land!" cried Lou, growing more excited every minute. "Did n't all the land come out of the homestead? It was bought with money borrowed on the homestead, and Oscar and me worked ourselves to the bone paying interest on it."

"Yes, you paid the interest. But when you married we made a division of the land, and you were satisfied. I've made more on my farms since I've been alone than when we all worked together."

"Everything you've made has come out of the original land that us boys worked for, has n't it? The farms and all that comes out of them belongs to us as a family."

Alexandra waved her hand impatiently. "Come now, Lou. Stick to the facts. You are talking nonsense. Go to the county clerk and ask him who owns my land, and whether my titles are good."

Lou turned to his brother. "This is what comes of letting a woman meddle in business," he said bitterly. "We ought to have taken things in our own hands years ago. But she liked to run things, and we humored her. We thought you had good sense, Alexandra. We never thought you'd do anything foolish."

Alexandra rapped impatiently on her desk with her knuckles. "Listen, Lou. Don't talk wild. You say you ought to have taken things into your own hands years ago. I suppose you mean before you left home. But how could you take hold of what was n't there? I've got most of what I have now since we divided the property; I've built it up myself, and it has nothing to do with you."

Oscar spoke up solemnly. "The property of a family really belongs to the men of the family, no matter about the title. If anything goes wrong, it's the men that are held responsible."

"Yes, of course," Lou broke in. "Everybody knows that. Oscar and me have always been easy-going and we've never made any fuss. We were willing you should hold the land and have the good of it, but you got no right to part with any of it. We worked in the fields to pay for the first land you bought, and whatever's come out of it has got to be kept in the family."

Oscar reinforced his brother, his mind fixed on the one point he could see. "The property of a family belongs to the men of the family, because they are held responsible, and because they do the work."

Alexandra looked from one to the other, her eyes full of indignation. She had been impatient before, but now she was beginning to feel angry. "And what about my work?" she asked in an unsteady voice.

Lou looked at the carpet. "Oh, now, Alexandra, you always took it pretty easy! Of course we wanted you to. You liked to manage round, and we always humored you. We realize you were a great deal of help to us. There's no woman anywhere around that knows as much about business as you do, and we've always been proud of that, and thought you were pretty smart. But, of course, the real work always fell on us. Good advice is all right, but it don't get the weeds out of the corn."

"Maybe not, but it sometimes puts in the crop, and it sometimes keeps the fields for corn to grow in," said Alexandra dryly. "Why, Lou, I can remember when you and Oscar wanted to sell this homestead and all the improvements to old preacher Ericson for two thousand dollars. If I'd consented, you'd have gone down to the river and scraped along on poor farms for the rest of your lives. When I put in our first field of alfalfa you both opposed me, just because I first heard about it from a young man who had been to the University. You said I was being taken in then, and all the neighbors said so. You know as well as I do that alfalfa has been the salvation of this country. You all laughed at me when I said our land here was about ready for wheat, and I had to raise three big wheat crops before the neighbors quit putting all their land in corn. Why, I remember you cried, Lou, when we put in the first big wheat-planting, and said everybody was laughing at us."

Lou turned to Oscar. "That's the woman of it; if she tells you to put in a crop, she thinks she's put it in. It makes women conceited to meddle in business. I should n't think you'd want to remind us how hard you were on us, Alexandra, after the way you baby Emil."

"Hard on you? I never meant to be hard. Conditions were hard. Maybe I would never have been very soft, anyhow; but I certainly did n't choose to be the kind of girl I was. If you take even a vine and cut it back again and again, it grows hard, like a tree."

Lou felt that they were wandering from the point, and that in digression Alexandra might unnerve him.

He wiped his forehead with a jerk of his handkerchief. "We never doubted you, Alexandra. We never questioned anything you did. You've always had your own way. But you can't expect us to sit like stumps and see you done out of the property by any loafer who happens along, and making yourself ridiculous into the bargain."

Oscar rose. "Yes," he broke in, "everybody's laughing to see you get took in; at your age, too. Everybody knows he's nearly five years younger than you, and is after your money. Why, Alexandra, you are forty years old!"

"All that does n't concern anybody but Carl and me. Go to town and ask your lawyers what you can do to restrain me from disposing of my own property. And I advise you to do what they tell you; for the authority you can exert by law is the only influence you will ever have over me again." Alexandra rose. "I think I would rather not have lived to find out what I have to-day," she said quietly, closing her desk.

Lou and Oscar looked at each other questioningly. There seemed to be nothing to do but to go, and they walked out.

"You can't do business with women," Oscar said heavily as he clambered into the cart. "But anyhow, we've had our say, at last."

Lou scratched his head. "Talk of that kind might come too high, you know; but she's apt to be sensible. You had n't ought to said that about her age, though, Oscar. I'm afraid that hurt her feelings; and the worst thing we can do is to make her sore at us. She'd marry him out of contrariness."

"I only meant," said Oscar, "that she is old enough to know better, and she is. If she was going to marry, she ought to done it long ago, and not go making a fool of herself now."

Lou looked anxious, nevertheless. "Of course," he reflected hopefully and inconsistently, "Alexandra ain't much like other women-folks. Maybe it won't make her sore. Maybe she'd as soon be forty as not!"

XI

Emil came home at about half-past seven o'clock that evening. Old Ivar met him at the windmill and took his horse, and the young man went directly into the house. He called to his sister and she answered from her bedroom, behind the sitting-room, saying that she was lying down.

Emil went to her door.

"Can I see you for a minute?" he asked. "I want to talk to you about something before Carl comes."

Alexandra rose quickly and came to the door. "Where is Carl?"

"Lou and Oscar met us and said they wanted to talk to him, so he rode over to Oscar's with them. Are you coming out?" Emil asked impatiently.

"Yes, sit down. I'll be dressed in a moment."

Alexandra closed her door, and Emil sank down on the old slat lounge and sat with his head in his hands. When his sister came out, he looked up, not knowing whether the interval had been short or long, and he was surprised to see that the room had grown quite dark. That was just as well; it would be easier to talk if he

157

were not under the gaze of those clear, deliberate eyes, that saw so far in some directions and were so blind in others. Alexandra, too, was glad of the dusk. Her face was swollen from crying.

Emil started up and then sat down again. "Alexandra," he said slowly, in his deep young baritone, "I don't want to go away to law school this fall. Let me put it off another year. I want to take a year off and look around. It's awfully easy to rush into a profession you don't really like, and awfully hard to get out of it. Linstrum and I have been talking about that."

"Very well, Emil. Only don't go off looking for land." She came up and put her hand on his shoulder. "I've been wishing you could stay with me this winter."

"That's just what I don't want to do, Alexandra. I'm restless. I want to go to a new place. I want to go down to the City of Mexico to join one of the University fellows who's at the head of an electrical plant. He wrote me he could give me a little job, enough to pay my way, and I could look around and see what I want to do. I want to go as soon as harvest is over. I guess Lou and Oscar will be sore about it."

"I suppose they will." Alexandra sat down on the lounge beside him. "They are very angry with me, Emil. We have had a quarrel. They will not come here again."

Emil scarcely heard what she was saying; he did not notice the sadness of her tone. He was thinking about the reckless life he meant to live in Mexico.

"What about?" he asked absently.

"About Carl Linstrum. They are afraid I am going to marry him, and that some of my property will get away from them."

Emil shrugged his shoulders. "What nonsense!" he murmured. "Just like them."

Alexandra drew back. "Why nonsense, Emil?"

"Why, you've never thought of such a thing, have you? They always have to have something to fuss about."

"Emil," said his sister slowly, "you ought not to take things for granted. Do you agree with them that I have no right to change my way of living?"

Emil looked at the outline of his sister's head in the dim light. They were sitting close together and he somehow felt that she could hear his thoughts. He was silent for a moment, and then said in an embarrassed tone, "Why, no, certainly not. You ought to do whatever you want to. I'll always back you."

"But it would seem a little bit ridiculous to you if I married Carl?"

Emil fidgeted. The issue seemed to him too far-fetched to warrant discussion. "Why, no. I should be surprised if you wanted to. I can't see exactly why. But that's none of my business. You ought to do as you please. Certainly you ought not to pay any attention to what the boys say."

Alexandra sighed. "I had hoped you might understand, a little, why I do want to. But I suppose that's too much to expect. I've had a pretty lonely life, Emil. Besides Marie, Carl is the only friend I have ever had."

Emil was awake now; a name in her last sentence roused him. He put out his hand and took his sister's awkwardly. "You ought to do just as you wish, and I think Carl's a fine fellow. He and I would always get on. I don't believe any of the things the boys say about him, honest I don't. They are suspicious of him because he's intelligent. You know their way. They've been sore at me ever since you let me go away to college. They're always trying to catch me up. If I were you, I would n't pay any attention to them. There's nothing to get upset about. Carl's a sensible fellow. He won't mind them."

"I don't know. If they talk to him the way they did to me, I think he'll go away."

Emil grew more and more uneasy. "Think so? Well, Marie said it would serve us all right if you walked off with him."

"Did she? Bless her little heart! *She* would." Alexandra's voice broke.

Emil began unlacing his leggings. "Why don't you talk to her about it? There's Carl, I hear his horse. I guess I'll go upstairs and get my boots off. No, I don't want any supper. We had supper at five o'clock, at the fair."

Emil was glad to escape and get to his own room. He was a little ashamed for his sister, though he had tried not to show it. He felt that there was something indecorous in her proposal, and she did seem to him somewhat ridiculous. There was trouble enough in the world, he reflected, as he threw himself upon his bed, without people who were forty years old imagining they wanted to get married. In the darkness and silence Emil was not likely to think long about Alexandra. Every image slipped away but one. He had seen Marie in the crowd that afternoon. She sold candy at the fair. *Why* had she ever run away with Frank Shabata, and how could she go on laughing and working and taking an interest in things? Why did she like so many people, and why had she seemed pleased when all the French and Bohemian boys, and the priest himself, crowded round her candy stand? Why did she care about any one but him? Why could he never, never find the thing he looked for in her playful, affectionate eyes?

Then he fell to imagining that he looked once more and found it there, and what it would be like if she loved him, — she who, as Alexandra said, could give her whole heart. In that dream he could lie for hours, as if in a trance. His spirit went out of his body and crossed the fields to Marie Shabata.

At the University dances the girls had often looked wonderingly at the tall young Swede with the fine head, leaning against the wall and frowning, his arms folded, his eyes fixed on the ceiling or the floor. All the girls were a little afraid of him. He was distinguished-looking, and not the jollying kind. They felt that he was too intense and preoccupied. There was something queer about him. Emil's fraternity rather prided itself upon its dances, and sometimes he did his duty and danced every dance. But whether he was on the floor or brooding in a corner, he was always thinking about Marie Shabata. For two years the storm had been gathering in him.

XII

CARL came into the sitting-room while Alexandra was lighting the lamp. She looked up at him as she adjusted the shade. His sharp shoulders stooped as if he were very tired, his face was pale, and there were bluish shadows under his dark eyes. His anger had burned itself out and left him sick and disgusted.

"You have seen Lou and Oscar?" Alexandra asked.

"Yes." His eyes avoided hers.

Alexandra took a deep breath. "And now you are going away. I thought so."

Carl threw himself into a chair and pushed the dark lock back from his forehead with his white, nervous hand. "What a hopeless position you are in, Alexandra!" he exclaimed feverishly. "It is your fate to be always surrounded by little men. And I am no better than the rest. I am too little to face the criticism of even such men as Lou and Oscar. Yes, I am going away; to-morrow. I cannot even ask you to give me a promise until I have something to offer you. I thought, perhaps, I could do that; but I find I can't."

"What good comes of offering people things they

163

don't need?" Alexandra asked sadly. "I don't need money. But I have needed you for a great many years. I wonder why I have been permitted to prosper, if it is only to take my friends away from me."

"I don't deceive myself," Carl said frankly. "I know that I am going away on my own account. I must make the usual effort. I must have something to show for myself. To take what you would give me, I should have to be either a very large man or a very small one, and I am only in the middle class."

Alexandra sighed. "I have a feeling that if you go away, you will not come back. Something will happen to one of us, or to both. People have to snatch at happiness when they can, in this world. It is always easier to lose than to find. What I have is yours, if you care enough about me to take it."

Carl rose and looked up at the picture of John Bergson. "But I can't, my dear, I can't! I will go North at once. Instead of idling about in California all winter, I shall be getting my bearings up there. I won't waste another week. Be patient with me, Alexandra. Give me a year!"

"As you will," said Alexandra wearily. "All at once, in a single day, I lose everything; and I do not know why. Emil, too, is going away." Carl was still studying John

Bergson's face and Alexandra's eyes followed his. "Yes," she said, "if he could have seen all that would come of the task he gave me, he would have been sorry. I hope he does not see me now. I hope that he is among the old people of his blood and country, and that tidings do not reach him from the New World."

PART III

Winter Memories

PART III

Winter Memories

I

WINTER has settled down over the Divide again; the season in which Nature recuperates, in which she sinks to sleep between the fruitfulness of autumn and the passion of spring. The birds have gone. The teeming life that goes on down in the long grass is exterminated. The prairie-dog keeps his hole. The rabbits run shivering from one frozen garden patch to another and are hard put to it to find frost-bitten cabbage-stalks. At night the coyotes roam the wintry waste, howling for food. The variegated fields are all one color now; the pastures, the stubble, the roads, the sky are the same leaden gray. The hedgerows and trees are scarcely perceptible against the bare earth, whose slaty hue they have taken on. The ground is frozen so hard that it bruises the foot to walk in the roads or in the ploughed fields. It is like an iron country, and the spirit is oppressed by its rigor and melancholy. One could easily believe that in that dead landscape the germs of life and fruitfulness were extinct forever.

Alexandra has settled back into her old routine. There are weekly letters from Emil. Lou and Oscar she has not seen since Carl went away. To avoid awkward encounters in the presence of curious spectators, she has stopped going to the Norwegian Church and drives up to the Reform Church at Hanover, or goes with Marie Shabata to the Catholic Church, locally known as "the French Church." She has not told Marie about Carl, or her differences with her brothers. She was never very communicative about her own affairs, and when she came to the point, an instinct told her that about such things she and Marie would not understand one another.

Old Mrs. Lee had been afraid that family misunderstandings might deprive her of her yearly visit to Alexandra. But on the first day of December Alexandra telephoned Annie that to-morrow she would send Ivar over for her mother, and the next day the old lady arrived with her bundles. For twelve years Mrs. Lee had always entered Alexandra's sitting-room with the same exclamation, "Now we be yust-a like old times!" She enjoyed the liberty Alexandra gave her, and hearing her own language about her all day long. Here she could wear her nightcap and sleep with all her windows shut, listen to Ivar reading the Bible, and here she could run about among the stables in a pair of Emil's old boots. Though she was bent almost double, she was as spry as a gopher. Her face was as brown as if it had been varnished, and as full of wrinkles as a washerwoman's hands. She had three jolly old teeth left in the front of her mouth, and when she grinned she looked very knowing, as if when you found out how to take it, life was n't half bad. While she and Alexandra patched and pieced and quilted, she talked incessantly about stories she read in a Swedish family paper, telling the plots in great detail; or about her life on a dairy farm in Gottland when she was a girl. Sometimes she forgot which were the printed stories and which were the real stories, it all seemed so far away. She loved to take a little brandy, with hot water and sugar, before she went to bed, and Alexandra always had it ready for her. "It sends good dreams," she would say with a twinkle in her eye.

When Mrs. Lee had been with Alexandra for a week, Marie Shabata telephoned one morning to say that Frank had gone to town for the day, and she would like them to come over for coffee in the afternoon. Mrs. Lee hurried to wash out and iron her new cross-stitched apron, which she had finished only the night before;

a checked gingham apron worked with a design ten inches broad across the bottom; a hunting scene, with fir trees and a stag and dogs and huntsmen. Mrs. Lee was firm with herself at dinner, and refused a second helping of apple dumplings. "I ta-ank I save up," she said with a giggle.

At two o'clock in the afternoon Alexandra's cart drove up to the Shabatas' gate, and Marie saw Mrs. Lee's red shawl come bobbing up the path. She ran to the door and pulled the old woman into the house with a hug, helping her to take off her wraps while Alexandra blanketed the horse outside. Mrs. Lee had put on her best black sateen dress — she abominated woolen stuffs, even in winter — and a crocheted collar, fastened with a big pale gold pin, containing faded daguerreotypes of her father and mother. She had not worn her apron for fear of rumpling it, and now she shook it out and tied it round her waist with a conscious air. Marie drew back and threw up her hands, exclaiming, "Oh, what a beauty! I've never seen this one before, have I, Mrs. Lee?"

The old woman giggled and ducked her head. "No, yust las' night I ma-ake. See dis tread; verra strong, no wa-ash out, no fade. My sister send from Sveden. I yust-a ta-ank you like dis."

Marie ran to the door again. "Come in, Alexandra. I have been looking at Mrs. Lee's apron. Do stop on your way home and show it to Mrs. Hiller. She's crazy about cross-stitch."

While Alexandra removed her hat and veil, Mrs. Lee went out to the kitchen and settled herself in a wooden rocking-chair by the stove, looking with great interest at the table, set for three, with a white cloth, and a pot of pink geraniums in the middle. "My, a-an't you gotta fine plants; such-a much flower. How you keep from freeze?"

She pointed to the window-shelves, full of blooming fuchsias and geraniums.

"I keep the fire all night, Mrs. Lee, and when it's very cold I put them all on the table, in the middle of the room. Other nights I only put newspapers behind them. Frank laughs at me for fussing, but when they don't bloom he says, 'What's the matter with the darned things?' — What do you hear from Carl, Alexandra?"

"He got to Dawson before the river froze, and now I suppose I won't hear any more until spring. Before he left California he sent me a box of orange flowers, but they did n't keep very well. I have brought a bunch of Emil's letters for you." Alexandra came out from the sitting-room and pinched Marie's cheek playfully. "You don't look as if the weather ever froze you up. Never have colds, do you? That's a good girl. She had dark red cheeks like this when she was a little girl, Mrs. Lee. She looked like some queer foreign kind of a doll. I've never forgot the first time I saw you in Mieklejohn's store, Marie, the time father was lying sick. Carl and I were talking about that before he went away."

"I remember, and Emil had his kitten along. When are you going to send Emil's Christmas box?"

"It ought to have gone before this. I'll have to send it by mail now, to get it there in time."

Marie pulled a dark purple silk necktie from her workbasket. "I knit this for him. It's a good color, don't you think? Will you please put it in with your things and tell him it's from me, to wear when he goes serenading."

Alexandra laughed. "I don't believe he goes serenading much. He says in one letter that the Mexican ladies are said to be very beautiful, but that don't seem to me very warm praise."

Marie tossed her head. "Emil can't fool me. If he's bought a guitar, he goes serenading. Who would n't, with all those Spanish girls dropping flowers down from their windows! I'd sing to them every night, would n't you, Mrs. Lee?"

The old lady chuckled. Her eyes lit up as Marie bent down and opened the oven door. A delicious hot fragrance blew out into the tidy kitchen. "My, somet'ing smell good!" She turned to Alexandra with a wink, her three yellow teeth making a brave show, "I ta-ank dat stop my yaw from ache no more!" she said contentedly.

Marie took out a pan of delicate little rolls, stuffed with stewed apricots, and began to dust them over with powdered sugar. "I hope you'll like these, Mrs. Lee; Alexandra does. The Bohemians always like them with their coffee. But if you don't, I have a coffee-cake with nuts and poppy seeds. Alexandra, will you get the cream jug? I put it in the window to keep cool."

"The Bohemians," said Alexandra, as they drew up to the table, "certainly know how to make more kinds of bread than any other people in the world. Old Mrs. Hiller told me once at the church supper that she could make seven kinds of fancy bread, but Marie could make a dozen."

Mrs. Lee held up one of the apricot rolls between her brown thumb and forefinger and weighed it critically. "Yust like-a fedders," she pronounced with satisfaction. "My, a-an't dis nice!" she exclaimed as she stirred her coffee. "I yust ta-ake a liddle yelly now, too, I ta-ank."

Alexandra and Marie laughed at her forehandedness,

175

and fell to talking of their own affairs. "I was afraid you had a cold when I talked to you over the telephone the other night, Marie. What was the matter, had you been crying?"

"Maybe I had," Marie smiled guiltily. "Frank was out late that night. Don't you get lonely sometimes in the winter, when everybody has gone away?"

"I thought it was something like that. If I had n't had company, I'd have run over to see for myself. If you get down-hearted, what will become of the rest of us?" Alexandra asked.

"I don't, very often. There's Mrs. Lee without any coffee!"

Later, when Mrs. Lee declared that her powers were spent, Marie and Alexandra went upstairs to look for some crochet patterns the old lady wanted to borrow. "Better put on your coat, Alexandra. It's cold up there, and I have no idea where those patterns are. I may have to look through my old trunks." Marie caught up a shawl and opened the stair door, running up the steps ahead of her guest. "While I go through the bureau drawers, you might look in those hat-boxes on the closet-shelf, over where Frank's clothes hang. There are a lot of odds and ends in them."

She began tossing over the contents of the drawers,

and Alexandra went into the clothes-closet. Presently she came back, holding a slender elastic yellow stick in her hand.

"What in the world is this, Marie? You don't mean to tell me Frank ever carried such a thing?"

Marie blinked at it with astonishment and sat down on the floor. "Where did you find it? I did n't know he had kept it. I have n't seen it for years."

"It really is a cane, then?"

"Yes. One he brought from the old country. He used to carry it when I first knew him. Is n't it foolish? Poor Frank!"

Alexandra twirled the stick in her fingers and laughed. "He must have looked funny!"

Marie was thoughtful. "No, he did n't, really. It did n't seem out of place. He used to be awfully gay like that when he was a young man. I guess people always get what's hardest for them, Alexandra." Marie gathered the shawl closer about her and still looked hard at the cane. "Frank would be all right in the right place," she said reflectively. "He ought to have a different kind of wife, for one thing. Do you know, Alexandra, I could pick out exactly the right sort of woman for Frank — now. The trouble is you almost have to marry a man before you can find out the sort of wife he needs; and usually it's exactly the sort you are not. Then what are you going to do about it?" she asked candidly.

Alexandra confessed she did n't know. "However," she added, "it seems to me that you get along with Frank about as well as any woman I've ever seen or heard of could."

Marie shook her head, pursing her lips and blowing her warm breath softly out into the frosty air. "No; I was spoiled at home. I like my own way, and I have a quick tongue. When Frank brags, I say sharp things, and he never forgets. He goes over and over it in his mind; I can feel him. Then I'm too giddy. Frank's wife ought to be timid, and she ought not to care about another living thing in the world but just Frank! I did n't, when I married him, but I suppose I was too young to stay like that." Marie sighed.

Alexandra had never heard Marie speak so frankly about her husband before, and she felt that it was wiser not to encourage her. No good, she reasoned, ever came from talking about such things, and while Marie was thinking aloud, Alexandra had been steadily searching the hat-boxes. "Are n't these the patterns, Maria?"

Marie sprang up from the floor. "Sure enough, we were looking for patterns, were n't we? I'd forgot about everything but Frank's other wife. I'll put that away."

She poked the cane behind Frank's Sunday clothes, and though she laughed, Alexandra saw there were tears in her eyes.

When they went back to the kitchen, the snow had begun to fall, and Marie's visitors thought they must be getting home. She went out to the cart with them, and tucked the robes about old Mrs. Lee while Alexandra took the blanket off her horse. As they drove away, Marie turned and went slowly back to the house. She took up the package of letters Alexandra had brought, but she did not read them. She turned them over and looked at the foreign stamps, and then sat watching the flying snow while the dusk deepened in the kitchen and the stove sent out a red glow.

Marie knew perfectly well that Emil's letters were written more for her than for Alexandra. They were not the sort of letters that a young man writes to his sister. They were both more personal and more painstaking; full of descriptions of the gay life in the old Mexican capital in the days when the strong hand of Porfirio Díaz was still strong. He told about bull-fights and cock-fights, churches and *fiestas*, the flower-markets and the fountains, the music and dancing, the people of all nations he met in the Italian restaurants on San Francisco Street. In short, they were the kind of letters

179

a young man writes to a woman when he wishes himself and his life to seem interesting to her, when he wishes to enlist her imagination in his behalf.

Marie, when she was alone or when she sat sewing in the evening, often thought about what it must be like down there where Emil was; where there were flowers and street bands everywhere, and carriages rattling up and down, and where there was a little blind bootblack in front of the cathedral who could play any tune you asked for by dropping the lids of blacking-boxes on the stone steps. When everything is done and over for one at twenty-three, it is pleasant to let the mind wander forth and follow a young adventurer who has life before him. "And if it had not been for me," she thought, "Frank might still be free like that, and having a good time making people admire him. Poor Frank, getting married was n't very good for him either. I'm afraid I do set people against him, as he says. I seem, somehow, to give him away all the time. Perhaps he would try to be agreeable to people again, if I were not around. It seems as if I always make him just as bad as he can be."

Later in the winter, Alexandra looked back upon that afternoon as the last satisfactory visit she had had with Marie. After that day the younger woman seemed to shrink more and more into herself. When she was with

Alexandra she was not spontaneous and frank as she used to be. She seemed to be brooding over something, and holding something back. The weather had a good deal to do with their seeing less of each other than usual. There had not been such snowstorms in twenty years, and the path across the fields was drifted deep from Christmas until March. When the two neighbors went to see each other, they had to go round by the wagon-road, which was twice as far. They telephoned each other almost every night, though in January there was a stretch of three weeks when the wires were down, and when the postman did not come at all.

Marie often ran in to see her nearest neighbor, old Mrs. Hiller, who was crippled with rheumatism and had only her son, the lame shoemaker, to take care of her; and she went to the French Church, whatever the weather. She was a sincerely devout girl. She prayed for herself and for Frank, and for Emil, among the temptations of that gay, corrupt old city. She found more comfort in the Church that winter than ever before. It seemed to come closer to her, and to fill an emptiness that ached in her heart. She tried to be patient with her husband. He and his hired man usually played California Jack in the evening. Marie sat sewing or crocheting and tried to take a friendly interest in the game, but she was always thinking about the wide fields outside, where the snow was drifting over the fences; and about the orchard, where the snow was falling and packing, crust over crust. When she went out into the dark kitchen to fix her plants for the night, she used to stand by the window and look out at the white fields, or watch the currents of snow whirling over the orchard. She seemed to feel the weight of all the snow that lay down there. The branches had become so hard that they wounded your hand if you but tried to break a twig. And yet, down under the frozen crusts, at the roots of the trees, the secret of life was still safe, warm as the blood in one's heart; and the spring would come again! Oh, it would come again!

II

IF Alexandra had had much imagination she might have guessed what was going on in Marie's mind, and she would have seen long before what was going on in Emil's. But that, as Emil himself had more than once reflected, was Alexandra's blind side, and her life had not been of the kind to sharpen her vision. Her training had all been toward the end of making her proficient in what she had undertaken to do. Her personal life, her own realization of herself, was almost a subconscious existence; like an underground river that came to the surface only here and there, at intervals months apart, and then sank again to flow on under her own fields. Nevertheless, the underground stream was there, and it was because she had so much personality to put into her enterprises and succeeded in putting it into them so completely, that her affairs prospered better than those of her neighbors.

There were certain days in her life, outwardly uneventful, which Alexandra remembered as peculiarly happy; days when she was close to the flat, fallow world about her, and felt, as it were, in her own body the joyous germination in the soil. There were days, too, which she and Emil had spent together, upon which she loved to look back. There had been such a day when they were down on the river in the dry year, looking over the land. They had made an early start one morning and had driven a long way before noon. When Emil said he was hungry, they drew back from the road, gave Brigham his oats among the bushes, and climbed up to the top of a grassy bluff to eat their lunch under the shade of some little elm trees. The river was clear there, and shallow, since there had been no rain, and it ran in ripples over the sparkling sand. Under the overhanging willows of the opposite bank there was an inlet where the water was deeper and flowed so slowly that it seemed to sleep in the sun. In this little bay a single wild duck was swimming and diving and preening her feathers, disporting herself very happily in the flickering light and shade. They sat for a long time, watching the solitary bird take its pleasure. No living thing had ever seemed to Alexandra as beautiful as that wild duck. Emil must have felt about it as she did, for afterward, when they were at home, he used sometimes to say, "Sister, you know our duck down there — " Alexandra remembered that day as one of the happiest in her life. Years afterward she thought of the duck as still there, swimming and diving all by herself in the sunlight, a kind of enchanted bird that did not know age or change.

Most of Alexandra's happy memories were as impersonal as this one; yet to her they were very personal. Her mind was a white book, with clear writing about weather and beasts and growing things. Not many people would have cared to read it; only a happy few. She had never been in love, she had never indulged in sentimental reveries. Even as a girl she had looked upon men as work-fellows. She had grown up in serious times.

There was one fancy indeed, which persisted through her girlhood. It most often came to her on Sunday mornings, the one day in the week when she lay late abed listening to the familiar morning sounds; the windmill singing in the brisk breeze, Emil whistling as he blacked his boots down by the kitchen door. Sometimes, as she lay thus luxuriously idle, her eyes closed, she used to have an illusion of being lifted up bodily and carried lightly by some one very strong. It was a man, certainly, who carried her, but he was like no man she knew; he was much larger and stronger and swifter, and he carried her as easily as if she were a sheaf of wheat. She never saw him, but, with eyes closed, she could feel that he was yellow like the sunlight, and there was the smell of ripe cornfields about him. She could feel him approach, bend over her and lift her, and then she could feel herself being carried swiftly off across the fields. After such a reverie she would rise hastily, angry with herself, and go down to the bath-house that was partitioned off the kitchen shed. There she would stand in a tin tub and prosecute her bath with vigor, finishing it by pouring buckets of cold well-water over her gleaming white body which no man on the Divide could have carried very far.

As she grew older, this fancy more often came to her when she was tired than when she was fresh and strong. Sometimes, after she had been in the open all day, overseeing the branding of the cattle or the loading of the pigs, she would come in chilled, take a concoction of spices and warm home-made wine, and go to bed with her body actually aching with fatigue. Then, just before she went to sleep, she had the old sensation of being lifted and carried by a strong being who took from her all her bodily weariness.

PART IV

The White
Mulberry
Tree

PART IV

The White Mulberry Tree

I

THE French Church, properly the Church of
Sainte-Agnès, stood upon a hill. The high, narrow, red-brick building, with its tall steeple and steep
roof, could be seen for miles across the wheatfields,
though the little town of Sainte-Agnès was completely
hidden away at the foot of the hill. The church looked
powerful and triumphant there on its eminence, so high
above the rest of the landscape, with miles of warm
color lying at its feet, and by its position and setting it
reminded one of some of the churches built long ago in
the wheat-lands of middle France.

Late one June afternoon Alexandra Bergson was
driving along one of the many roads that led through
the rich French farming country to the big church. The
sunlight was shining directly in her face, and there was a
blaze of light all about the red church on the hill. Beside
Alexandra lounged a strikingly exotic figure in a tall

Mexican hat, a silk sash, and a black velvet jacket sewn with silver buttons. Emil had returned only the night before, and his sister was so proud of him that she decided at once to take him up to the church supper, and to make him wear the Mexican costume he had brought home in his trunk. "All the girls who have stands are going to wear fancy costumes," she argued, "and some of the boys. Marie is going to tell fortunes, and she sent to Omaha for a Bohemian dress her father brought back from a visit to the old country. If you wear those clothes, they will all be pleased. And you must take your guitar. Everybody ought to do what they can to help along, and we have never done much. We are not a talented family."

The supper was to be at six o'clock, in the basement of the church, and afterward there would be a fair, with charades and an auction. Alexandra had set out from home early, leaving the house to Signa and Nelse Jensen, who were to be married next week. Signa had shyly asked to have the wedding put off until Emil came home.

Alexandra was well satisfied with her brother. As they drove through the rolling French country toward the westering sun and the stalwart church, she was thinking of that time long ago when she and Emil drove back from the river valley to the still unconquered Divide. Yes, she told herself, it had been worth while; both Emil and the country had become what she had hoped. Out of her father's children there was one who was fit to cope with the world, who had not been tied to the plow, and who had a personality apart from the soil. And that, she reflected, was what she had worked for. She felt well satisfied with her life.

When they reached the church, a score of teams were hitched in front of the basement doors that opened from the hillside upon the sanded terrace, where the boys wrestled and had jumping-matches. Amédée Chevalier, a proud father of one week, rushed out and embraced Emil. Amédée was an only son, — hence he was a very rich young man, — but he meant to have twenty children himself, like his uncle Xavier. "Oh, Emil," he cried, hugging his old friend rapturously, "why ain't you been up to see my boy? You come to-morrow, sure? Emil, you wanna get a boy right off! It's the greatest thing ever! No, no, no! Angel not sick at all. Everything just fine. That boy he come into this world laughin', and he been laughin' ever since. You come an' see!" He pounded Emil's ribs to emphasize each announcement.

Emil caught his arms. "Stop, Amédée. You're knocking the wind out of me. I brought him cups and spoons and blankets and moccasins enough for an orphan asylum. I'm awful glad it's a boy, sure enough!"

The young men crowded round Emil to admire his costume and to tell him in a breath everything that had happened since he went away. Emil had more friends up here in the French country than down on Norway Creek. The French and Bohemian boys were spirited and jolly, liked variety, and were as much pre-disposed to favor anything new as the Scandinavian boys were to reject it. The Norwegian and Swedish lads were much more self-centred, apt to be egotistical and jealous. They were cautious and reserved with Emil because he had been away to college, and were prepared to take him down if he should try to put on airs with them. The French boys liked a bit of swagger, and they were always delighted to hear about anything new: new clothes, new games, new songs, new dances. Now they carried Emil off to show him the club room they had just fitted up over the post-office, down in the village. They ran down the hill in a drove, all laughing and chattering at once, some in French, some in English.

Alexandra went into the cool, whitewashed basement where the women were setting the tables. Marie was standing on a chair, building a little tent of shawls where she was to tell fortunes. She sprang down and

ran toward Alexandra, stopping short and looking at
her in disappointment. Alexandra nodded to her en-
couragingly.

"Oh, he will be here, Marie. The boys have taken
him off to show him something. You won't know him.
He is a man now, sure enough. I have no boy left. He
smokes terrible-smelling Mexican cigarettes and talks
Spanish. How pretty you look, child. Where did you
get those beautiful earrings?"

"They belonged to father's mother. He always prom-
ised them to me. He sent them with the dress and said I
could keep them."

Marie wore a short red skirt of stoutly woven cloth, a
white bodice and kirtle, a yellow silk turban wound
low over her brown curls, and long coral pendants in
her ears. Her ears had been pierced against a piece of
cork by her great-aunt when she was seven years old. In
those germless days she had worn bits of broom-straw,
plucked from the common sweeping-broom, in the
lobes until the holes were healed and ready for little
gold rings.

When Emil came back from the village, he lingered
outside on the terrace with the boys. Marie could hear
him talking and strumming on his guitar while Raoul
Marcel sang falsetto. She was vexed with him for stay-

ing out there. It made her very nervous to hear him and not to see him; for, certainly, she told herself, she was not going out to look for him. When the supper bell rang and the boys came trooping in to get seats at the first table, she forgot all about her annoyance and ran to greet the tallest of the crowd, in his conspicuous attire. She did n't mind showing her embarrassment at all. She blushed and laughed excitedly as she gave Emil her hand, and looked delightedly at the black velvet coat that brought out his fair skin and fine blond head. Marie was incapable of being lukewarm about anything that pleased her. She simply did not know how to give a half-hearted response. When she was delighted, she was as likely as not to stand on her tip-toes and clap her hands. If people laughed at her, she laughed with them.

"Do the men wear clothes like that every day, in the street?" She caught Emil by his sleeve and turned him about. "Oh, I wish I lived where people wore things like that! Are the buttons real silver? Put on the hat, please. What a heavy thing! How do you ever wear it? Why don't you tell us about the bull-fights?"

She wanted to wring all his experiences from him at once, without waiting a moment. Emil smiled tolerantly and stood looking down at her with his old, brooding gaze, while the French girls fluttered about him in their white dresses and ribbons, and Alexandra watched the scene with pride. Several of the French girls, Marie knew, were hoping that Emil would take them to supper, and she was relieved when he took only his sister. Marie caught Frank's arm and dragged him to the same table, managing to get seats opposite the Bergsons, so that she could hear what they were talking about. Alexandra made Emil tell Mrs. Xavier Chevalier, the mother of the twenty, about how he had seen a famous matador killed in the bull-ring. Marie listened to every word, only taking her eyes from Emil to watch Frank's plate and keep it filled. When Emil finished his account, — bloody enough to satisfy Mrs. Xavier and to make her feel thankful that she was not a matador, — Marie broke out with a volley of questions. How did the women dress when they went to bull-fights? Did they wear *mantillas*? Did they never wear hats?

After supper the young people played charades for the amusement of their elders, who sat gossiping between their guesses. All the shops in Sainte-Agnès were closed at eight o'clock that night, so that the merchants and their clerks could attend the fair. The auction was the liveliest part of the entertainment, for the French boys always lost their heads when they began to bid, satisfied that their extravagance was in a good cause.

After all the pincushions and sofa pillows and embroidered slippers were sold, Emil precipitated a panic by taking out one of his turquoise shirt studs, which every one had been admiring, and handing it to the auctioneer. All the French girls clamored for it, and their sweethearts bid against each other recklessly. Marie wanted it, too, and she kept making signals to Frank, which he took a sour pleasure in disregarding. He did n't see the use of making a fuss over a fellow just because he was dressed like a clown. When the turquoise went to Malvina Sauvage, the French banker's daughter, Marie shrugged her shoulders and betook herself to her little tent of shawls, where she began to shuffle her cards by the light of a tallow candle, calling out, "Fortunes, fortunes!"

The young priest, Father Duchesne, went first to have his fortune read. Marie took his long white hand, looked at it, and then began to run off her cards. "I see a long journey across water for you, Father. You will go to a town all cut up by water; built on islands, it seems to be, with rivers and green fields all about. And you will visit an old lady with a white cap and gold hoops in her ears, and you will be very happy there."

"*Mais, oui,*" said the priest, with a melancholy smile. "*C'est L'Isle-Adam, chez ma mère. Vous êtes très savante, ma fille.*" He patted her yellow turban, calling, "*Venez donc, mes garçons! Il y a ici une véritable clairvoyante!*"

Marie was clever at fortune-telling, indulging in a light irony that amused the crowd. She told old Brunot, the miser, that he would lose all his money, marry a girl of sixteen, and live happily on a crust. Sholte, the fat Russian boy, who lived for his stomach, was to be disappointed in love, grow thin, and shoot himself from despondency. Amédée was to have twenty children, and nineteen of them were to be girls. Amédée slapped Frank on the back and asked him why he did n't see what the fortune-teller would promise him. But Frank shook off his friendly hand and grunted, "She tell my fortune long ago; bad enough!" Then he withdrew to a corner and sat glowering at his wife.

Frank's case was all the more painful because he had no one in particular to fix his jealousy upon. Sometimes he could have thanked the man who would bring him evidence against his wife. He had discharged a good farm-boy, Jan Smirka, because he thought Marie was fond of him; but she had not seemed to miss Jan when he was gone, and she had been just as kind to the next boy. The farm-hands would always do anything for Marie; Frank could n't find one so surly that he would not make an effort to please her. At the bottom of his heart Frank knew well enough that if he could once give up his grudge, his wife would come back to him. But he could never in the world do that. The grudge was fundamental. Perhaps he could not have given it up if he had tried. Perhaps he got more satisfaction out of feeling himself abused than he would have got out of being loved. If he could once have made Marie thoroughly unhappy, he might have relented and raised her from the dust. But she had never humbled herself. In the first days of their love she had been his slave; she had admired him abandonedly. But the moment he began to bully her and to be unjust, she began to draw away; at first in tearful amazement, then in quiet, unspoken disgust. The distance between them had widened and hardened. It no longer contracted and brought them suddenly together. The spark of her life went somewhere else, and he was always watching to surprise it. He knew that somewhere she must get a feeling to live upon, for she was not a woman who could live without loving. He wanted to prove to himself the wrong he felt. What did she hide in her heart? Where did it go? Even Frank had his churlish delicacies; he never reminded her of how much she had once loved him. For that Marie was grateful to him.

While Marie was chattering to the French boys,

The White Mulberry Tree

Amédée called Emil to the back of the room and whispered to him that they were going to play a joke on the girls. At eleven o'clock, Amédée was to go up to the switchboard in the vestibule and turn off the electric lights, and every boy would have a chance to kiss his sweetheart before Father Duchesne could find his way up the stairs to turn the current on again. The only difficulty was the candle in Marie's tent; perhaps, as Emil had no sweetheart, he would oblige the boys by blowing out the candle. Emil said he would undertake to do that.

At five minutes to eleven he sauntered up to Marie's booth, and the French boys dispersed to find their girls. He leaned over the card-table and gave himself up to looking at her. "Do you think you could tell my fortune?" he murmured. It was the first word he had had alone with her for almost a year. "My luck has n't changed any. It's just the same."

Marie had often wondered whether there was any one else who could look his thoughts to you as Emil could. To-night, when she met his steady, powerful eyes, it was impossible not to feel the sweetness of the dream he was dreaming; it reached her before she could shut it out, and hid itself in her heart. She began to shuffle her cards furiously. "I'm angry with you, Emil," she broke out with petulance. "Why did you give them that lovely blue stone to sell? You might have known Frank would n't buy it for me, and I wanted it awfully!"

Emil laughed shortly. "People who want such little things surely ought to have them," he said dryly. He thrust his hand into the pocket of his velvet trousers and brought out a handful of uncut turquoises, as big as marbles. Leaning over the table he dropped them into her lap. "There, will those do? Be careful, don't let any one see them. Now, I suppose you want me to go away and let you play with them?"

Marie was gazing in rapture at the soft blue color of the stones. "Oh, Emil! Is everything down there beautiful like these? How could you ever come away?"

At that instant Amédée laid hands on the switchboard. There was a shiver and a giggle, and every one looked toward the red blur that Marie's candle made in the dark. Immediately that, too, was gone. Little shrieks and currents of soft laughter ran up and down the dark hall. Marie started up, — directly into Emil's arms. In the same instant she felt his lips. The veil that had hung uncertainly between them for so long was dissolved. Before she knew what she was doing, she had committed herself to that kiss that was at once a boy's and a man's, as timid as it was tender; so like Emil and so unlike any one else in the world. Not until it was over did she realize what it meant. And Emil, who had so often imagined the shock of this first kiss, was surprised at its gentleness and naturalness. It was like a sigh which they had breathed together; almost sorrowful, as if each were afraid of wakening something in the other.

When the lights came on again, everybody was laughing and shouting, and all the French girls were rosy and shining with mirth. Only Marie, in her little tent of shawls, was pale and quiet. Under her yellow turban the red coral pendants swung against white cheeks. Frank was still staring at her, but he seemed to see nothing. Years ago, he himself had had the power to take the blood from her cheeks like that. Perhaps he did not remember — perhaps he had never noticed! Emil was already at the other end of the hall, walking about with the shoulder-motion he had acquired among the Mexicans, studying the floor with his intent, deep-set eyes. Marie began to take down and fold her shawls. She did not glance up again. The young people drifted to the other end of the hall where the guitar was sounding. In a moment she heard Emil and Raoul singing: —

"Across the Rio Grand-e
There lies a sunny land-e,
My bright-eyed Mexico!"

Alexandra Bergson came up to the card booth. "Let me help you, Marie. You look tired."

She placed her hand on Marie's arm and felt her shiver. Marie stiffened under that kind, calm hand. Alexandra drew back, perplexed and hurt.

There was about Alexandra something of the impervious calm of the fatalist, always disconcerting to very young people, who cannot feel that the heart lives at all unless it is still at the mercy of storms; unless its strings can scream to the touch of pain.

II

SIGNA'S wedding supper was over. The guests, and
the tiresome little Norwegian preacher who had
performed the marriage ceremony, were saying good-
night. Old Ivar was hitching the horses to the wagon to
take the wedding presents and the bride and groom up
to their new home, on Alexandra's north quarter. When
Ivar drove up to the gate, Emil and Marie Shabata began to carry out the presents, and Alexandra went into
her bedroom to bid Signa good-bye and to give her a
few words of good counsel. She was surprised to find
that the bride had changed her slippers for heavy shoes
and was pinning up her skirts. At that moment Nelse
appeared at the gate with the two milk cows that Alexandra had given Signa for a wedding present.

Alexandra began to laugh. "Why, Signa, you and
Nelse are to ride home. I'll send Ivar over with the cows
in the morning."

Signa hesitated and looked perplexed. When her
husband called her, she pinned her hat on resolutely. "I
ta-ank I better do yust like he say," she murmured in
confusion.

Alexandra and Marie accompanied Signa to the gate and saw the party set off, old Ivar driving ahead in the wagon and the bride and groom following on foot, each leading a cow. Emil burst into a laugh before they were out of hearing.

"Those two will get on," said Alexandra as they turned back to the house. "They are not going to take any chances. They will feel safer with those cows in their own stable. Marie, I am going to send for an old woman next. As soon as I get the girls broken in, I marry them off."

"I've no patience with Signa, marrying that grumpy fellow!" Marie declared. "I wanted her to marry that nice Smirka boy who worked for us last winter. I think she liked him, too."

"Yes, I think she did," Alexandra assented, "but I suppose she was too much afraid of Nelse to marry any one else. Now that I think of it, most of my girls have married men they were afraid of. I believe there is a good deal of the cow in most Swedish girls. You high-strung Bohemians can't understand us. We're a terribly practical people, and I guess we think a cross man makes a good manager."

Marie shrugged her shoulders and turned to pin up a lock of hair that had fallen on her neck. Somehow

Alexandra had irritated her of late. Everybody irritated
her. She was tired of everybody. "I'm going home alone,
Emil, so you need n't get your hat," she said as she
wound her scarf quickly about her head. "Good-night,
Alexandra," she called back in a strained voice, running
down the gravel walk.

Emil followed with long strides until he overtook
her. Then she began to walk slowly. It was a night of
warm wind and faint starlight, and the fireflies were
glimmering over the wheat.

"Marie," said Emil after they had walked for a while,
"I wonder if you know how unhappy I am?"

Marie did not answer him. Her head, in its white
scarf, drooped forward a little.

Emil kicked a clod from the path and went on: —

"I wonder whether you are really shallow-hearted,
like you seem? Sometimes I think one boy does just as
well as another for you. It never seems to make much
difference whether it is me or Raoul Marcel or Jan
Smirka. Are you really like that?"

"Perhaps I am. What do you want me to do? Sit
round and cry all day? When I've cried until I can't cry
any more, then — then I must do something else."

"Are you sorry for me?" he persisted.

"No, I'm not. If I were big and free like you, I would

n't let anything make me unhappy. As old Napoléon Brunot said at the fair, I would n't go lovering after no woman. I'd take the first train and go off and have all the fun there is."

"I tried that, but it did n't do any good. Everything reminded me. The nicer the place was, the more I wanted you." They had come to the stile and Emil pointed to it persuasively. "Sit down a moment, I want to ask you something." Marie sat down on the top step and Emil drew nearer. "Would you tell me something that's none of my business if you thought it would help me out? Well, then, tell me, *please* tell me, why you ran away with Frank Shabata!"

Marie drew back. "Because I was in love with him," she said firmly.

"Really?" he asked incredulously.

"Yes, indeed. Very much in love with him. I think I was the one who suggested our running away. From the first it was more my fault than his."

Emil turned away his face.

"And now," Marie went on, "I've got to remember that. Frank is just the same now as he was then, only then I would see him as I wanted him to be. I would have my own way. And now I pay for it."

"You don't do all the paying."

"That's it. When one makes a mistake, there's no telling where it will stop. But you can go away; you can leave all this behind you."

"Not everything. I can't leave you behind. Will you go away with me, Marie?"

Marie started up and stepped across the stile. "Emil! How wickedly you talk! I am not that kind of a girl, and you know it. But what am I going to do if you keep tormenting me like this!" she added plaintively.

"Marie, I won't bother you any more if you will tell me just one thing. Stop a minute and look at me. No, nobody can see us. Everybody's asleep. That was only a firefly. Marie, *stop* and tell me!"

Emil overtook her and catching her by the shoulders shook her gently, as if he were trying to awaken a sleep-walker.

Marie hid her face on his arm. "Don't ask me anything more. I don't know anything except how miserable I am. And I thought it would be all right when you came back. Oh, Emil," she clutched his sleeve and began to cry, "what am I to do if you don't go away? I can't go, and one of us must. Can't you see?"

Emil stood looking down at her, holding his shoulders stiff and stiffening the arm to which she clung. Her white dress looked gray in the darkness. She seemed like a troubled spirit, like some shadow out of the earth, clinging to him and entreating him to give her peace. Behind her the fireflies were weaving in and out over the wheat. He put his hand on her bent head. "On my honor, Marie, if you will say you love me, I will go away."

She lifted her face to his. "How could I help it? Did n't you know?"

Emil was the one who trembled, through all his frame. After he left Marie at her gate, he wandered about the fields all night, till morning put out the fireflies and the stars.

III

ONE evening, a week after Signa's wedding, Emil was kneeling before a box in the sitting-room, packing his books. From time to time he rose and wandered about the house, picking up stray volumes and bringing them listlessly back to his box. He was packing without enthusiasm. He was not very sanguine about his future. Alexandra sat sewing by the table. She had helped him pack his trunk in the afternoon. As Emil came and went by her chair with his books, he thought to himself that it had not been so hard to leave his sister since he first went away to school. He was going directly to Omaha, to read law in the office of a Swedish lawyer until October, when he would enter the law school at Ann Arbor. They had planned that Alexandra was to come to Michigan — a long journey for her — at Christmas time, and spend several weeks with him. Nevertheless, he felt that this leavetaking would be more final than his earlier ones had been; that it meant a definite break with his old home and the beginning of something new — he did not know what. His ideas about the future would not crystallize; the more he tried to think about it, the vaguer his conception of it became. But one thing was clear, he told himself; it was high time that he made good to Alexandra, and that ought to be incentive enough to begin with.

As he went about gathering up his books he felt as if he were uprooting things. At last he threw himself down on the old slat lounge where he had slept when he was little, and lay looking up at the familiar cracks in the ceiling.

"Tired, Emil?" his sister asked.

"Lazy," he murmured, turning on his side and looking at her. He studied Alexandra's face for a long time in the lamplight. It had never occurred to him that his sister was a handsome woman until Marie Shabata had told him so. Indeed, he had never thought of her as being a woman at all, only a sister. As he studied her bent head, he looked up at the picture of John Bergson above the lamp. "No," he thought to himself, "she did n't get it there. I suppose I am more like that."

"Alexandra," he said suddenly, "that old walnut secretary you use for a desk was father's, was n't it?"

Alexandra went on stitching. "Yes. It was one of the first things he bought for the old log house. It was a great extravagance in those days. But he wrote a great many letters back to the old country. He had many friends there, and they wrote to him up to the time he died. No one ever blamed him for grandfather's disgrace. I can see him now, sitting there on Sundays, in his white shirt, writing pages and pages, so carefully. He wrote a fine, regular hand, almost like engraving. Yours is something like his, when you take pains."

"Grandfather was really crooked, was he?"

"He married an unscrupulous woman, and then — then I'm afraid he was really crooked. When we first came here father used to have dreams about making a great fortune and going back to Sweden to pay back to the poor sailors the money grandfather had lost."

Emil stirred on the lounge. "I say, that would have been worth while, would n't it? Father was n't a bit like Lou or Oscar, was he? I can't remember much about him before he got sick."

"Oh, not at all!" Alexandra dropped her sewing on her knee. "He had better opportunities; not to make money, but to make something of himself. He was a quiet man, but he was very intelligent. You would have been proud of him, Emil."

Alexandra felt that he would like to know there had been a man of his kin whom he could admire. She knew that Emil was ashamed of Lou and Oscar, because they were bigoted and self-satisfied. He never said much about them, but she could feel his disgust. His brothers had shown their disapproval of him ever since he first went away to school. The only thing that would have satisfied them would have been his failure at the University. As it was, they resented every change in his speech, in his dress, in his point of view; though the latter they had to conjecture, for Emil avoided talking to them about any but family matters. All his interests they treated as affectations.

Alexandra took up her sewing again. "I can remember father when he was quite a young man. He belonged to some kind of a musical society, a male chorus, in Stockholm. I can remember going with mother to hear them sing. There must have been a hundred of them, and they all wore long black coats and white neckties. I was used to seeing father in a blue coat, a sort of jacket, and when I recognized him on the platform, I was very proud. Do you remember that Swedish song he taught you, about the ship boy?"

"Yes. I used to sing it to the Mexicans. They like anything different." Emil paused. "Father had a hard fight here, did n't he?" he added thoughtfully.

"Yes, and he died in a dark time. Still, he had hope. He believed in the land."

"And in you, I guess," Emil said to himself. There

was another period of silence; that warm, friendly silence, full of perfect understanding, in which Emil and Alexandra had spent many of their happiest half-hours.

At last Emil said abruptly, "Lou and Oscar would be better off if they were poor, would n't they?"

Alexandra smiled. "Maybe. But their children would n't. I have great hopes of Milly."

Emil shivered. "I don't know. Seems to me it gets worse as it goes on. The worst of the Swedes is that they're never willing to find out how much they don't know. It was like that at the University. Always so pleased with themselves! There's no getting behind that conceited Swedish grin. The Bohemians and Germans were so different."

"Come, Emil, don't go back on your own people. Father was n't conceited, Uncle Otto was n't. Even Lou and Oscar were n't when they were boys."

Emil looked incredulous, but he did not dispute the point. He turned on his back and lay still for a long time, his hands locked under his head, looking up at the ceiling. Alexandra knew that he was thinking of many things. She felt no anxiety about Emil. She had always believed in him, as she had believed in the land. He had been more like himself since he got back from Mexico; seemed glad to be at home, and talked to her as he used to do. She had no doubt that his wandering fit was over, and that he would soon be settled in life.

"Alexandra," said Emil suddenly, "do you remember the wild duck we saw down on the river that time?"

His sister looked up. "I often think of her. It always seems to me she's there still, just like we saw her."

"I know. It's queer what things one remembers and what things one forgets." Emil yawned and sat up. "Well, it's time to turn in." He rose, and going over to Alexandra stooped down and kissed her lightly on the cheek. "Good-night, sister. I think you did pretty well by us."

Emil took up his lamp and went upstairs. Alexandra sat finishing his new nightshirt, that must go in the top tray of his trunk.

IV

THE next morning Angélique, Amédée's wife, was in the kitchen baking pies, assisted by old Mrs. Chevalier. Between the mixing-board and the stove stood the old cradle that had been Amédée's, and in it was his black-eyed son. As Angélique, flushed and excited, with flour on her hands, stopped to smile at the baby, Emil Bergson rode up to the kitchen door on his mare and dismounted.

" 'Médée is out in the field, Emil," Angélique called as she ran across the kitchen to the oven. "He begins to cut his wheat to-day; the first wheat ready to cut anywhere about here. He bought a new header, you know, because all the wheat's so short this year. I hope he can rent it to the neighbors, it cost so much. He and his cousins bought a steam thresher on shares. You ought to go out and see that header work. I watched it an hour this morning, busy as I am with all the men to feed. He has a lot of hands, but he's the only one that knows how to drive the header or how to run the engine, so he has to be everywhere at once. He's sick, too, and ought to be in his bed."

O Pioneers!

Emil bent over Hector Baptiste, trying to make him blink his round, bead-like black eyes. "Sick? What's the matter with your daddy, kid? Been making him walk the floor with you?"

Angélique sniffed. "Not much! We don't have that kind of babies. It was his father that kept Baptiste awake. All night I had to be getting up and making mustard plasters to put on his stomach. He had an awful colic. He said he felt better this morning, but I don't think he ought to be out in the field, overheating himself."

Angélique did not speak with much anxiety, not because she was indifferent, but because she felt so secure in their good fortune. Only good things could happen to a rich, energetic, handsome young man like Amédée, with a new baby in the cradle and a new header in the field.

Emil stroked the black fuzz on Baptiste's head. "I say, Angélique, one of 'Médée's grandmothers, 'way back, must have been a squaw. This kid looks exactly like the Indian babies."

Angélique made a face at him, but old Mrs. Chevalier had been touched on a sore point, and she let out such a stream of fiery *patois* that Emil fled from the kitchen and mounted his mare.

Opening the pasture gate from the saddle, Emil rode

across the field to the clearing where the thresher stood, driven by a stationary engine and fed from the header boxes. As Amédée was not on the engine, Emil rode on to the wheatfield, where he recognized, on the header, the slight, wiry figure of his friend, coatless, his white shirt puffed out by the wind, his straw hat stuck jauntily on the side of his head. The six big work-horses that drew, or rather pushed, the header, went abreast at a rapid walk, and as they were still green at the work they required a good deal of management on Amédée's part; especially when they turned the corners, where they divided, three and three, and then swung round into line again with a movement that looked as complicated as a wheel of artillery. Emil felt a new thrill of admiration for his friend, and with it the old pang of envy at the way in which Amédée could do with his might what his hand found to do, and feel that, whatever it was, it was the most important thing in the world. "I'll have to bring Alexandra up to see this thing work," Emil thought; "it's splendid!"

When he saw Emil, Amédée waved to him and called to one of his twenty cousins to take the reins. Stepping off the header without stopping it, he ran up to Emil who had dismounted. "Come along," he called. "I have to go over to the engine for a minute. I gotta a green man running it, and I gotta to keep an eye on him."

Emil thought the lad was unnaturally flushed and more excited than even the cares of managing a big farm at a critical time warranted. As they passed behind a last year's stack, Amédée clutched at his right side and sank down for a moment on the straw.

"Ouch! I got an awful pain in me, Emil. Something's the matter with my insides, for sure."

Emil felt his fiery cheek. "You ought to go straight to bed, 'Médée, and telephone for the doctor; that's what you ought to do."

Amédée staggered up with a gesture of despair. "How can I? I got no time to be sick. Three thousand dollars' worth of new machinery to manage, and the wheat so ripe it will begin to shatter next week. My wheat's short, but it's gotta grand full berries. What's he slowing down for? We have n't got header boxes enough to feed the thresher, I guess."

Amédée started hot-foot across the stubble, leaning a little to the right as he ran, and waved to the engineer not to stop the engine.

Emil saw that this was no time to talk about his own affairs. He mounted his mare and rode on to Sainte-Agnès, to bid his friends there good-bye. He went first to see Raoul Marcel, and found him innocently practising the "Gloria" for the big confirmation service on

Sunday while he polished the mirrors of his father's saloon.

As Emil rode homewards at three o'clock in the afternoon, he saw Amédée staggering out of the wheatfield, supported by two of his cousins. Emil stopped and helped them put the boy to bed.

V

WHEN Frank Shabata came in from work at five
o'clock that evening, old Moïse Marcel, Raoul's
father, telephoned him that Amédée had had a seizure
in the wheatfield, and that Doctor Paradis was going to
operate on him as soon as the Hanover doctor got there
to help. Frank dropped a word of this at the table,
bolted his supper, and rode off to Sainte-Agnès, where
there would be sympathetic discussion of Amédée's case
at Marcel's saloon.

As soon as Frank was gone, Marie telephoned Alexandra. It was a comfort to hear her friend's voice. Yes,
Alexandra knew what there was to be known about
Amédée. Emil had been there when they carried him
out of the field, and had stayed with him until the doctors operated for appendicitis at five o'clock. They were
afraid it was too late to do much good; it should have
been done three days ago. Amédée was in a very bad
way. Emil had just come home, worn out and sick himself. She had given him some brandy and put him to
bed.

The White Mulberry Tree

Marie hung up the receiver. Poor Amédée's illness had taken on a new meaning to her, now that she knew Emil had been with him. And it might so easily have been the other way — Emil who was ill and Amédée who was sad! Marie looked about the dusky sitting-room. She had seldom felt so utterly lonely. If Emil was asleep, there was not even a chance of his coming; and she could not go to Alexandra for sympathy. She meant to tell Alexandra everything, as soon as Emil went away. Then whatever was left between them would be honest.

But she could not stay in the house this evening. Where should she go? She walked slowly down through the orchard, where the evening air was heavy with the smell of wild cotton. The fresh, salty scent of the wild roses had given way before this more powerful perfume of midsummer. Wherever those ashes-of-rose balls hung on their milky stalks, the air about them was saturated with their breath. The sky was still red in the west and the evening star hung directly over the Bergsons' windmill. Marie crossed the fence at the wheatfield corner, and walked slowly along the path that led to Alexandra's. She could not help feeling hurt that Emil had not come to tell her about Amédée. It seemed to her most unnatural that he should not have come. If she were in trouble, certainly he was the one person in the world she would want to see. Perhaps he wished her to understand that for her he was as good as gone already.

Marie stole slowly, flutteringly, along the path, like a white night-moth out of the fields. The years seemed to stretch before her like the land; spring, summer, autumn, winter, spring; always the same patient fields, the patient little trees, the patient lives; always the same yearning, the same pulling at the chain — until the instinct to live had torn itself and bled and weakened for the last time, until the chain secured a dead woman, who might cautiously be released. Marie walked on, her face lifted toward the remote, inaccessible evening star.

When she reached the stile she sat down and waited. How terrible it was to love people when you could not really share their lives!

Yes, in so far as she was concerned, Emil was already gone. They could n't meet any more. There was nothing for them to say. They had spent the last penny of their small change; there was nothing left but gold. The day of love-tokens was past. They had now only their hearts to give each other. And Emil being gone, what was her life to be like? In some ways, it would be easier.

She would not, at least, live in perpetual fear. If Emil were once away and settled at work, she would not have the feeling that she was spoiling his life. With the memory he left her, she could be as rash as she chose. Nobody could be the worse for it but herself; and that, surely, did not matter. Her own case was clear. When a girl had loved one man, and then loved another while that man was still alive, everybody knew what to think of her. What happened to her was of little consequence, so long as she did not drag other people down with her. Emil once away, she could let everything else go and live a new life of perfect love.

Marie left the stile reluctantly. She had, after all, thought he might come. And how glad she ought to be, she told herself, that he was asleep. She left the path and went across the pasture. The moon was almost full. An owl was hooting somewhere in the fields. She had scarcely thought about where she was going when the pond glittered before her, where Emil had shot the ducks. She stopped and looked at it. Yes, there would be a dirty way out of life, if one chose to take it. But she did not want to die. She wanted to live and dream — a hundred years, forever! As long as this sweetness welled up in her heart, as long as her breast could hold this treasure of pain! She felt as the pond must feel when it held the moon like that; when it encircled and swelled with that image of gold.

In the morning, when Emil came downstairs, Alexandra met him in the sitting-room and put her hands on his shoulders. "Emil, I went to your room as soon as it was light, but you were sleeping so sound I hated to wake you. There was nothing you could do, so I let you sleep. They telephoned from Sainte-Agnès that Amédée died at three o'clock this morning."

VI

THE Church has always held that life is for the living. On Saturday, while half the village of Sainte-Agnès was mourning for Amédée and preparing the funeral black for his burial on Monday, the other half was busy with white dresses and white veils for the great confirmation service to-morrow, when the bishop was to confirm a class of one hundred boys and girls. Father Duchesne divided his time between the living and the dead. All day Saturday the church was a scene of bustling activity, a little hushed by the thought of Amédée. The choir were busy rehearsing a mass of Rossini, which they had studied and practised for this occasion. The women were trimming the altar, the boys and girls were bringing flowers.

On Sunday morning the bishop was to drive overland to Sainte-Agnès from Hanover, and Emil Bergson had been asked to take the place of one of Amédée's cousins in the cavalcade of forty French boys who were to ride across country to meet the bishop's carriage. At six o'clock on Sunday morning the boys met at the church. As they stood holding their horses by the bridle, they talked in low tones of their dead comrade. They kept repeating that Amédée had always been a good boy, glancing toward the red-brick church which had played so large a part in Amédée's life, had been the scene of his most serious moments and of his happiest hours. He had played and wrestled and sung and courted under its shadow. Only three weeks ago he had proudly carried his baby there to be christened. They could not doubt that that invisible arm was still about Amédée; that through the church on earth he had passed to the church triumphant, the goal of the hopes and faith of so many hundred years.

When the word was given to mount, the young men rode at a walk out of the village; but once out among the wheatfields in the morning sun, their horses and their own youth got the better of them. A wave of zeal and fiery enthusiasm swept over them. They longed for a Jerusalem to deliver. The thud of their galloping hoofs interrupted many a country breakfast and brought many a woman and child to the door of the farmhouses as they passed. Five miles east of Sainte-Agnès they met the bishop in his open carriage, attended by two priests. Like one man the boys swung off their hats in a broad salute, and bowed their heads as the handsome old man lifted his two fingers in the episcopal blessing. The horsemen closed about the carriage like a guard, and whenever a restless horse broke from control and shot down the road ahead of the body, the bishop laughed and rubbed his plump hands together. "What fine boys!" he said to his priests. "The Church still has her cavalry."

As the troop swept past the graveyard half a mile east of the town, — the first frame church of the parish had stood there, — old Pierre Séguin was already out with his pick and spade, digging Amédée's grave. He knelt and uncovered as the bishop passed. The boys with one accord looked away from old Pierre to the red church on the hill, with the gold cross flaming on its steeple.

Mass was at eleven. While the church was filling, Emil Bergson waited outside, watching the wagons and buggies drive up the hill. After the bell began to ring, he saw Frank Shabata ride up on horseback and tie his horse to the hitch-bar. Marie, then, was not coming. Emil turned and went into the church. Amédée's was the only empty pew, and he sat down in it. Some of Amédée's cousins were there, dressed in black and weeping. When all the pews were full, the old men and boys packed the open space at the back of the church, kneeling on the floor. There was scarcely a family in town that was not represented in the confirmation class, by a cousin, at least. The new communicants, with their clear, reverent faces, were beautiful to look upon as they entered in a body and took the front benches reserved for them. Even before the Mass began, the air was charged with feeling. The choir had never sung so well and Raoul Marcel, in the "Gloria," drew even the bishop's eyes to the organ loft. For the offertory he sang Gounod's "Ave Maria,"—always spoken of in Sainte-Agnès as "the Ave Maria."

Emil began to torture himself with questions about Marie. Was she ill? Had she quarreled with her husband? Was she too unhappy to find comfort even here? Had she, perhaps, thought that he would come to her? Was she waiting for him? Overtaxed by excitement and sorrow as he was, the rapture of the service took hold upon his body and mind. As he listened to Raoul, he seemed to emerge from the conflicting emotions which had been whirling him about and sucking him under. He felt as if a clear light broke upon his mind, and with it a conviction that good was, after all, stronger than evil, and that good was possible to men. He seemed to discover that there was a kind of rapture in which he could love forever without faltering and without sin. He looked across the heads of the people at Frank Shabata with calmness. That rapture was for those who could feel it; for people who could not, it was non-existent. He coveted nothing that was Frank Shabata's. The spirit he had met in music was his own. Frank Shabata had never found it; would never find it if he lived beside it a thousand years; would have destroyed it if he had found it, as Herod slew the innocents, as Rome slew the martyrs.

San — cta Mari-i-i-a,

wailed Raoul from the organ loft;

O — ra pro no-o-bis!

And it did not occur to Emil that any one had ever reasoned thus before, that music had ever before given a man this equivocal revelation.

The confirmation service followed the Mass. When it was over, the congregation thronged about the newly confirmed. The girls, and even the boys, were kissed and embraced and wept over. All the aunts and grand-mothers wept with joy. The housewives had much ado to tear themselves away from the general rejoicing and hurry back to their kitchens. The country parishioners were staying in town for dinner, and nearly every house in Sainte-Agnès entertained visitors that day. Father Duchesne, the bishop, and the visiting priests dined with Fabien Sauvage, the banker. Emil and Frank Shabata were both guests of old Moïse Marcel. After dinner Frank and old Moïse retired to the rear room of the saloon to play California Jack and drink their cognac, and Emil went over to the banker's with Raoul, who had been asked to sing for the bishop.

At three o'clock, Emil felt that he could stand it no longer. He slipped out under cover of "The Holy City," followed by Malvina's wistful eye, and went to the stable for his mare. He was at that height of excitement from which everything is foreshortened, from which life seems short and simple, death very near, and the soul seems to soar like an eagle. As he rode past the graveyard he looked at the brown hole in the earth where Amédée was to lie, and felt no horror. That, too, was beautiful, that simple doorway into forgetfulness. The heart, when it is too much alive, aches for that brown earth, and ecstasy has no fear of death. It is the old and the poor and the maimed who shrink from that brown hole; its wooers are found among the young, the passionate, the gallant-hearted. It was not until he had passed the graveyard that Emil realized where he was going. It was the hour for saying good-bye. It might be the last time that he would see her alone, and to-day he could leave her without rancor, without bitterness.

Everywhere the grain stood ripe and the hot afternoon was full of the smell of the ripe wheat, like the smell of bread baking in an oven. The breath of the wheat and the sweet clover passed him like pleasant things in a dream. He could feel nothing but the sense of diminishing distance. It seemed to him that his mare was flying, or running on wheels, like a railway train. The sunlight, flashing on the window-glass of the big red barns, drove him wild with joy. He was like an arrow shot from the bow. His life poured itself out along the road before him as he rode to the Shabata farm.

When Emil alighted at the Shabatas' gate, his horse was in a lather. He tied her in the stable and hurried to the house. It was empty. She might be at Mrs. Hiller's or with Alexandra. But anything that reminded him of her would be enough, the orchard, the mulberry tree . . . When he reached the orchard the sun was hanging low over the wheatfield. Long fingers of light reached through the apple branches as through a net; the orchard was riddled and shot with gold; light was the reality, the trees were merely interferences that reflected and refracted light. Emil went softly down between the cherry trees toward the wheatfield. When he came to the corner, he stopped short and put his hand over his mouth. Marie was lying on her side under the white mulberry tree, her face half hidden in the grass,

231

her eyes closed, her hands lying limply where they had happened to fall. She had lived a day of her new life of perfect love, and it had left her like this. Her breast rose and fell faintly, as if she were asleep. Emil threw himself down beside her and took her in his arms. The blood came back to her cheeks, her amber eyes opened slowly, and in them Emil saw his own face and the orchard and the sun. "I was dreaming this," she whispered, hiding her face against him, "don't take my dream away!"

VII

WHEN Frank Shabata got home that night, he found Emil's mare in his stable. Such an impertinence amazed him. Like everybody else, Frank had had an exciting day. Since noon he had been drinking too much, and he was in a bad temper. He talked bitterly to himself while he put his own horse away, and as he went up the path and saw that the house was dark he felt an added sense of injury. He approached quietly and listened on the doorstep. Hearing nothing, he opened the kitchen door and went softly from one room to another. Then he went through the house again, upstairs and down, with no better result. He sat down on the bottom step of the box stairway and tried to get his wits together. In that unnatural quiet there was no sound but his own heavy breathing. Suddenly an owl began to hoot out in the fields. Frank lifted his head. An idea flashed into his mind, and his sense of injury and outrage grew. He went into his bedroom and took his murderous .405 Winchester from the closet.

When Frank took up his gun and walked out of the house, he had not the faintest purpose of doing anything with it. He did not believe that he had any real grievance. But it gratified him to feel like a desperate man. He had got into the habit of seeing himself always in desperate straits. His unhappy temperament was like a cage; he could never get out of it; and he felt that other people, his wife in particular, must have put him there. It had never more than dimly occurred to Frank that he made his own unhappiness. Though he took up his gun with dark projects in his mind, he would have been paralyzed with fright had he known that there was the slightest probability of his ever carrying any of them out.

Frank went slowly down to the orchard gate, stopped and stood for a moment lost in thought. He retraced his steps and looked through the barn and the hayloft. Then he went out to the road, where he took the foot-path along the outside of the orchard hedge. The hedge was twice as tall as Frank himself, and so dense that one could see through it only by peering closely between the leaves. He could see the empty path a long way in the moonlight. His mind traveled ahead to the stile, which he always thought of as haunted by Emil Bergson. But why had he left his horse?

At the wheatfield corner, where the orchard hedge ended and the path led across the pasture to the Bergsons', Frank stopped. In the warm, breathless night air he heard a murmuring sound, perfectly inarticulate, as low as the sound of water coming from a spring, where there is no fall, and where there are no stones to fret it. Frank strained his ears. It ceased. He held his breath and began to tremble. Resting the butt of his gun on the ground, he parted the mulberry leaves softly with his fingers and peered through the hedge at the dark figures on the grass, in the shadow of the mulberry tree. It seemed to him that they must feel his eyes, that they must hear him breathing. But they did not. Frank, who had always wanted to see things blacker than they were, for once wanted to believe less than he saw. The woman lying in the shadow might so easily be one of the Bergsons' farm-girls. . . . Again the murmur, like water welling out of the ground. This time he heard it more distinctly, and his blood was quicker than his brain. He began to act, just as a man who falls into the fire begins to act. The gun sprang to his shoulder, he sighted mechanically and fired three times without stopping, stopped without knowing why. Either he shut his eyes or he had vertigo. He did not see anything while he was firing. He thought he heard a cry simultaneous with the second report, but he was not sure. He peered again through the hedge, at the two dark figures under the tree. They had fallen a little apart from each other, and were perfectly still — No, not quite; in a white patch of light, where the moon shone through the branches, a man's hand was plucking spasmodically at the grass.

Suddenly the woman stirred and uttered a cry, then another, and another. She was living! She was dragging herself toward the hedge! Frank dropped his gun and ran back along the path, shaking, stumbling, gasping. He had never imagined such horror. The cries followed him. They grew fainter and thicker, as if she were choking. He dropped on his knees beside the hedge and crouched like a rabbit, listening; fainter, fainter; a sound like a whine; again — a moan — another — silence. Frank scrambled to his feet and ran on, groaning and praying. From habit he went toward the house, where he was used to being soothed when he had worked himself into a frenzy, but at the sight of the black, open door, he started back. He knew that he had murdered somebody, that a woman was bleeding and moaning in the orchard, but he had not realized before that it was his wife. The gate stared him in the face. He threw his hands over his head. Which way to turn? He lifted his tormented face and looked at the sky. "Holy Mother of God, not to suffer! She was a good girl — not to suffer!"

Frank had been wont to see himself in dramatic situations; but now, when he stood by the windmill, in the bright space between the barn and the house, facing his own black doorway, he did not see himself at all. He stood like the hare when the dogs are approaching from all sides. And he ran like a hare, back and forth about that moonlit space, before he could make up his mind to go into the dark stable for a horse. The thought of going into a doorway was terrible to him. He caught Emil's horse by the bit and led it out. He could not have buckled a bridle on his own. After two or three attempts, he lifted himself into the saddle and started for Hanover. If he could catch the one-o'clock train, he had money enough to get as far as Omaha.

While he was thinking dully of this in some less sensitized part of his brain, his acuter faculties were going over and over the cries he had heard in the orchard. Terror was the only thing that kept him from going back to her, terror that she might still be she, that she might still be suffering. A woman, mutilated and bleeding in his orchard — it was because it was a woman that he was so afraid. It was inconceivable that he should have hurt a woman. He would rather be eaten by wild beasts than see her move on the ground as she had moved in the orchard. Why had she been so careless? She knew he was like a crazy man when he was angry.

She had more than once taken that gun away from him and held it, when he was angry with other people. Once it had gone off while they were struggling over it. She was never afraid. But, when she knew him, why had n't she been more careful? Did n't she have all summer before her to love Emil Bergson in, without taking such chances? Probably she had met the Smirka boy, too, down there in the orchard. He did n't care. She could have met all the men on the Divide there, and welcome, if only she had n't brought this horror on him.

There was a wrench in Frank's mind. He did not honestly believe that of her. He knew that he was doing her wrong. He stopped his horse to admit this to himself the more directly, to think it out the more clearly. He knew that he was to blame. For three years he had been trying to break her spirit. She had a way of making the best of things that seemed to him a sentimental affectation. He wanted his wife to resent that he was wasting his best years among these stupid and unappreciative people; but she had seemed to find the people quite good enough. If he ever got rich he meant to buy her pretty clothes and take her to California in a Pullman car, and treat her like a lady; but in the mean time he wanted her to feel that life was as ugly and as unjust as he felt it. He had tried to make her life ugly.

He had refused to share any of the little pleasures she was so plucky about making for herself. She could be gay about the least thing in the world; but she must be gay! When she first came to him, her faith in him, her adoration — Frank struck the mare with his fist. Why had Marie made him do this thing; why had she brought this upon him? He was overwhelmed by sickening misfortune. All at once he heard her cries again — he had forgotten for a moment. "Maria," he sobbed aloud, "Maria!"

When Frank was halfway to Hanover, the motion of his horse brought on a violent attack of nausea. After it had passed, he rode on again, but he could think of nothing except his physical weakness and his desire to be comforted by his wife. He wanted to get into his own bed. Had his wife been at home, he would have turned and gone back to her meekly enough.

VIII

WHEN old Ivar climbed down from his loft at four o'clock the next morning, he came upon Emil's mare, jaded and lather-stained, her bridle broken, chewing the scattered tufts of hay outside the stable door. The old man was thrown into a fright at once. He put the mare in her stall, threw her a measure of oats, and then set out as fast as his bow-legs could carry him on the path to the nearest neighbor.

"Something is wrong with that boy. Some misfortune has come upon us. He would never have used her so, in his right senses. It is not his way to abuse his mare," the old man kept muttering, as he scuttled through the short, wet pasture grass on his bare feet.

While Ivar was hurrying across the fields, the first long rays of the sun were reaching down between the orchard boughs to those two dew-drenched figures. The story of what had happened was written plainly on the orchard grass, and on the white mulberries that had fallen in the night and were covered with dark stain. For Emil the chapter had been short. He was shot in the heart, and had rolled over on his back and died. His face was turned up to the sky and his brows were drawn in a frown, as if he had realized that something had befallen him. But for Marie Shabata it had not been so easy. One ball had torn through her right lung, another had shattered the carotid artery. She must have started up and gone toward the hedge, leaving a trail of blood. There she had fallen and bled. From that spot there was another trail, heavier than the first, where she must have dragged herself back to Emil's body. Once there, she seemed not to have struggled any more. She had lifted her head to her lover's breast, taken his hand in both her own, and bled quietly to death. She was lying on her right side in an easy and natural position, her cheek on Emil's shoulder. On her face there was a look of ineffable content. Her lips were parted a little; her eyes were lightly closed, as if in a day-dream or a light slumber. After she lay down there, she seemed not to have moved an eyelash. The hand she held was covered with dark stains, where she had kissed it.

But the stained, slippery grass, the darkened mulberries, told only half the story. Above Marie and Emil, two white butterflies from Frank's alfalfa-field were fluttering in and out among the interlacing shadows; diving and soaring, now close together, now far apart; and in the long grass by the fence the last wild roses of the year opened their pink hearts to die.

When Ivar reached the path by the hedge, he saw Shabata's rifle lying in the way. He turned and peered through the branches, falling upon his knees as if his legs had been mowed from under him. "Merciful God!" he groaned; "merciful, merciful God!"

Alexandra, too, had risen early that morning, because of her anxiety about Emil. She was in Emil's room upstairs when, from the window, she saw Ivar coming along the path that led from the Shabatas'. He was running like a spent man, tottering and lurching from side to side. Ivar never drank, and Alexandra thought at once that one of his spells had come upon him, and that he must be in a very bad way indeed. She ran downstairs and hurried out to meet him, to hide his infirmity from the eyes of her household. The old man fell in the road at her feet and caught her hand, over which he bowed his shaggy head. "Mistress, mistress," he sobbed, "it has fallen! Sin and death for the young ones! God have mercy upon us!"

PART V

Alexandra

PART V

Alexandra

I

IVAR was sitting at a cobbler's bench in the barn, mending harness by the light of a lantern and repeating to himself the 101st Psalm. It was only five o'clock of a mid-October day, but a storm had come up in the afternoon, bringing black clouds, a cold wind and torrents of rain. The old man wore his buffalo-skin coat, and occasionally stopped to warm his fingers at the lantern. Suddenly a woman burst into the shed, as if she had been blown in, accompanied by a shower of rain-drops. It was Signa, wrapped in a man's overcoat and wearing a pair of boots over her shoes. In time of trouble Signa had come back to stay with her mistress, for she was the only one of the maids from whom Alexandra would accept much personal service. It was three months now since the news of the terrible thing that had happened in Frank Shabata's orchard had first run like a fire over the Divide. Signa and Nelse were staying on with Alexandra until winter.

"Ivar," Signa exclaimed as she wiped the rain from her face, "do you know where she is?"

The old man put down his cobbler's knife. "Who, the mistress?"

"Yes. She went away about three o'clock. I happened to look out of the window and saw her going across the fields in her thin dress and sun-hat. And now this storm has come on. I thought she was going to Mrs. Hiller's, and I telephoned as soon as the thunder stopped, but she had not been there. I'm afraid she is out somewhere and will get her death of cold."

Ivar put on his cap and took up the lantern. "*Ja, ja*, we will see. I will hitch the boy's mare to the cart and go."

Signa followed him across the wagon-shed to the horses' stable. She was shivering with cold and excitement. "Where do you suppose she can be, Ivar?"

The old man lifted a set of single harness carefully from its peg. "How should I know?"

"But you think she is at the graveyard, don't you?" Signa persisted. "So do I. Oh, I wish she would be more like herself! I can't believe it's Alexandra Bergson come to this, with no head about anything. I have to tell her when to eat and when to go to bed."

"Patience, patience, sister," muttered Ivar as he settled the bit in the horse's mouth. "When the eyes of the flesh are shut, the eyes of the spirit are open. She will have a message from those who are gone, and that will bring her peace. Until then we must bear with her. You and I are the only ones who have weight with her. She trusts us."

"How awful it's been these last three months." Signa held the lantern so that he could see to buckle the straps. "It don't seem right that we must all be so miserable. Why do we all have to be punished? Seems to me like good times would never come again."

Ivar expressed himself in a deep sigh, but said nothing. He stooped and took a sandburr from his toe.

"Ivar," Signa asked suddenly, "will you tell me why you go barefoot? All the time I lived here in the house I wanted to ask you. Is it for a penance, or what?"

"No, sister. It is for the indulgence of the body. From my youth up I have had a strong, rebellious body, and have been subject to every kind of temptation. Even in age my temptations are prolonged. It was necessary to make some allowances; and the feet, as I understand it, are free members. There is no divine prohibition for them in the Ten Commandments. The hands, the tongue, the eyes, the heart, all the bodily desires we are commanded to subdue; but the feet are free members. I indulge them without harm to any one, even to tram-

247

pling in filth when my desires are low. They are quickly cleaned again."

Signa did not laugh. She looked thoughtful as she followed Ivar out to the wagon-shed and held the shafts up for him, while he backed in the mare and buckled the hold-backs. "You have been a good friend to the mistress, Ivar," she murmured.

"And you, God be with you," replied Ivar as he clambered into the cart and put the lantern under the oilcloth lap-cover. "Now for a ducking, my girl," he said to the mare, gathering up the reins.

As they emerged from the shed, a stream of water, running off the thatch, struck the mare on the neck. She tossed her head indignantly, then struck out bravely on the soft ground, slipping back again and again as she climbed the hill to the main road. Between the rain and the darkness Ivar could see very little, so he let Emil's mare have the rein, keeping her head in the right direction. When the ground was level, he turned her out of the dirt road upon the sod, where she was able to trot without slipping.

Before Ivar reached the graveyard, three miles from the house, the storm had spent itself, and the downpour had died into a soft, dripping rain. The sky and the land were a dark smoke color, and seemed to be coming together, like two waves. When Ivar stopped at the gate and swung out his lantern, a white figure rose from beside John Bergson's white stone.

The old man sprang to the ground and shuffled toward the gate calling, "Mistress, mistress!"

Alexandra hurried to meet him and put her hand on his shoulder. "*Tyst!* Ivar. There's nothing to be worried about. I'm sorry if I've scared you all. I did n't notice the storm till it was on me, and I could n't walk against it. I'm glad you've come. I am so tired I did n't know how I'd ever get home."

Ivar swung the lantern up so that it shone in her face. "*Gud!* You are enough to frighten us, mistress. You look like a drowned woman. How could you do such a thing!"

Groaning and mumbling he led her out of the gate and helped her into the cart, wrapping her in the dry blankets on which he had been sitting.

Alexandra smiled at his solicitude. "Not much use in that, Ivar. You will only shut the wet in. I don't feel so cold now; but I'm heavy and numb. I'm glad you came."

Ivar turned the mare and urged her into a sliding trot. Her feet sent back a continual spatter of mud.

Alexandra spoke to the old man as they jogged along through the sullen gray twilight of the storm. "Ivar, I

249

think it has done me good to get cold clear through like this, once. I don't believe I shall suffer so much any more. When you get so near the dead, they seem more real than the living. Worldly thoughts leave one. Ever since Emil died, I've suffered so when it rained. Now that I've been out in it with him, I shan't dread it. After you once get cold clear through, the feeling of the rain on you is sweet. It seems to bring back feelings you had when you were a baby. It carries you back into the dark, before you were born; you can't see things, but they come to you, somehow, and you know them and are n't afraid of them. Maybe it's like that with the dead. If they feel anything at all, it's the old things, before they were born, that comfort people like the feeling of their own bed does when they are little."

"Mistress," said Ivar reproachfully, "those are bad thoughts. The dead are in Paradise."

Then he hung his head, for he did not believe that Emil was in Paradise.

When they got home, Signa had a fire burning in the sitting-room stove. She undressed Alexandra and gave her a hot footbath, while Ivar made ginger tea in the kitchen. When Alexandra was in bed, wrapped in hot blankets, Ivar came in with his tea and saw that she drank it. Signa asked permission to sleep on the slat lounge outside her door. Alexandra endured their attentions patiently, but she was glad when they put out the lamp and left her. As she lay alone in the dark, it occurred to her for the first time that perhaps she was actually tired of life. All the physical operations of life seemed difficult and painful. She longed to be free from her own body, which ached and was so heavy. And longing itself was heavy: she yearned to be free of that.

As she lay with her eyes closed, she had again, more vividly than for many years, the old illusion of her girlhood, of being lifted and carried lightly by some one very strong. He was with her a long while this time, and carried her very far, and in his arms she felt free from pain. When he laid her down on her bed again, she opened her eyes, and, for the first time in her life, she saw him, saw him clearly, though the room was dark, and his face was covered. He was standing in the doorway of her room. His white cloak was thrown over his face, and his head was bent a little forward. His shoulders seemed as strong as the foundations of the world. His right arm, bared from the elbow, was dark and gleaming, like bronze, and she knew at once that it was the arm of the mightiest of all lovers. She knew at last for whom it was she had waited, and where he would carry her. That, she told herself, was very well. Then she went to sleep.

Alexandra wakened in the morning with nothing worse than a hard cold and a stiff shoulder. She kept her bed for several days, and it was during that time that she formed a resolution to go to Lincoln to see Frank Shabata. Ever since she last saw him in the courtroom, Frank's haggard face and wild eyes had haunted her. The trial had lasted only three days. Frank had given himself up to the police in Omaha and pleaded guilty of killing without malice and without premeditation. The gun was, of course, against him, and the judge had given him the full sentence, — ten years. He had now been in the State Penitentiary for a month.

Frank was the only one, Alexandra told herself, for whom anything could be done. He had been less in the wrong than any of them, and he was paying the heaviest penalty. She often felt that she herself had been more to blame than poor Frank. From the time the Shabatas had first moved to the neighboring farm, she had omitted no opportunity of throwing Marie and Emil together. Because she knew Frank was surly about doing little things to help his wife, she was always sending Emil over to spade or plant or carpenter for Marie. She was glad to have Emil see as much as possible of an intelligent, city-bred girl like their neighbor; she noticed that it improved his manners. She knew that

Emil was fond of Marie, but it had never occurred to her that Emil's feeling might be different from her own. She wondered at herself now, but she had never thought of danger in that direction. If Marie had been unmarried,—oh, yes! Then she would have kept her eyes open. But the mere fact that she was Shabata's wife, for Alexandra, settled everything. That she was beautiful, impulsive, barely two years older than Emil, these facts had had no weight with Alexandra. Emil was a good boy, and only bad boys ran after married women.

Now, Alexandra could in a measure realize that Marie was, after all, Marie; not merely a "married woman." Sometimes, when Alexandra thought of her, it was with an aching tenderness. The moment she had reached them in the orchard that morning, everything was clear to her. There was something about those two lying in the grass, something in the way Marie had settled her cheek on Emil's shoulder, that told her everything. She wondered then how they could have helped loving each other; how she could have helped knowing that they must. Emil's cold, frowning face, the girl's content— Alexandra had felt awe of them, even in the first shock of her grief.

The idleness of those days in bed, the relaxation of body which attended them, enabled Alexandra to think more calmly than she had done since Emil's death. She and Frank, she told herself, were left out of that group of friends who had been overwhelmed by disaster. She must certainly see Frank Shabata. Even in the courtroom her heart had grieved for him. He was in a strange country, he had no kinsmen or friends, and in a moment he had ruined his life. Being what he was, she felt, Frank could not have acted otherwise. She could understand his behavior more easily than she could understand Marie's. Yes, she must go to Lincoln to see Frank Shabata.

The day after Emil's funeral, Alexandra had written to Carl Linstrum; a single page of note-paper, a bare statement of what had happened. She was not a woman who could write much about such a thing, and about her own feelings she could never write very freely. She knew that Carl was away from post-offices, prospecting somewhere in the interior. Before he started he had written her where he expected to go, but her ideas about Alaska were vague. As the weeks went by and she heard nothing from him, it seemed to Alexandra that her heart grew hard against Carl. She began to wonder whether she would not do better to finish her life alone. What was left of life seemed unimportant.

II

LATE in the afternoon of a brilliant October day, Alexandra Bergson, dressed in a black suit and traveling-hat, alighted at the Burlington depot in Lincoln. She drove to the Lindell Hotel, where she had stayed two years ago when she came up for Emil's Commencement. In spite of her usual air of sureness and self-possession, Alexandra felt ill at ease in hotels, and she was glad, when she went to the clerk's desk to register, that there were not many people in the lobby. She had her supper early, wearing her hat and black jacket down to the dining-room and carrying her handbag. After supper she went out for a walk.

It was growing dark when she reached the university campus. She did not go into the grounds, but walked slowly up and down the stone walk outside the long iron fence, looking through at the young men who were running from one building to another, at the lights shining from the armory and the library. A squad of cadets were going through their drill behind the armory, and the commands of their young officer rang out at regular intervals, so sharp and quick that Alexandra

255

could not understand them. Two stalwart girls came down the library steps and out through one of the iron gates. As they passed her, Alexandra was pleased to hear them speaking Bohemian to each other. Every few moments a boy would come running down the flagged walk and dash out into the street as if he were rushing to announce some wonder to the world. Alexandra felt a great tenderness for them all. She wished one of them would stop and speak to her. She wished she could ask them whether they had known Emil.

As she lingered by the south gate she actually did encounter one of the boys. He had on his drill cap and was swinging his books at the end of a long strap. It was dark by this time; he did not see her and ran against her. He snatched off his cap and stood bareheaded and panting. "I'm awfully sorry," he said in a bright, clear voice, with a rising inflection, as if he expected her to say something.

"Oh, it was my fault!" said Alexandra eagerly. "Are you an old student here, may I ask?"

"No, ma'am. I'm a Freshie, just off the farm. Cherry County. Were you hunting somebody?"

"No, thank you. That is — " Alexandra wanted to detain him. "That is, I would like to find some of my brother's friends. He graduated two years ago."

"Then you'd have to try the Seniors, would n't you? Let's see; I don't know any of them yet, but there'll be sure to be some of them around the library. That red building, right there," he pointed.

"Thank you, I'll try there," said Alexandra lingeringly.

"Oh, that's all right! Good-night." The lad clapped his cap on his head and ran straight down Eleventh Street. Alexandra looked after him wistfully.

She walked back to her hotel unreasonably comforted. "What a nice voice that boy had, and how polite he was. I know Emil was always like that to women." And again, after she had undressed and was standing in her nightgown, brushing her long, heavy hair by the electric light, she remembered him and said to herself: "I don't think I ever heard a nicer voice than that boy had. I hope he will get on well here. Cherry County; that's where the hay is so fine, and the coyotes can scratch down to water."

At nine o'clock the next morning Alexandra presented herself at the warden's office in the State Penitentiary. The warden was a German, a ruddy, cheerful-looking man who had formerly been a harness-maker. Alexandra had a letter to him from the German banker in Hanover. As he glanced at the letter, Mr. Schwartz put away his pipe.

"That big Bohemian, is it? Sure, he's gettin' along fine," said Mr. Schwartz cheerfully.

"I am glad to hear that. I was afraid he might be quarrelsome and get himself into more trouble. Mr. Schwartz, if you have time, I would like to tell you a little about Frank Shabata, and why I am interested in him."

The warden listened genially while she told him briefly something of Frank's history and character, but he did not seem to find anything unusual in her account.

"Sure, I'll keep an eye on him. We'll take care of him all right," he said, rising. "You can talk to him here, while I go to see to things in the kitchen. I'll have him sent in. He ought to be done washing out his cell by this time. We have to keep 'em clean, you know."

The warden paused at the door, speaking back over his shoulder to a pale young man in convicts' clothes who was seated at a desk in the corner, writing in a big ledger.

"Bertie, when 1037 is brought in, you just step out and give this lady a chance to talk."

The young man bowed his head and bent over his ledger again.

When Mr. Schwartz disappeared, Alexandra thrust

her black-edged handkerchief nervously into her hand-bag. Coming out on the street-car she had not had the least dread of meeting Frank. But since she had been here the sounds and smells in the corridor, the look of the men in convicts' clothes who passed the glass door of the warden's office, affected her unpleasantly.

The warden's clock ticked, the young convict's pen scratched busily in the big book, and his sharp shoulders were shaken every few seconds by a loose cough which he tried to smother. It was easy to see that he was a sick man. Alexandra looked at him timidly, but he did not once raise his eyes. He wore a white shirt under his striped jacket, a high collar, and a necktie, very carefully tied. His hands were thin and white and well cared for, and he had a seal ring on his little finger. When he heard steps approaching in the corridor, he rose, blotted his book, put his pen in the rack, and left the room without raising his eyes. Through the door he opened a guard came in, bringing Frank Shabata.

"You the lady that wanted to talk to 1037? Here he is. Be on your good behavior, now. He can set down, lady," seeing that Alexandra remained standing. "Push that white button when you're through with him, and I'll come."

The guard went out and Alexandra and Frank were left alone.

Alexandra tried not to see his hideous clothes. She tried to look straight into his face, which she could scarcely believe was his. It was already bleached to a chalky gray. His lips were colorless, his fine teeth looked yellowish. He glanced at Alexandra sullenly, blinked as if he had come from a dark place, and one eyebrow twitched continually. She felt at once that this interview was a terrible ordeal to him. His shaved head, showing the conformation of his skull, gave him a criminal look which he had not had during the trial.

Alexandra held out her hand. "Frank," she said, her eyes filling suddenly, "I hope you'll let me be friendly with you. I understand how you did it. I don't feel hard toward you. They were more to blame than you."

Frank jerked a dirty blue handkerchief from his trousers pocket. He had begun to cry. He turned away from Alexandra. "I never did mean to do not'ing to dat woman," he muttered. "I never mean to do not'ing to dat boy. I ain't had not'ing ag'in' dat boy. I always like dat boy fine. An' then I find him — " He stopped. The feeling went out of his face and eyes. He dropped into a chair and sat looking stolidly at the floor, his hands hanging loosely between his knees, the handkerchief lying across his striped leg. He seemed to have stirred up in his mind a disgust that had paralyzed his faculties.

"I have n't come up here to blame you, Frank. I think they were more to blame than you." Alexandra, too, felt benumbed.

Frank looked up suddenly and stared out of the office window. "I guess dat place all go to hell what I work so hard on," he said with a slow, bitter smile. "I not care a damn." He stopped and rubbed the palm of his hand over the light bristles on his head with annoyance. "I no can t'ink without my hair," he complained. "I forget English. We not talk here, except swear."

Alexandra was bewildered. Frank seemed to have undergone a change of personality. There was scarcely anything by which she could recognize her handsome Bohemian neighbor. He seemed, somehow, not altogether human. She did not know what to say to him.

"You do not feel hard to me, Frank?" she asked at last.

Frank clenched his fist and broke out in excitement. "I not feel hard at no woman. I tell you I not that kind-a man. I never hit my wife. No, never I hurt her when she devil me something awful!" He struck his fist down on the warden's desk so hard that he afterward stroked it absently. A pale pink crept over his neck and face. "Two, t'ree years I know dat woman don' care no more 'bout me, Alexandra Bergson. I know she after some other man. I know her, oo-oo! An' I ain't never hurt her. I never would-a done dat, if I ain't had dat gun along. I don' know what in hell make me take dat gun. She always say I ain't no man to carry gun. If she been in dat house, where she ought-a been — But das a foolish talk."

Frank rubbed his head and stopped suddenly, as he had stopped before. Alexandra felt that there was something strange in the way he chilled off, as if something came up in him that extinguished his power of feeling or thinking.

"Yes, Frank," she said kindly. "I know you never meant to hurt Marie."

Frank smiled at her queerly. His eyes filled slowly with tears. "You know, I most forgit dat woman's name. She ain't got no name for me no more. I never hate my wife, but dat woman what make me do dat— Honest to God, but I hate her! I no man to fight. I don' want to kill no boy and no woman. I not care how many men she take under dat tree. I not care for not'ing but dat fine boy I kill, Alexandra Bergson. I guess I go crazy sure 'nough."

Alexandra remembered the little yellow cane she had found in Frank's clothes-closet. She thought of how he had come to this country a gay young fellow, so attractive that the prettiest Bohemian girl in Omaha had run away with him. It seemed unreasonable that life should have landed him in such a place as this. She blamed Marie bitterly. And why, with her happy, affectionate nature, should she have brought destruction and sorrow to all who had loved her, even to poor old Joe Tovesky, the uncle who used to carry her about so proudly when she was a little girl? That was the strangest thing of all. Was there, then, something wrong in being warm-hearted and impulsive like that? Alexandra hated to think so. But there was Emil, in the Norwegian graveyard at home, and here was Frank Shabata. Alexandra rose and took him by the hand.

"Frank Shabata, I am never going to stop trying until I get you pardoned. I'll never give the Governor any peace. I know I can get you out of this place."

Frank looked at her distrustfully, but he gathered confidence from her face. "Alexandra," he said earnestly, "if I git out-a here, I not trouble dis country no more. I go back where I come from; see my mother."

Alexandra tried to withdraw her hand, but Frank held on to it nervously. He put out his finger and absently touched a button on her black jacket. "Alexandra," he said in a low tone, looking steadily at the button, "you ain' t'ink I use dat girl awful bad before — "

"No, Frank. We won't talk about that," Alexandra said, pressing his hand. "I can't help Emil now, so I'm going to do what I can for you. You know I don't go away from home often, and I came up here on purpose to tell you this."

The warden at the glass door looked in inquiringly. Alexandra nodded, and he came in and touched the white button on his desk. The guard appeared, and with a sinking heart Alexandra saw Frank led away down the corridor. After a few words with Mr. Schwartz, she left the prison and made her way to the street-car. She had refused with horror the warden's cordial invitation to "go through the institution." As the car lurched over its uneven roadbed, back toward Lincoln, Alexandra thought of how she and Frank had been wrecked by the same storm and of how, although she could come out into the sunlight, she had not much more left in her life than he. She remembered some lines from a poem she had liked in her schooldays: —

> Henceforth the world will only be
> A wider prison-house to me, —

and sighed. A disgust of life weighed upon her heart; some such feeling as had twice frozen Frank Shabata's features while they talked together. She wished she were back on the Divide.

Alexandra

When Alexandra entered her hotel, the clerk held up one finger and beckoned to her. As she approached his desk, he handed her a telegram. Alexandra took the yellow envelope and looked at it in perplexity, then stepped into the elevator without opening it. As she walked down the corridor toward her room, she reflected that she was, in a manner, immune from evil tidings. On reaching her room she locked the door, and sitting down on a chair by the dresser, opened the telegram. It was from Hanover, and it read: —

ARRIVED HANOVER LAST NIGHT. SHALL WAIT HERE UNTIL YOU COME. PLEASE HURRY.

CARL LINSTRUM.

Alexandra put her head down on the dresser and burst into tears.

III

THE next afternoon Carl and Alexandra were walking across the fields from Mrs. Hiller's. Alexandra had left Lincoln after midnight, and Carl had met her at the Hanover station early in the morning. After they reached home, Alexandra had gone over to Mrs. Hiller's to leave a little present she had bought for her in the city. They stayed at the old lady's door but a moment, and then came out to spend the rest of the afternoon in the sunny fields.

Alexandra had taken off her black traveling-suit and put on a white dress; partly because she saw that her black clothes made Carl uncomfortable and partly because she felt oppressed by them herself. They seemed a little like the prison where she had worn them yesterday, and to be out of place in the open fields. Carl had changed very little. His cheeks were browner and fuller. He looked less like a tired scholar than when he went away a year ago, but no one, even now, would have taken him for a man of business. His soft, lustrous black eyes, his whimsical smile, would be less against him

266

in the Klondike than on the Divide. There are always dreamers on the frontier.

Carl and Alexandra had been talking since morning. Her letter had never reached him. He had first learned of her misfortune from a San Francisco paper, four weeks old, which he had picked up in a saloon, and which contained a brief account of Frank Shabata's trial. When he put down the paper, he had already made up his mind that he could reach Alexandra as quickly as a letter could; and ever since he had been on the way; day and night, by the fastest boats and trains he could catch. His steamer had been held back two days by rough weather.

As they came out of Mrs. Hiller's garden they took up their talk again where they had left it.

"But could you come away like that, Carl, without arranging things? Could you just walk off and leave your business?" Alexandra asked.

Carl laughed. "Prudent Alexandra! You see, my dear, I happen to have an honest partner. I trust him with everything. In fact, it's been his enterprise from the beginning, you know. I'm in it only because he took me in. I'll have to go back in the spring. Perhaps you will want to go with me then. We have n't turned up millions yet, but we've got a start that's worth following.

But this winter I'd like to spend with you. You won't feel that we ought to wait longer, on Emil's account, will you, Alexandra?"

Alexandra shook her head. "No, Carl; I don't feel that way about it. And surely you need n't mind anything Lou and Oscar say now. They are much angrier with me about Emil, now, than about you. They say it was all my fault. That I ruined him by sending him to college."

"No, I don't care a button for Lou or Oscar. The moment I knew you were in trouble, the moment I thought you might need me, it all looked different. You've always been a triumphant kind of person." Carl hesitated, looking sidewise at her strong, full figure. "But you do need me now, Alexandra?"

She put her hand on his arm. "I needed you terribly when it happened, Carl. I cried for you at night. Then everything seemed to get hard inside of me, and I thought perhaps I should never care for you again. But when I got your telegram yesterday, then — then it was just as it used to be. You are all I have in the world, you know."

Carl pressed her hand in silence. They were passing the Shabatas' empty house now, but they avoided the orchard path and took one that led over by the pasture pond.

"Can you understand it, Carl?" Alexandra murmured. "I have had nobody but Ivar and Signa to talk to. Do talk to me. Can you understand it? Could you have believed that of Marie Tovesky? I would have been cut to pieces, little by little, before I would have betrayed her trust in me!"

Carl looked at the shining spot of water before them. "Maybe she was cut to pieces, too, Alexandra. I am sure she tried hard; they both did. That was why Emil went to Mexico, of course. And he was going away again, you tell me, though he had only been home three weeks. You remember that Sunday when I went with Emil up to the French Church fair? I thought that day there was some kind of feeling, something unusual, between them. I meant to talk to you about it. But on my way back I met Lou and Oscar and got so angry that I forgot everything else. You must n't be hard on them, Alexandra. Sit down here by the pond a minute. I want to tell you something."

They sat down on the grass-tufted bank and Carl told her how he had seen Emil and Marie out by the pond that morning, more than a year ago, and how young and charming and full of grace they had seemed to him. "It happens like that in the world sometimes, Alexandra," he added earnestly. "I've seen it before. There are women who spread ruin around them through no fault of theirs, just by being too beautiful, too full of life and love. They can't help it. People come to them as people go to a warm fire in winter. I used to feel that in her when she was a little girl. Do you remember how all the Bohemians crowded round her in the store that day, when she gave Emil her candy? You remember those yellow sparks in her eyes?"

Alexandra sighed. "Yes. People could n't help loving her. Poor Frank does, even now, I think; though he's got himself in such a tangle that for a long time his love has been bitterer than his hate. But if you saw there was anything wrong, you ought to have told me, Carl."

Carl took her hand and smiled patiently. "My dear, it was something one felt in the air, as you feel the spring coming, or a storm in summer. I did n't *see* anything. Simply, when I was with those two young things, I felt my blood go quicker, I felt — how shall I say it? — an acceleration of life. After I got away, it was all too delicate, too intangible, to write about."

Alexandra looked at him mournfully. "I try to be more liberal about such things than I used to be. I try to realize that we are not all made alike. Only, why could n't it have been Raoul Marcel, or Jan Smirka? Why did it have to be my boy?"

"Because he was the best there was, I suppose. They were both the best you had here."

The sun was dropping low in the west when the two friends rose and took the path again. The straw-stacks were throwing long shadows, the owls were flying home to the prairie-dog town. When they came to the corner where the pastures joined, Alexandra's twelve young colts were galloping in a drove over the brow of the hill.

"Carl," said Alexandra, "I should like to go up there with you in the spring. I have n't been on the water since we crossed the ocean, when I was a little girl. After we first came out here I used to dream sometimes about the shipyard where father worked, and a little sort of inlet, full of masts." Alexandra paused. After a moment's thought she said, "But you would never ask me to go away for good, would you?"

"Of course not, my dearest. I think I know how you feel about this country as well as you do yourself." Carl took her hand in both his own and pressed it tenderly.

"Yes, I still feel that way, though Emil is gone. When I was on the train this morning, and we got near Hanover, I felt something like I did when I drove back with

Emil from the river that time, in the dry year. I was glad to come back to it. I've lived here a long time. There is great peace here, Carl, and freedom. . . . I thought when I came out of that prison, where poor Frank is, that I should never feel free again. But I do, here." Alexandra took a deep breath and looked off into the red west.

"You belong to the land," Carl murmured, "as you have always said. Now more than ever."

"Yes, now more than ever. You remember what you once said about the graveyard, and the old story writing itself over? Only it is we who write it, with the best we have."

They paused on the last ridge of the pasture, over-looking the house and the windmill and the stables that marked the site of John Bergson's homestead. On every side the brown waves of the earth rolled away to meet the sky.

"Lou and Oscar can't see those things," said Alexandra suddenly. "Suppose I do will my land to their children, what difference will that make? The land belongs to the future, Carl; that's the way it seems to me. How many of the names on the county clerk's plat will be there in fifty years? I might as well try to will the sunset over there to my brothers' children. We come and go, but the land is always here. And the people who love it and understand it are the people who own it—for a little while."

Carl looked at her wonderingly. She was still gazing into the west, and in her face there was that exalted serenity that sometimes came to her at moments of deep feeling. The level rays of the sinking sun shone in her clear eyes.

"Why are you thinking of such things now, Alexandra?"

"I had a dream before I went to Lincoln—But I will tell you about that afterward, after we are married. It will never come true, now, in the way I thought it might." She took Carl's arm and they walked toward the gate. "How many times we have walked this path together, Carl. How many times we will walk it again! Does it seem to you like coming back to your own place? Do you feel at peace with the world here? I think we shall be very happy. I have n't any fears. I think when friends marry, they are safe. We don't suffer like—those young ones." Alexandra ended with a sigh.

They had reached the gate. Before Carl opened it, he drew Alexandra to him and kissed her softly, on her lips and on her eyes.

She leaned heavily on his shoulder. "I am tired," she murmured. "I have been very lonely, Carl."

O Pioneers!

They went into the house together, leaving the Divide behind them, under the evening star. Fortunate country, that is one day to receive hearts like Alexandra's into its bosom, to give them out again in the yellow wheat, in the rustling corn, in the shining eyes of youth!

THE END

Acknowledgments

T HE textual editing of *O Pioneers!* is the result of con-
tributions from many members of the Cather Edition
staff, among whom we wish to acknowledge especially Erin
Marcus and, during the initial year of the project, Kathryn A.
Bellman. Numerous graduate students contributed to the
project, among whom James Cihlar, Ray Korpi, Judy Krier,
Tim Tostengard, and Kelly Utley-Wouthtiwongprecha provided major assistance; among numerous undergraduates,
Christie Long provided major assistance.

Three people were especially helpful at different stages of
the preparation of this edition. Joan Crane (University of
Virginia) in *Willa Cather: A Bibliography* (Lincoln: U of Nebraska P, 1982) provided an authoritative starting place for
our identifying and assembling of basic materials, then in
correspondence was unfailingly generous with her expertise.
David J. Nordloh (Indiana University) provided invaluable
advice as we established policies and procedures and wrote
our editorial manual. Noel Polk (University of Southern
Mississippi) brought knowledge and grace, as well as interest

in Cather, to his inspection of our materials on behalf of the Committee on Scholarly Editions.

Consultations early in the project were helpful as we charted our course. Fredson Bowers (University of Virginia) advised us about the steps necessary to organize the project. As editor of the Lewis and Clark journals, Gary Moulton (University of Nebraska–Lincoln) generously provided expertise and encouragement. Conversations with Richard Rust (University of North Carolina–Chapel Hill) were helpful in refining procedures concerning variants.

Kathleen Danker and Emily Levine assisted David Stouck in preparing the explanatory notes, and also assembled materials concerning Nebraska history, geography, fauna, and flora, while Kari Ronning was especially helpful in locating and securing illustrations. Those who helped in locating and interpreting materials for the explanatory notes also include Joseph Svoboda and Lynn R. Beideck-Porn, Archives and Special Collections of Love Library, University of Nebraska–Lincoln; Patricia Phillips, director, Willa Cather Pioneer Memorial and Educational Foundation, Red Cloud; Anne Billesbach, first at the Cather Historical Center, Red Cloud, and later at the Nebraska State Historical Society, Lincoln; and John Lindall, Cather Historical Center. In assembling the materials, we were assisted also by numerous graduate students, to all of whom we are grateful. We wish to thank in particular Susan Moss.

We relied upon many people who generously contributed their specialized knowledge: Paul A. Olson, for his expertise in plains culture; Kay Young, for her knowledge of plains flora; Andrea Pinto Lebowitz, for the further identification of flora; Paul Johnsgard, for his knowledge of birds of the Great Plains; and Donald F. Danker and Richard Sutton, for their assistance with the geography of Webster County. We are grateful to the staffs of Love Library, University of Nebraska–Lincoln; the Nebraska State Historical Society, Lincoln; Bennett Martin Public Library, Lincoln; Houghton Library, Harvard University, especially Melanee Wisner; the University of Vermont Library; The Beinecke Rare Book and Manuscript Library, Yale University; The Pierpont Morgan Library, New York; Columbia University Library; The Newberry Library, Chicago; and the Henry E. Huntington Library, San Marino, California. We acknowledge with thanks Houghton Mifflin Company and the Houghton Library, Harvard University, for permission to quote from the letters of Ferris Greenslet.

We wish to express our special gratitude to Helen Cather Southwick for her assistance and encouragement throughout the project, and to acknowledge our indebtedness to the late Mildred R. Bennett, whose work as founder and president of the Willa Cather Pioneer Memorial and Educational Foundation ensured that Cather-related materials in Webster County would be preserved, and whose knowledge guided us through those materials.

For their administrative support at the University of Nebraska–Lincoln, we thank Gerry Meisels and John G. Peters, deans of arts and sciences; John Yost, vice chancellor for research; and Frederick C. Luebke, director of the Center for Great Plains Studies. We are especially grateful to

Frederick M. Link, who, as chair of the Department of English, provided support for the project in innumerable ways, both tangible and intangible.

For a major grant that supported our initial year on this edition, we are most grateful to the Woods Charitable Fund; for research grants, we thank the Nebraska Council for the Humanities; and for material assistance throughout the project, the Research Council, the College of Arts and Sciences, the Office of the Vice Chancellor for Research, and the Department of English, University of Nebraska–Lincoln.

Historical Apparatus

Historical Essay

WILLA Cather liked to think of *O Pioneers!* as her first novel. When she sent a copy of the book to her friend Carrie Miner Sherwood in Red Cloud, Nebraska, she wrote on the flyleaf, "This was the first time I walked off on my own feet — everything before was half real and half an imitation of writers whom I admired. In this one I hit the home pasture and found that I was Yance Sorgensen and not Henry James."* *O Pioneers!*, published in 1913, was in fact Cather's second novel, preceded by *Alexander's Bridge* in 1912. Her feeling, however, that her career as a novelist really began with *O Pioneers!* was an abiding one and was restated in an essay she wrote in 1931 for *The Colophon* titled "My First Novels [There Were Two]." There she describes *Alexander's Bridge* with its transatlantic setting and sophisticated drawing-room characters as a studio picture, done according to

---

*Reproduced in facsimile in Mildred Bennett's *The World of Willa Cather* (222–23). Yance Sorgensen, originally from Norway, was a prosperous Nebraska farmer who refused to modernize his home, preferring the old way of doing things (see Bennett 200).

the best standards of the day, but conventional and shallow. She wrote it, she says, in the manner of Henry James and Edith Wharton but without their qualifications. *O Pioneers!*, on the other hand, she wrote for herself, and her subjects were her old neighbors and the Nebraska farm country where she had grown up. The book contained not only her true subject matter but was written in her own style. "Here," she said, "there was no arranging or 'inventing'; everything was spontaneous and took its own place." Writing the book "was like taking a ride through a familiar country on a horse that knew the way" (92–93). When Houghton Mifflin brought out the Autograph Edition of her works in 1937, she placed *O Pioneers!* at the beginning of the series.

Composition

Although Willa Cather was always secretive about the writing of her books, we have from her letters, her essay "My First Novels," and the memoirs of her friends a considerable amount of information about the composition of *O Pioneers!* The work had its genesis in two Nebraska stories that she had written separately. In the autumn of 1911, on leave from her post as managing editor at *McClure's Magazine*, she spent three productive months with her friend Isabelle McClung at Cherry Valley in upstate New York; there she revised the initial magazine installment of *Alexander's Bridge;* wrote one of her best short stories, "The Bohemian Girl"; and completed a story about a Swedish farm woman titled "Alexandra," which according to Edith Lewis she had begun some time previously (Lewis 79). The following spring Cather made a lengthy trip to the Southwest. Before she left, she took out the Alexandra story and read it to Lewis, but was dissatisfied and made no attempt to publish it. By Lewis's account "Alexandra" began where *O Pioneers!* starts; continued almost unchanged through Part I of the novel, "The Wild Land"; and concluded with Alexandra's dream, which now appears at the end of Part III.

On her return from the Southwest, Cather spent five weeks in June and July in Red Cloud, where she visited with old neighbors and watched the wheat harvest for the first time in several years. She wrote to Elizabeth Sergeant saying that on the edge of a wheat field she had the idea for another story — she was going to call it "The White Mulberry Tree" (5 July 1913). She enclosed in the letter a copy of a poem she had written titled "Prairie Spring," which *McClure's* published the following December and which Cather eventually placed at the beginning of *O Pioneers!* The mood and theme of the novel are anticipated by the poem's depiction of the flat and somber land, the epic labors of the pioneers, and the romantic exaltation of youth. In Pittsburgh, in her sewing-room study at the McClung residence, she set about in August writing the new story, which James Woodress has described as a Nebraska version of Dante's story of Paolo and Francesca (*Willa Cather* 231). In Cather's story, a Bohemian farmer surprises and kills his wife and her lover, who are lying together in his orchard under a white mulberry tree.

At some point, however, in the writing of this second

story, Cather suddenly had the idea that "Alexandra" and "The White Mulberry Tree" belonged together. Later, to Elizabeth Sergeant, she described this coming together of the two parts of the book "as a sudden inner explosion and enlightenment," something she had experienced before only in the writing of a poem. This was an important creative experience because the inner explosion seemed to dictate the form the novel would take, a work with "inevitable shape that is not plotted but designs itself" (Sergeant 116). Cather would henceforth believe in organic form, letting the materials of the work dictate the structure, form rising from function. Nonetheless, it took five months for her to work out the details of the design, and the manuscript for *O Pioneers!* was not completed until December 1912. "Alexandra" was still the backbone of the story, lengthened by some fifty percent, into which was spliced the story of the lovers, "The White Mulberry Tree." Referring to its rural subject matter, Cather described her new book as "a two-part pastoral" (Sergeant 86).

Cather sent the manuscript to Houghton Mifflin, but she also sent a copy to Elizabeth Sergeant early in 1913, asking for an opinion. She expressed her own reservations, feeling that there was some hasty writing and wondering if it was too much about crops and farming. She told Sergeant that as she wrote, the country insisted on being the hero and she did not interfere because the story had come out of the long grasses, like Dvořák's *New World Symphony*, which Dvořák had composed after spending several weeks in Nebraska in the 1880s.

What she feared, however, was that there might be emotional writing, something she dreaded, and she asked Sergeant to come down hard on any such passages. She also asked Sergeant's advice about publishing *O Pioneers!* in the same volume with "The Bohemian Girl" (Sergeant 91–92). Sergeant's side of the correspondence has not survived, so we do not know what advice she may have offered. Her enthusiasm for the manuscript, however, was such that it is not likely that she suggested any significant changes. Ferris Greenslet, Cather's friend at Houghton Mifflin, was equally enthusiastic. He reported to his associates that the novel "ought to . . . definitely establish the author as a novelist of the first rank" (Brown 179), and accordingly, in March 1913, the company offered her a contract for publication.

Materials

Willa Cather's fiction is autobiographical to an uncommon degree, her characters suggested by actual people she had known. *My Ántonia*, for example, follows closely the life of her old Nebraska friend Anna Pavelka, while *A Lost Lady* is based on the author's impressions of Lyra Garber, the wife of a former governor of Nebraska. But for *O Pioneers!* no specific prototypes have ever been identified. Elizabeth Sergeant, with whom Cather communicated most about the composing of the novel, has written, "How 'close to life' the characters in *O Pioneers!* were I was never to know with exactitude from herself, in spite of our many conversations and talks about the book" (Sergeant 90). Cather said the book was about old neighbors, and it seems likely that she had the Lambrechts, German-speaking neighbors in Catherton precinct, in mind when she composed this novel. Elsewhere, however, she insisted that in all her fiction her characters were composites, and probably this is particularly true of *O Pioneers!* She also said to both Elizabeth Sergeant and Zoë Akins that the land was the hero, and perhaps that is why residents in Webster County, Nebraska, point to certain features of the terrain — a slough, a duck pond, the river, a rise in the land — as the identifiable originals for the novel.

In an interview she gave for the *Philadelphia Record* in August 1913, Cather described some of the experiences that she had transmuted into fiction. She told about the Cather family's move west in 1883 from Virginia's Shenandoah Valley when she was nine years old. Although her grandparents had arrived eight years before, the country "was still wild and bleak enough" when they reached Nebraska, "the roads . . . mostly faint trails over the bunch grass." In a particularly vivid phrase, she said it was "a country as bare as a piece of sheet iron." She was homesick, but her father told her that one had to show grit in a new country. She saw her feelings of displacement and the need for courage reflected especially in the lives of the immigrants:

> We had very few American neighbors — they were mostly Swedes and Danes, Norwegians and Bohemians. I liked them from the first and they made up for what I missed in the country. I particularly liked the old women, they understood my homesickness and were kind to me. I had met "traveled"

people in Virginia and Washington, but these old women on the farms were the first people who ever gave me the real feeling of an older world across the sea. Even when they spoke very little English, the old women somehow managed to tell me a great many stories about the old country. They talk more freely to a child than to grown people, and I always felt as if every word they said to me counted for twenty. (Bohlke 10)

In an interview for the *Bookman* eight years later, Cather credited the immigrant women and their stories as a direct source of inspiration for *O Pioneers!* and *My Ántonia:*

I grew fond of some of these immigrants — particularly the old women, who used to tell me of their home country. I used to think them underrated, and wanted to explain them to their neighbors. Their stories used to go round and round in my head at night. This was, with me, the initial impulse. I didn't know any writing people. I had an enthusiasm for a kind of country and a kind of people. (Bohlke 20)

She found her subject in the memories of her youth — the pioneers' struggle to tame a wild land, the storms of winter, the heat and drought of summer, the tending of livestock, the exhilarating labors of harvest time. These she focused in the story of Alexandra Bergson, the leader of the Scandinavian farming community, who embodies the creative instincts, the will, and the foresight necessary to bring the unbroken country into prosperous cultivation. These materials were remembered, not documented. Cather told the reviewer for the *Bookman:*

If I had made notes, or should make them now, the material collected would be dead. No, it's memory — the memory that goes with the vocation. When I sit down to write, turns of phrase I've forgotten for years come back like white ink before fire. I think that most of the basic material a writer works with is acquired before the age of fifteen. That's the important period: when one's not writing. Those years determine whether one's work will be poor and thin or rich and fine. (Bohlke 20)

Cather's approach to her materials is suggested by the epigraph to *O Pioneers!*, which is from Adam Mickiewicz's *Pan Tadeusz*, an epic poem first published in 1834. It reads simply "Those fields, colored by various grain!"* but evokes the long perspective of the history and literature of the Old World. *Pan Tadeusz*, a narrative about the old order in Polish Lithuania, is a nostalgic account of a courteous way of life lived close to the land. Cather used it perhaps to signal continuity between old and new civilizations, but she probably also used it to indicate an aesthetic approach to a similar subject: that is, rural labors, youthful romance, the role of the church, the love of one's country. Like Mickiewicz, Cather was remembering her early life as a work of art. She wrote to Sergeant that the people and places she knew in Nebraska continued on for her like scenes from *War and Peace*, always

---

*Cather apparently altered the 1885 English translation by Maude Ashurst Biggs, which reads "those fields, rich hued with various grain." For a discussion of Cather and Mickiewicz, see Slote 12–16.

more dramatic and interesting than anything she could have invented (10 August 1914).

The influence of Russian literature is especially strong in Cather's early work. In a letter to H. L. Mencken, Cather writes that when she was fourteen she came upon four of Tolstoy's works — *Anna Karenina*, *The Cossacks*, *The Death of Ivan Ilyich*, and *The Kreutzer Sonata* — and for the next three years read them over and over again. She says that this reading so strongly colored the way she saw her own world in America that she eventually turned to a long apprenticeship with Henry James and Mrs. Wharton to get over it. Yet in writing *O Pioneers!*, she wonders if she has really recovered from the Russian influence (6 February 1922). What the Russian writers gave her, especially Tolstoy and Turgenev, was a precedent for the artistic treatment of great continental plains — the lands of wheat fields and pastures and meadows, great expanses of sky, and climatic extremes. Just as she maintained of *O Pioneers!* that the land was the hero, of Russian literature she said that there "the earth speaks louder than the people" (Bohlke 170). The Russian writers also gave her a precedent for the presentation of an immigrant folk, a peasantry. In *O Pioneers!* we see a people at their labors and at play together, experiencing joys and sorrows that are communal: the French church fair, the grain harvest, the mourning of the people for Amédée Chevalier, the confirmation service. In this stylized presentation of a land and its people, Cather's Nebraska experience and her reading fuse together as dynamic elements of her art.

291

O Pioneers! is dedicated to the memory of Sarah Orne Jewett, and this dedication directs the reader to another important influence on Cather's art. The tribute is a meaningful one because it was Jewett who advised Cather that the things "which haunt the mind for years" are the proper material for serious literature (Bohlke 9). Cather had written *Alexander's Bridge* according to the popular literary interests and conventions of her day, but the unfashionable story of Nebraska immigrants was one she had wanted to write for a long time. "Don't try to write the kind of short story that this or that magazine wants," said Jewett. "Write the truth, and let them take it or leave it" (Bohlke 11). Cather met Jewett in February 1908 at the home of Mrs. James T. Fields, widow of the Boston publisher. The friendship lasted only sixteen months, cut short by Jewett's death at the age of sixty, but it was one of the most important factors in Cather's literary development (see O'Brien 334–63). A writer in the pastoral mode and a woman, Jewett was for Cather a model of the woman as artist. Jewett had written about the landscape and people of Maine in a way that Cather would do of Nebraska. When Cather edited a collection of Jewett's best stories in the twenties, she wrote of *The Country of the Pointed Firs* that the sketches in that book were "living things caught in the open, with light and freedom and air-spaces about them. They melt into the land and the life of the land until they are not stories at all, but life itself" (*On Writing* 49). This is a good account of what Cather succeeded in doing herself in *O Pioneers!*

When she was interviewed for the *Philadelphia Record*

shortly after the novel's publication, Cather described the intellectual excitement she had felt as a girl after watching the immigrant women at their baking and butter making: "I used to ride home in the most unreasonable state of excitement; I always felt as if they told me so much more than they said — as if I had actually got inside another person's skin" (Bohlke 10). Years later, again in her celebration of Jewett's work, Cather described something similar that could be likened to Keats's "negative capability." Describing the artist's relation to his work she wrote, "If he achieves anything noble, anything enduring, it must be by giving himself absolutely to his material. And this gift of sympathy is his great gift; it is the fine thing in him that alone can make his work fine. He fades away into the land and people of his heart, he dies of love only to be born again" (*On Writing* 51).

These lines could also describe the poetry of Walt Whitman, whose "Pioneers! O Pioneers!" provided Cather with her title. Certain lines of Whitman's poem anticipate scenes in the novel:

> Life's involv'd and varied pageants,
> All the forms and shows, all the workmen at their work,
> All the seamen and the landsmen, all the masters with
>   their slaves,
> Pioneers! O pioneers!
>
> All the hapless silent lovers,
> All the prisoners in the prisons, all the righteous and
>   the wicked,

> All the joyous, all the sorrowing, all the living, all
>   the dying,
> Pioneers! O pioneers! (lines 61–68)

Reference to Whitman's poem sounds the epic theme that is taken up in Cather's poem "Prairie Spring," written in Whitman's free-verse manner and placed like an epigraph at the opening of the text. For *O Pioneers!*, like Whitman's poem, celebrates the dynamic growth of the American democracy as experienced by the immigrant settlers of the pioneer west. It also embodies the Emersonian transcendentalism that reverberates through Whitman's "Song of Myself." If Whitman's readers ask where the dead have gone, he assures them that "they are alive and well somewhere / The smallest sprout shows there is really no death" (sec. 6, lines 27–28); and if the readers ask specifically after the poet, he says, "I bequeath myself to the dirt to grow from the grass I love, / If you want me again look for me under your bootsoles" (sec. 52, lines 9–10). Cather evokes this same transcendental theme in the final rhythmic lines of her story: "They went into the house together, leaving the Divide behind them, under the evening star. Fortunate country, that is one day to receive hearts like Alexandra's into its bosom, to give them out again in the yellow wheat, in the rustling corn, in the shining eyes of youth!" (274).

Publication and Reception

Cather signed a contract for *O Pioneers!* with Houghton Mifflin on March 29, 1913, and the book was published

June 28, 1913 (Crane 30). Whether she offered it to *Mc-Clure's Magazine* for serialization is not known, but it was not published in magazine form. When she sent the manuscript to Elizabeth Sergeant, she requested that Sergeant pass it on to an American agent in Paris who might get a translation for it, but apparently the agent turned it down (Sergeant 92–93). William Heinemann, however, published the book simultaneously in England, which pleased Cather a great deal because she had met Heinemann several times in London when she was on the editorial staff for *McClure's* and she had a very high opinion of his taste and judgment.

When Cather wrote about *O Pioneers!* in her essay "My First Novels," she claimed that a New York critic voiced a general opinion, saying, "I simply don't care a damn what happens in Nebraska, no matter who writes about it" (94). Perhaps she was thinking back to the review by Frederick Taber Cooper in the *Bookman*, who found the novel very regional, slow-moving, and "frankly depressing." Although he commended the author on her gift of observation, he says, "Somehow the reader cannot bring himself to care keenly whether the young neighbour returns or not, whether Alexandra is eventually happy or not, —whether, indeed, the farm itself prospers or not." He found the whole thing predictable, loosely constructed, and boring (Murphy 112–13).

Cooper's review, however, was an exception; most of the reviews were enthusiastic. The notice in the *Boston Evening Transcript* said that with *O Pioneers!* Cather introduced a new kind of story and a new part of the country into American fiction, commending especially Cather's disclosure of the splendid resources of the immigrant population and the changing face of the country (16 July 1913). Similarly, the reviewer for the *New York Herald Tribune* was impressed by the originality and significance of Cather's subject matter: "With a steady hand this author holds up the mirror of fiction to a people of our land little, if at all, seen therein before: the Scandinavian and Bohemian pioneers. . . . In her clear, smooth glass, we see these Old World pioneers adapting themselves to new conditions, identifying themselves with the prairie soil and becoming a voice in our national life. . . . This is a novel of considerable substance" (18 July 1913). The review in the *Nation* began with "Few American novels of recent years have impressed us so strongly as this" and concluded on the same high note of praise: "The sureness of feeling and touch, the power without strain, which mark this book, lift it far above the ordinary product of contemporary novelists" (14 September 1913). The reviewer for the *Boston Evening Transcript* had also made an acute observation on the book's artistry: "The novel has great dramatic power; it is deep, thrilling, intense — and this intensity comes through the simplicity — one might almost say severity, of treatment."

The notice in the *New York Times Book Review* would surely have interested and pleased the author, for it echoed some of the things that Cather had written to her friends while composing the novel. As importantly as the characters, the reviewer writes, "looms large the earth, the land, patient and bountiful source of all things." The reviewer praises

Cather for this attitude, which, he says, is not characteristically American:

> The average American does not have any deep instinct for the land or vital consciousness of the value and dignity of the life that may be lived upon it. But *O Pioneers!* is filled with this instinct and consciousness. It is a tale of the old wood and field worshipping races, Swedes and Bohemians transplanted to the uplands of Nebraska, and of their struggle with the untamed soil. . . . A thread of symbolism runs through it, in which the goddess of fertility once more subdues the barren and stubborn earth. (30 November 1913)

The most valuable review perhaps, for Cather's career, appeared in the *Chicago Evening Post*. There Floyd Dell, who would later become a novelist of some note himself, wrote that *O Pioneers!* was "touched with genius" and was "worthy of being recognized as the most vital, subtle, and artistic piece of the year's fiction." He despaired, however, of being able to explain to his readers why the novel impressed him so much, because it didn't deal with any large ideas, nor did it dazzle by means of style. In this long review Dell recounted much of the novel's plot, pointing out as well that it is an ordinary story, yet the novel somehow has, in his estimation, richness, charm, and dignity. He urged the American Academy of Arts and Letters to justify its existence by recognizing and acclaiming this early production of genius by Willa Cather (Dell, 25 July 1913).

There was also a good notice in the *Lincoln Journal*, which described the novel as true to life, "at once homely and beautiful and strange" (3 August 1913). Cather seems to have responded to this review when interviewed for the *Philadelphia Record* a week later:

> What has pleased me most in the cordial reception the West has given this new book of mine, is that the reviewers in all those Western States say the thing seems to them true to the country and the people. That is a great satisfaction. The reviews have concerned themselves a good deal more with the subject matter of the story than with my way of telling it, and I am glad of that. I care a lot more about the country and the people than I care about my own way of writing or anybody else's way of writing. (Bohlke 11)

She did of course think about the book's structure and style a great deal, for this novel's success represented a significant turning point in her artistic development. But in this case she found that structure was something dictated by the subject and was not a matter of literary conventions. In "My First Novels" she wrote that being in the West for six months in 1912, in a part of the country and among people she really cared about, changed her point of view. She no longer felt the need to write according to prescription. In writing *O Pioneers!*, she ignored all the conventional situations and accents that were then thought necessary. This was a story without action, humor, or a conventional hero—"a story concerned entirely with heavy farming people, with cornfields and pasture lands and pig yards" (94). And in her

1922 preface to *Alexander's Bridge* she said that when a writer begins to work with his own material "he has less and less power of choice about the moulding of it. It seems to be there of itself, already moulded." The writer contrives "only as regards mechanical details, and questions of effective presentation, always debatable. About the essential matter of his story he cannot argue" (viii–ix). Elizabeth Sergeant's one criticism of *O Pioneers!*, when she read it in manuscript, concerned structure; she felt that the book had no strong, definite skeleton. Cather agreed, but defended this lack of structure on the grounds that the country she was writing about was itself soft and fluid; there were no rocks or mountain ridges (22 April 1913). The book's critical and popular success encouraged Cather to follow this road again in the writing of *My Ántonia.*

The enthusiastic response to *O Pioneers!* by generations of readers in this century was anticipated in 1913 by readers to whom Elizabeth Sergeant showed the novel in manuscript form. One was an old Bostonian with wide-ranging intellectual interests. She told Sergeant that the book made her very proud, as an American, to think that the European immigrants, with their own culture and ideals, had so quickly blended their lives with the soil of Nebraska. More importantly, she praised the author for creating "such rare and measured visual images" of this new world with its "almost cosmic vistas, overtones, and undertones." She marveled that "though the story unfolded with deceptive simplicity, it had majesty, even terror." The author, she told Sergeant, "seemed to be looking through objective lenses at something new God had made" (Sergeant 95–96). The other readers were the widow and family of the French medieval scholar Gaston Paris, with whom Sergeant was then living in France. After dinner Sergeant would read the manuscript out loud when the women gathered about the salon fire for an hour of needlework and conversation. *"Très original,"* they thought. Although no French woman for centuries had seen virgin soil, they were thrilled by this account of the birth of a new country. They said to Sergeant, "We French who love the land, have it in our bones, can see the quality of her writing." Alexandra's return from the river farms singing a Swedish hymn, sure of the future of wheat on the Divide, was a scene they felt belonged to poetry and legend (Sergeant 93).

That is how Cather's readers have continued to view the book, as a unique and poetic blending of New World experience and Old World cultural and literary traditions, as a myth-making text (see Woodress in *The Art of Willa Cather* 43–62). Alexandra exists wholly and specifically in her relation to the farm on the Divide, but when she finally makes it yield its bounty, she becomes a larger-than-life figure of myth, a corn goddess. The moment when she envisions the future stirring under the shaggy ridges of the Divide is described, as Sergeant's Boston friend observed, in almost cosmic language:

> Her face was so radiant. . . . For the first time, perhaps, since that land emerged from the waters of geologic ages, a human

face was set toward it with love and yearning. It seemed beautiful to her, rich and strong and glorious. Her eyes drank in the breadth of it, until her tears blinded her. Then the Genius of the Divide, the great, free spirit which breathes across it, must have bent lower than it ever bent to a human will before. The history of every country begins in the heart of a man or a woman. (64)

When Carl Linstrum, who will eventually marry Alexandra, comes back to the Divide and sees what Alexandra and his old neighbors have made out of the land, he says, "Isn't it queer: there are only two or three human stories, and they go on repeating themselves as fiercely as if they had never happened before" (110). The two stories woven together in *O Pioneers!* stretch back to Genesis. Alexandra's is the story of creation, the story of a human civilization being shaped out of a land as flat and formless as the sea. Emil and Marie's is the story of lovers cast from the earth's garden through sin. The timeless, ever-recurring nature of these stories is secured by literary allusion. Alexandra's heroic character and actions are enriched by her connection with the old Swedish legends of Tegner's *Frithiofs Saga*. Emil and Marie's story acquires a universal pathos by its association with Ovid's story of Pyramus and Thisbe, whose blood stains the fruit of the white mulberry tree. And there is a suggestion of the Endymion story when Marie resolves in the moonlight that to dream of her lover will henceforth be enough. There are hidden but strong parallels between characters and episodes in *O Pioneers!* and Virgil's *Eclogues* (see Rosowski 46–48, 60–61). The two stories of the novel are brought together in a

301

nexus of creation and destruction as Alexandra's servant, old Ivar, repeats to himself Psalm 101, a song of "mercy and judgment" in which the psalmist promises to remember the faithful of the land and to destroy all evil doers.

When she wrote *O Pioneers!* Willa Cather achieved what Virgil wrote of in those lines that she quoted in *My Ántonia*, *"Primus ego in patriam mecum . . . deducam Musas,"* and which she translated as "I shall be the first, if I live, to bring the Muse into my country" (264). *O Pioneers!* was not Willa Cather's first published novel, but it was certainly the novel in which she first brought the muse into her country.

Works Cited

Bennett, Mildred. *The World of Willa Cather.* 1951. Lincoln: U of Nebraska P, 1961.

Bohlke, L. Brent, ed. *Willa Cather in Person: Interviews, Speeches, and Letters.* Lincoln: U of Nebraska P, 1986.

Brown, E. K., completed by Leon Edel. *Willa Cather: A Critical Biography.* 1953. Lincoln: U of Nebraska P, 1987.

Cather, Willa. Letter to H. L. Mencken. 6 Feb. 1922. Enoch Pratt Library, Baltimore.

——. Letters to Elizabeth Shepley Sergeant. Pierpont Morgan Library, New York.

——. *My Ántonia.* 1918. Boston: Houghton Mifflin, 1977.

——. "My First Novels [There Were Two]." *On Writing* 89–98.

——. *On Writing: Critical Studies on Writing as an Art.* 1949. New York: Knopf, 1968.

——. "Preface" to *Alexander's Bridge.* Boston: Houghton Mifflin, 1922.

Crane, Joan. *Willa Cather: A Bibliography.* Lincoln: U of Nebraska P, 1982.

Dell, Floyd. Rev. of *O Pioneers!* *Chicago Evening Post* 25 July 1913. Rpt. in part in *Dictionary of Literary Biography, Documentary Series.* Vol. I. Detroit: Gale Research Co. 1982, 67–69.

Lewis, Edith. *Willa Cather Living: A Personal Record.* 1953. Lincoln: U of Nebraska P, 1976.

Murphy, John J., ed. *Critical Essays on Willa Cather.* Boston: G. K. Hall, 1984.

O'Brien, Sharon. *Willa Cather: The Emerging Voice.* New York: Oxford U P, 1987.

Rev. of *O Pioneers!* *Boston Evening Transcript* 16 July 1913: 18.

——. *Lincoln Journal* 3 Aug. 1913, sec. a: 7.

——. *Nation* 14 Sept. 1913: 210–11.

——. *New York Herald Tribune* 18 July 1913: 8.

——. *New York Times Book Review* 30 Nov. 1913: 664.

Rosowski, Susan J. *The Voyage Perilous: Willa Cather's Romanticism.* Lincoln: U of Nebraska P, 1986.

Sergeant, Elizabeth Shepley. *Willa Cather: A Memoir.* 1953. Lincoln: U of Nebraska P, 1963.

Slote, Bernice. "The Secret Web." *Five Essays on Willa Cather: The Merrimack Symposium.* Ed. John J. Murphy. North Andover: Merrimack College, 1974.

Whitman, Walt. *Leaves of Grass.* Philadelphia: McKay, 1891–92.

Woodress, James. "Willa Cather: American Experience and European Tradition." *The Art of Willa Cather.* Ed. Bernice Slote and Virginia Faulkner. Lincoln: U of Nebraska P, 1974.

——. *Willa Cather: A Literary Life.* Lincoln: U of Nebraska P, 1963.

Illustrations

1. Opposite: The frontispiece of *O Pioneers!*, in color in the first impression, by Clarence F. Underwood (1871–1929). Cather considered the picture inappropriate and asked that it be removed. Underwood illustrated popular fiction and advertisements; the foreword to his book of drawings, *American Types* (1912), asserted that he expressed an American ideal of womanly beauty — "clear-eyed out-of-doors girls, unspoiled by the artificial restraints of ceremonious Europe."

ALEXANDRA

2. Opposite: The title page from the first printing of the first edition of *O Pioneers!* (actual size 4⅞ x 7¼ inches).

The epigraph is a paraphrasing of "those fields, rich hued with various grain," from the 1885 translation of *Master Thaddeus, or The Last Foray in Lithuania,* the 1834 epic poem by Polish Romantic poet Adam Mickie-wicz (1798–1855).

Apart from the Black Letter (Old English) of the Riverside Press imprint on the title page, the types employed throughout the book are variants of Caslon, an eighteenth-century face which had recently returned to favor, partly because of its adoption by *Vogue* magazine.

O PIONEERS!

BY

WILLA SIBERT CATHER

"Those fields, colored by various grain!"
MICKIEWICZ

BOSTON AND NEW YORK
HOUGHTON MIFFLIN COMPANY
The Riverside Press Cambridge
1913

3–4. Opposite: The text opening page from the first printing of the first edition of *O Pioneers!* Overleaf: facing text pages from the first chapter.

The text face closely resembles 12 pt Monotype Caslon English 37, though a few letters differ from the standard font. It is tempting to speculate that this may be the special cutting that the Riverside Press is known to have commissioned from the Monotype Corporation. It is superior to many versions of Caslon for its evenness of color — a product of consistent spacing within and between letters and its harmonious, understated stroke weight.

The heavy, rough-textured paper of the first edition was an excellent vehicle for letterpress printing, particularly for a version of Caslon that was designed to gain weight when impressed into the sheet.

The Riverside Press is remembered partly because of its association with the great typographer Bruce Rogers. In some ways Rogers's career paralleled that of Cather. Rogers first became established at the Riverside Press and worked for the company between 1896 and 1912, the year before the publication of *O Pioneers!* It was Rogers who had encouraged the use of Caslon types at Riverside. Later, Cather and Rogers were to be directly associated in the publication of the Houghton Mifflin Autograph Edition, printed at Riverside. Those handsome volumes testify to the cordiality of their relationship.

O PIONEERS!

PART I

THE WILD LAND

I

ONE January day, thirty years ago, the little town of Hanover, anchored on a windy Nebraska tableland, was trying not to be blown away. A mist of fine snowflakes was curling and eddying about the cluster of low drab buildings huddled on the gray prairie, under a gray sky. The dwelling-houses were set about haphazard on the tough prairie sod; some of them looked as if they had been moved in overnight, and others as if they were straying off by themselves, headed straight for the open plain. None of them had any appearance of permanence, and the howling wind blew under them as well as over them. The main street was a deeply rutted road, now frozen hard, which ran from the squat red railway station and the grain "elevator" at the north end of the town to the lumber yard and the horse pond at the south end. On either side of this road straggled two uneven rows of wooden buildings; the general merchandise stores, the two banks, the drug store, the feed store, the saloon, the post-office. The board sidewalks were gray with trampled snow, but at two o'clock in the afternoon the shopkeepers, having come back from dinner, were keeping well behind their frosty windows. The children were all in school, and there was nobody abroad in the streets but a few rough-looking countrymen in coarse overcoats, with their long caps pulled down to their noses. Some of them had brought their wives to town, and now and then a red or a plaid shawl flashed out of one store into the shelter of another. At the hitch-bars along the street a few heavy work-horses, harnessed to farm wagons, shivered under their blankets. About the station everything was quiet, for there would not be another train in until night.

On the sidewalk in front of one of the stores sat a little Swede boy, crying bitterly. He was about five years old. His black cloth coat was much too big for him and made him look like a little old man. His shrunken brown flannel dress had been washed many times and left a long stretch of stocking between the hem of his skirt and the tops of his clumsy, copper-toed shoes. His cap was pulled down over his ears; his nose and his chubby cheeks were chapped and red with cold. He cried quietly, and the few people who hurried by did not notice him. He was afraid to stop any one, afraid to go into the store and ask for help, so he sat wringing his long sleeves and looking up a telegraph pole beside him, whimpering, "My kitten, oh, my kitten! Her will fweeze!" At the top of the pole crouched a shivering gray kitten, mewing faintly and clinging desperately to the wood with her claws. The boy had been left at the store while his sister went to the doctor's office, and in her absence a dog had chased his kitten up the pole. The little creature had never been so high before, and she was too frightened to move. Her master was sunk in despair. He was a little country boy, and this village was to him a very strange and perplexing place, where

Evening and the flat land,
Rich and somber and always silent;
The miles of fresh-plowed soil,
Heavy and black, full of strength and harshness;
The growing wheat, the growing weeds,
The toiling horses, the tired men,
The long, empty roads,
The sullen fires of sunset dying;
The eternal, unresponsive sky.
Against all this, Youth,
Flaming like the wild roses,
Singing like the larks over the plowed fields,
Flashing like a star out of the twilight;
Youth, with its insupportable sweetness,
Its fierce necessity,
Its sharp desire;
Singing and singing,
Out of the lips of silence,
Out of the earthy dusk.

5. Above: Typescript page of "Prairie Spring,"
with holograph corrections. Courtesy of
The Pierpont Morgan Library, New York.
MA 1602.

6. Opposite: Willa Cather, c. 1911–12,
wearing a jade necklace given her by Sarah
Orne Jewett. Courtesy of the University
Archives, University of Nebraska–Lincoln.

7. Webster County, 1900. The northwest corner shows the Divide, the watershed between streams flowing north to the Little Blue River and those flowing south to the Republican River.

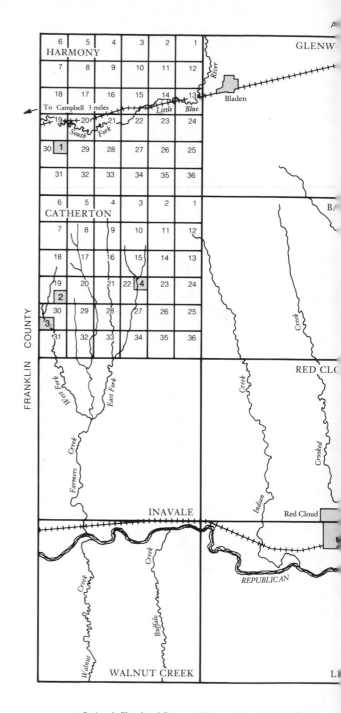

1 St. Anne's Church and Cemetery (Harmony Twp., Sec. 30, NE 1/4)
2 Zion Lutheran Norwegian Church (Catherton Twp., Sec. 19, SE 1/4)
3 Zion Lutheran Norwegian Cemetery (Catherton Twp., Sec. 30, SW 1/4)
4 Land on which Willa Cather lived (Catherton Twp., Sec. 22, NE 1/4)

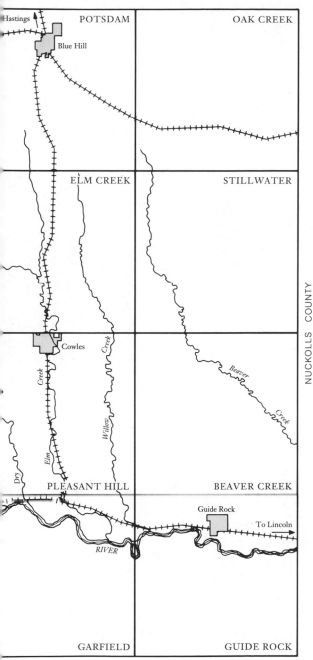

POTSDAM

Hastings

Blue Hill

OAK CREEK

ELM CREEK

STILLWATER

NUCKOLLS COUNTY

Cowles

Creek

Beaver

Creek

Willow

Creek

Elm

Dry

PLEASANT HILL

BEAVER CREEK

Guide Rock

To Lincoln

RIVER

GARFIELD

GUIDE ROCK

 Burlington and Missouri River Railroad

N

0   3 miles

8. Left top: Virgin prairie south of Red Cloud. Photograph by Lucia Woods. Courtesy of the University Archives, University of Nebraska–Lincoln.

9. Left bottom: (p.21) Farmstead in central Nebraska, c. 1890. Note sod house and windmill at right. Courtesy of the Nebraska State Historical Society.

10. Above: (p.25) Log house of the Warner family, overlooking the Little Blue River, c. 1873, Fillmore County, Nebraska. Courtesy of the Nebraska State Historical Society.

11. Above: (p.39) Dugout in western Nebraska. Courtesy of the Nebraska State Historical Society.

12. Opposite: (p.127) Music box owned by the Cook family and donated by them to the Willa Cather Pioneer Memorial and Educational Foundation, Red Cloud, Nebraska. Photograph by Lucia Woods. Courtesy of the University Archives, University of Nebraska–Lincoln.

13. Top left: (p.215) William Cooper's thresher, steam engine, and water wagon, c. 1900. Based in Catherton precinct, Cooper did custom threshing in Webster, Franklin, and Adams Counties until his death in 1920. Courtesy of the Nebraska State Historical Society. (Reproduced from a broken glass negative.)

14. Bottom left: (p.255) The Lindell Hotel, 1901. Located at 13th and M Streets, Lincoln, Nebraska, the Lindell was one of the earliest and finest of Lincoln's hotels. Courtesy of the Nebraska State Historical Society.

15. Above: (p.255) Library Hall, c. 1905, campus of the University of Nebraska, Lincoln. The iron fence was erected around the campus in 1891. Courtesy of the Nebraska State Historical Society.

16. (p.257) State Penitentiary, Lincoln, Nebraska, built in
1876 on a site then several miles south of town on 14th Street.
Courtesy of the Nebraska State Historical Society.

Explanatory Notes

T̲H̲E̲ explanatory notes are designed to assist the reader
in understanding the text by providing information on
persons, places, historical events, literary allusions, and specialized terminology that is not readily available elsewhere
such as in a standard desk dictionary or one-volume ency-
clopedic reference. Regional, occupational, religious, and
other specialized terms are similarly explained when more
information is needed than can be found in desk references. Cather often refers to well-known people by their real
names; because many of these have become obscure to modern readers, they have been briefly identified. Cather used
both real and fictional placenames; the notes identify both
types and give the likely prototype for the fictional name,
when known. Brief backgrounds for historical events are also
included. Sources of quotations are provided, as well as the
complete original quotation if different from that in the text,
and a translation if necessary.

Cather used common names for her references to local
flora and fauna; these have been glossed with the botanical
names and brief descriptions of the most likely species for the

325

novel's setting. Botanical information for Webster County was derived for the most part from the early biologists who surveyed Nebraska. Sources include Charles Bessey, *Preliminary Report on the Native Trees and Shrubs of Nebraska* (Lincoln: College of Agriculture Experiment Station, v. 4, Art. no. 4, n.d.); Niels F. Petersen, *Flora of Nebraska: A List of Conifers and Flowering Plants of the State with Keys for Their Determination* (Lincoln: The author, [c. 1912]); Raymond Pool, *Handbook of Nebraska Trees* (1919; Lincoln: University of Nebraska Conservation and Survey Division, 1951); and John M. Winter, *An Analysis of the Flowering Plants of Nebraska with Keys to the Families, Genera, and Species, with Notes Concerning their Occurrence, Range, and Frequency within the State* (Lincoln: Nebraska Conservation and Survey Division, 1936). Nomenclature and other information was cross-checked with current authorities such as Lauren Brown, *Grasslands*, Audubon Society Nature Guide (New York: Knopf, 1985); Robert Lomasson, *Nebraska Wildflowers* (Lincoln: U of Nebraska P, 1973); Nebraska Statewide Arboretum, *Common and Scientific Names of Nebraska Plants: Native and Introduced*, Publication No. 101 (Lincoln: Nebraska Statewide Arboretum, n.d.); and Theodore Van Bruggen, *Wildflowers, Grasses, and Other Plants of the Northern Plains and Black Hills* (Interior, SD: Badlands Natural History Association, 1983).

The outside column below lists the page and line numbers of each reading in *O Pioneers!* The inside column gives the reading, followed by the commentary on the reading.

Sarah Orne Jewett: Jewett (1849–1909) published 20 volumes of   3
fiction set in the rural regions of her native Maine. Cather met
Jewett the year before the latter's death and long viewed her writing
as a model for her own work.

"Prairie Spring": Cather's poem, first published in *McClure's Maga-*   5
zine 40 (Dec. 1912) and reprinted in her collection *April Twilights*
and Other Poems (New York: Alfred A. Knopf, 1923). See Illustration 5.

Hanover: Cather may have had aspects of Red Cloud, Nebraska, in   11.2
mind when she created Hanover, but the location of the fictional
town on windy tableland also suggests the smaller settlements of
Bladen and Blue Hill as historical prototypes. Bladen did not receive railroad service until 1886 (Cather opens the novel in roughly
1883), but it is closer than Red Cloud to Catherton, the precinct where the Cather family first homesteaded and where Cather
would likely have located her first memories of pioneering. Tableland is flat elevated terrain more exposed to the prevailing winds
than land at lower elevations.

sod: Sod is the upper stratum of soil packed with the fibrous root   11.7
systems of the prairie grasses, so dense that the steel plow was
needed to "break" it. The dominant grass was little bluestem (*An-*
dropogon scoparius), whose "roots are so abundant as to form a dense
sod, almost completely occupying good soil at least 2.5 feet in
depth." J. E. Weaver, *North American Prairie* (Lincoln: Johnsen,
1954), p. 97.

The main street . . . railway station . . . grain "elevator": The   11.12–14
railroad and grain elevators were necessary for agriculture on the
plains. Elevators were upright wooden structures into which con-
veyor belts lifted the grain and from which chutes carried it to

freight cars. In the 1880s their 30,000-bushel capacity necessitated elevators every 36 square miles. Railroad towns with elevators were close enough together that farmers could haul grain to town by wagon in a one-day round trip of 20 miles maximum. Towns that were not on the rail lines did not survive. When Cather lived in Red Cloud, eight passenger trains per day passed through the town.

16.2   chromo "studies": color lithographs. The process of chromolithography, patented in 1837, superimposed impressions of the three primary colors and black to print a wide range of colors. Although used as a medium by artists, in the nineteenth century chromolithography was used primarily to make inexpensive reproductions of famous works of art. "Chromos" came to be considered in bad taste by the end of the century.

17.24–25   Bohemian: Bohemia was historically an independent Slavic kingdom of central Europe. Ruled by the German Hapsburgs from 1526 to 1918, it joined Moravia and Slovakia to form the state of Czechoslovakia in 1918. All Slavic immigrants from this region, whether Czechs, Moravians, or Slovaks, were known in Nebraska as Bohemians.

18.12   "Kate Greenaway" manner: Catherine Greenaway (1846–1901) was an English painter and widely imitated illustrator of children's books. The clothing styles she painted (long dresses, high waists, high collars) were copied for real children.

18.14–15   poke bonnet: woman's bonnet with a projecting brim at the front.

20.2–3   raw alcohol . . . oil of cinnamon: Roger L. and Linda K. Welsch write that "raw spirits were sometimes doctored to imitate the *Kirsch*, *Schnapps*, or *Kummel* of the Old Country." *Cather's Kitchens: Foodways in Literature and Life* (Lincoln: U of Nebraska P, 1987), p. 140.

windmill: Windmills were necessary for pumping water in the 21.7 semi-arid environment of the plains, where wells were often several hundred feet deep. In the plains, the velocity of the wind was greater and more variable than in the east. Thus, the 1870s invention of light steel structures, whose blades were smaller than those of eastern windmills and would self-adjust to changes in wind direction and speed, was an important development. See Illustration 9.

sod house: There were few trees on the Nebraska plains, so early 21.7 settlers used the earth as a building material. Ribbons of plowed sod, 4 to 5 inches thick, were cut into rectangles roughly 18 by 24 inches, and the heavy sod strips were laid one on another with joints broken as in bricklaying. Corner posts took the weight of a log roof, which was covered with tar paper and earth. The walls inside were whitewashed or papered with old newspapers, while muslin was stretched across the ceiling to catch insects, rodents, falling bits of earth, even snakes. Rooms were created by hanging strips of canvas or blankets. Sod houses were dark and hard to keep clean—the earth floor was dusty in dry weather, muddy in wet—but they were fairly comfortable because they stayed cool in summer and held the heat in winter. See Illustration 9.

the Blue: The Little Blue River in south central Nebraska joins 21.19 with the Big Blue River and flows into the Kansas River. The Little Blue, approximately three to seven miles from the farms described in *O Pioneers!*, was a clear and fast-flowing stream and its banks were heavily wooded.

Norwegian graveyard: The Zion Lutheran Norwegian Cemetery is 22.3–4 located in Catherton Township, Webster County, Nebraska. See Illustration 7.

22.4–5 grass . . . shaggy and red: The dominant species of the tall-grass prairie, big bluestem (*Andropogon gerardii*), and of the mid-grass prairie, little bluestem (*Andropogon scoparius*), are known for their red bronze color in the fall after frost.

22.20–21 magic lantern: This popular child's toy was a primitive slide projector, consisting of a tin box with a simple lens and light source (a candle or kerosene lamp). The slides illustrated nursery tales and popular novels, historical subjects, and scenic wonders of the world.

23.4–5 Robinson Crusoe: The hero of Daniel Defoe's well-known 1719 novel about shipwreck on an uninhabited island.

23.6–7 Hans Andersen: Danish writer of fairy tales usually referred to by his full name, Hans Christian Andersen (1805–1875).

25.2 log house: Where timber was available, Scandinavians built log houses rather than dugouts since that was a type of construction they were familiar with. See Illustration 10.

25.4 Norway Creek: There is no creek of this name in the area Cather likely used as a model. In the Catherton area, the probable candidate would be Farmers Creek. See Illustration 7.

25.7–8 brush and cottonwoods and dwarf ash: Common shrubs along streams in the region include sandbar willow (*Salix interior*), chokecherry (*Prunus virginiana*), wild plum (*Prunus americana*), and smooth sumac (*Rhus glabra*). The cottonwoods would be the plains species (*Populus sargentii*), while the ash mentioned here is probably not a true ash (*Fraxinus*), but the prickly ash (*Zanthoxlum americanum*).

25.12 the Divide: The watershed referred to here is part of the seventy-mile-long plateau dividing the streams flowing south to the Republican River and those flowing north to the Little Blue River. The Divide crossed northern Webster County; its flattened top was one-fourth to one-half mile wide and about 300 feet higher than the Republican River valley, 10 to 12 miles to the south. See Illustration 7.

Genius: Cather suggests an animistic belief here, the idea of spirit or soul present in the natural world.   26.5

draw and gully: Gullies are deep, canyon-like trenches cut into the land by periodic torrential rains, whereas draws are simply low areas between ridges of land in rough country.   26.10

prairie-dog hole: The prairie-dog (*Cynomys*) is a burrowing squirrel-like rodent of the American plains, named for its sharp, barklike call. There are five species, but all are gregarious and live in underground colonies.   26.17

cholera: Cholera, a bacterial infection of the intestines, was the bane of the swine industry in the nineteenth century. Losses in Nebraska in the 1880s totaled over a million dollars annually.   26.18

crops had failed: Causes for crop failure in the late nineteenth century in Nebraska included drought, hail, chinch bugs, and grasshoppers.   26.20

He owned . . . adjoining: 640 acres is a section of land. The Homestead Act of 1862 offered, for a filing fee of 10 dollars, a quarter-section to anyone who would settle and develop the land for 5 years. Further land was available to settlers through the Timber Culture Act of 1873, whereby anyone who qualified for a homestead could make a "timber claim" and receive an additional 160 acres by planting 40 acres of it in trees and keeping them alive for 10 years. This act was amended in 1878, and the homesteader needed only plant   27.4–8

10 acres of trees (2,700 per acre) and only 675 of them had to be alive at the end of 10 years. The Timber Act was a failure because most farmers wanted land for crops, not trees.

27.11 Swedish athletic club: Scandinavian athletic clubs were organized for men to develop physical strength and to debate social issues, especially those touching matters of ethnicity and politics in America of the late nineteenth century.

27.19 how to farm it properly: Bergson's thoughts reflect the difficulties early pioneers experienced in finding the right crops for the land. Wheat growing, for example, was not successful until the introduction of winter wheat, particularly Turkey Red (see note 154.3–11). Spring wheat ripens late and is thus susceptible to insects, drought, and disease. The type of farming best suited to Webster County is a modified system of dry farming and stock raising.

32.11–12 eggs and butter: "The sale of butter and eggs seems to have provided a fairly steady source of income for women. These funds were especially important because of the chronic shortage of capital on the frontier. . . . Women often supported their families while their husbands learned to farm." Julie Roy Jeffrey, *Frontier Women: The Trans-Mississippi West, 1840–1880* (New York: Hill and Wang, 1979), p. 60. Eggs were also used to exchange for goods in town when there was no cash.

32.14 sod corn: "Sod corn was the crop planted when the ground was first broken. As the furrow was laid open, corn was planted by hand. When the next furrow was plowed, the sod was turned over the corn. Sod corn was no different from other corn and was so-called only the first year when the new ground was broken." Mildred Bennett, *The World of Willa Cather* (Lincoln: U of Nebraska P, 1961), p. 105.

channel cat: Channel catfish (*Ictaluras lacustris punctatus*), named for   33.17
the whisker-like barbels or feelers on the upper jaw, are found in
most of the rivers and streams in Nebraska, and are especially abundant in the Little Blue and Republican rivers.

fox grapes: By "fox grapes" Cather may have intended either *Vitis*   33.25
cinera or *Vitis vulpina*.

goose plums: Goose plums are probably *Prunus hortulana*, a small   34.1
wild tree with red or yellowish-red fruit, but could also be the wild
plum, *Prunus americana*.

ground-cherries: *Physalis heterophylla* has an orange berry inside an   34.2
inflated papery calyx.

buffalo-pea: The buffalo pea is *Astragalus crassicarpus*, but as Cather   34.5
describes it as "rank," she may be referring to the buffalo currant
(*Ribes odoratum*).

cave: food cellar.   34.18

dugout: The early plains settlers often lived for a year or two in   37.15
dugouts until a sod or log house could be built. These were dwelling places cut into the bank of a draw or ravine usually facing south,
with the north wall cut into the bank, the east and west walls partly
cut into the bank, and the rest of the shelter constructed of sod.
Inside, the walls were plastered and whitewashed, but muslin was
often stretched across the ceiling to catch loose earth, snakes, and
insects. These were uncomfortable, primitive dwellings that leaked
badly in the rain. See Illustration 8.

Russians . . . barracks: A group of German Russians came to Frank-   38.1–3
lin, Nebraska, in the fall of 1875. It was too late in the season for
them to build their homes, so they put together what they called a

settlement house near the Little Blue River and lived there together that winter.

38.11   coreopsis: *Coreopsis tinctoria* has a bright yellow cosmos-like flower on slender stalks that grow as high as four feet. Coreopsis is an attractive annual that grows in moist soils and along ditches in the Midwest.

38.12   wild ducks: The most likely species of wild duck in the region are the mallard (*Anas platyrhynchos*), the pintail (*Anas acuta*), and the blue-winged teal (*Anas discors*).

39.5–6   Crazy Ivar's country: Cather was likely describing the west branch of Thompson Creek in Franklin County, Nebraska. In this hilly region the soil is thin and not suitable for cultivation.

39.11   shoestring: Also known as lead plant (*Amorpha canescens*), this gray-colored shrub, one to three feet in height, with showy spikes of lavender flowers, is sometimes called shoestring because the pinnately compound leaves suggest the appearance of a laced shoestring.

39.11   ironweed: *Vernonia fasciculata* is a tall purple-flowered plant that grows in marshy areas.

39.11–12   snow-on-the-mountain: *Euphorbia marginata* grows in waste places and is a showy plant when in blossom because of the white-edged bracts surrounding the flower cluster.

41.11   lark: By referring to its song, Cather here designates the western meadowlark (*Sturnella neglecta*), whose rich song is described as "a variable song of seven to ten notes, flute-like, gurgling, and double-noted." Roger Tory Peterson, *A Field Guide to the Birds* (Boston: Houghton Mifflin, 1960), p. 210.

quail: The "drumming" quail in this passage is likely the greater   41.11
prairie chicken (*Tympanuchus cupido*), which gives a "booming" call
during its dancing courtships.

locust: Nebraska has more than 100 species of grasshoppers —   41.12
sometimes called locusts from the Latin word for grasshopper,
locusta. The family of *Acrididae* includes the short-horned grasshoppers and some of the destructive migratory grasshoppers. The male
produces a "burr" or buzzing sound by rubbing its front wings
together. Cather may also be referring to the cicada, also known as
the locust (*Cicadidae* family), which is known for the distinctive
sounds produced by vibrations of the male's sound organs.

He sendeth . . . conies: Ivar conflates lines 10, 11, 16, 17, and 18 of   41.17–26
Psalm 104.

snipe: The common snipe or Wilson's snipe (*Capella gallinago*), is a   42.16
brown long-billed bird, about 11 inches tall, that lives in marshy
habitats. It was a favored gamebird among nineteenth-century settlers.

crane: Most likely the greater sandhill crane (*Grus canadensis*), an   42.16
ash-colored bird about three feet tall, although it could possibly be
the larger and much rarer whooping crane (*Grus americana*).

sea gull: Most likely the herring gull (*Larus argentatus*), which is   42.22
ubiquitous in North America.

He watches over them and counts them: Matthew 10:29–31 reads   43.21–22
"Are not two sparrows sold for a farthing? and one of them shall not
fall on the ground without your Father. But the very hairs of your
head are all numbered. Fear ye not therefore, ye are of more value
than many sparrows." (This and all subsequent citations are from
the King James Version.) See also Luke 12:6–7.

46.20 hogs. . . . Bible: Ivar is referring to the Mosaic law against eating pork frequently announced in the Old Testament. For example, Deuteronomy 14:8 reads "And the swine, because it divideth the hoof, yet cheweth not the cud; it *is* unclean unto you; ye shall not eat of their flesh, nor touch their dead carcase."

47.23 prove up on his land because he worked it so little: "The land was given on the basis that the recipient intended to make it his home and that he would live on it and make substantial improvements. From the date of application, called filing, he was allowed six months to move onto the tract and begin his improvements. He was required to make it his continuous residence for five years from the time of filing. Any time after completing the five years' residence but before seven and a half years from the time of filing had passed, he could take out his final papers, a process known as proving up, and receive a patent or United States title for the land. Proving up consisted of giving evidence supported by two witnesses that the conditions had been fulfilled." Everett N. Dick, "Free Homes for the Millions," in *Nebraska History*, 43 (1962): 219.

50.16 citrons: *Citrullus citroides* is a small hard-fleshed melon, part of the watermelon family, used in pickles and preserves.

53.10–13 colic . . . horse: Flatulent colic in horses is caused by excessive fermentation of food in the stomach, which produces gas and can result in suffocation, rupturing of the stomach, or a fatal twisting of the bowel. In very severe distension it is necessary to "tap" the bowel with a trocar and cannula (a blade fitted with a tube), thereby releasing the gas from the abdomen.

60.2 chinch-bugs: The chinch bug (*Blissus leucopterus*) is a small (one-fifth inch) black insect with red legs and white forewings. A major grain and corn pest, the reddish-colored nymphs suck the sap from the young plants.

"Frithjof Saga": *Fritiofs Saga* (1825) was composed by the Swedish   60.22
professor and bishop Esaias Tegner (1782–1846). This cycle of
poems, based on an old Icelandic saga, looked to the heroism of the
late Middle Ages as a source of moral inspiration. Tegner's very
popular work was translated into English fifteen times between
1839 and 1924.

Longfellow's verse . . . "Golden Legend" and "The Spanish Stu-   60.24–25
dent": American poet Henry Wadsworth Longfellow (1807–1882)
translated some of Tegner's verse into English. "The Golden Legend" (1851), mentioned here, is a dramatic poem set in the Middle
Ages, celebrating the virtues of disinterestedness and self-sacrifice,
while "The Spanish Student" (1842), a lyric comedy based on Cer-
vantes's *La Gitanilla*, is about a Spanish student's love for a gypsy
girl. The two works by Longfellow, the heroic legend and the love
story, parallel the two strands of Cather's novel.

prince's feather: Cather may be referring to *Polygonum orientale*,   61.13
native to India and cultivated elsewhere for its crimson flower-
spikes. It often escaped cultivation and grew wild.

Hans Andersen book says . . . Swedes liking to buy Danish bread   62.6–8
and the Danes liking to buy Swedish bread: In the story "Holger
Danske" (Ogier the Dane) Andersen tells how in winter, when the
water of the narrow sound between the Danish island of Sjaelland
and the southern tip of Sweden freezes, the Danes and Swedes pass
each other, shaking hands and exchanging white bread and biscuits
because foreign articles taste better.

"The Swiss Family Robinson": This very popular book by Swiss   62.19–20
author Johann Rudolf Wyss (1782–1830) was published in 1813
and tells the story of a family shipwrecked on an uninhabited island.

337

63.6–7 new kind of clover hay: Cather is likely referring to red clover (*Trifolium pratense*), which was the subject of research at the Agricultural Experiment Station at the University of Nebraska in the 1880s and 1890s. Early in this period the station advocated red clover as a forage crop because it is rich in protein, calcium, and phosphorus, providing valuable nourishment for livestock in either the green or hay stage. Clover also adds nitrogen to the soil, thus enriching it. The hay, however, is not as palatable to livestock as alfalfa.

67.10 *dragharmonika:* concertina or accordion.

69.8 plover: The plover family (*Charadridriidae*) includes several species that appear in Nebraska; two that are noted for their vocal abilities are the killdeer, or pasture-bird (*Charadrius vociferus*), and the golden plover (*Pluvialis dominica*), also known as the pasture-bird or prairie-bird.

74.21 plains of Lombardy: Much of Lombardy, a region of northern Italy, is a flat grain-growing plain.

75.11 like the Gladiator's: This is a reference to the dying gladiator in Byron's *Childe Harold's Pilgrimage* (1812–18). The lines read ". . . he is gone, / Ere ceased the inhuman shout which hailed the wretch who won. / He heard it, but he heeded not—his eyes / Were with his heart, and that was far away; . . . where his rude hut by the Danube lay" (IV, stanzas 140–41).

75.21 the "Jewel" song: From Charles Gounod's opera *Faust* (1859). This is Marguerite's aria, sung as she adorns herself with the jewels Mephistopheles has provided Faust for her seduction.

77.12 "Free-thinkers": Many Czech immigrants, nominally members of the Catholic Church, abandoned their allegiance to the church and became secularists or free-thinkers. They rejected organized religion because in Bohemia the Catholic Church was used by the Hapsburgs to keep the Czechs in political subjugation and economic misery.

John Huss: Jan Hus (1372/73–1415) was a Bohemian religious   77.16
leader whose preaching anticipated the sixteenth-century Lutheran Reformation. He was arrested as a heretic and burned at the stake.

"Don't they ever teach you . . . Bohemians?": Marie is saying that it   77.19–21
was the Bohemians that prevented the expansion of the Ottoman Empire into Eastern and Central Europe in the seventeenth century. Actually it was a Polish king, Jan Sobieski, who stopped the advance of the Turks in 1683.

osage orange: The osage orange (*Maclura pomifera*) is a very thorny   80.8
medium-sized tree with smooth, shiny leaves and large wrinkled, inedible green fruit. It is native to the south central United States. Wood being scarce in Nebraska, osage orange was planted as a living fence before barbed wire became available.

silo: Wood-stave silos were built at the beginning of the century in   85.10
Nebraska to store and protect silage (partially fermented fodder), thus keeping it in a succulent and slightly sour condition for farm animals.

bloat: In cattle and horses, bloat, also called hoven or tympanites, is   85.18
a distention of the stomach from an accumulation of fermentation gas. If not relieved by means of trocar and cannula (see note 53.10), the animal can die from suffocation, rupture of the stomach, or blood poisoning from the gas.

"they would have taken me to Hastings": An asylum was built in   89.11–12
Hastings in 1887 and was called the Nebraska Hospital for the Incurable Insane.

93.2–3   "was not going anywhere just now": She was pregnant.

94.2   the malaria district of Missouri: Malaria was common along all the major river bottoms in Missouri, but the southeast corner of the state was swamp country and is probably the region being referred to here.

94.8   Lou speaks like anybody from Iowa: Iowa was settled chiefly by English-speaking Americans who moved west before the large waves of non-English-speaking immigrants came to Nebraska.

99.8   castor beans: *Ricinus communis*, a tropical perennial from which castor oil is derived, is grown as an annual in temperate zones for its giant showy, fanlike leaves. Growing as high as seven feet, it was an exotic curiosity in pioneer gardens.

104.19   William Jennings Bryan: Bryan (1860–1925) was a midwestern lawyer and political leader who ran unsuccessfully for the presidency in 1896, 1900, and 1908. His proposed cure for the depressed economic conditions of the 1890s, strongly opposed by Wall Street bankers, was an "easy money" policy based on unlimited coinage of silver. Bryan was enormously popular in Nebraska.

105.15   Morgan: J. Pierpont Morgan (1837–1913), New York banker and financier.

107.5   Norfolk coat: A type of tweed jacket popular in the Victorian period, so named for the kind of coat worn by the Prince of Wales when hunting in Norfolk.

110.7–8   *'Wo bist du, . . . mein geliebtest Land?'*: This is from the third stanza of Franz Schubert's song "Der Wanderer." It translates "Where are you, where are you, my beloved country?"

340

rosemary leaves: Rosemary (*Rosmarinus officinalis*) is a small ever-   124.1
green shrub whose leaves are used for scent and to flavor foods. In
literature and herbal folklore it is an emblem of remembrance and
fidelity. An old garden legend reads "Where rosemary thrives the
mistress is master."

white mulberry tree: The white mulberry (*Morus alba*), native to   124.10
Asia, was introduced to North America in an attempt to establish a
silk industry. The staining of the white mulberry fruit with the
lovers' blood later in the novel recalls the story of Pyramus and
Thisbe told by Ovid in his *Metamorphoses*. In that story parents
refuse a marriage, so the lovers arrange to flee and meet under a
mulberry tree. Thisbe, first to arrive, is frightened by the roar
of a lioness and runs away. But she leaves behind her veil, which
the lioness tears up with her blood-stained jaws. Pyramus arrives,
thinks that Thisbe has been eaten, and stabs himself. When Thisbe
returns and finds her lover mortally wounded, she puts an end to
her own life. Legend has it that the fruit of the mulberry, previously
white, was from that time forward always red.

a Turkish lady sitting on an ottoman: Cather's friends, the Cooks   127.11–12
of Red Cloud, owned such a music box. See Illustration 12.

Elbe valley: The Elbe valley is a region in northern Germany. The   131.16
Elbe River, however, does have its source in Czechoslovakia, although in that country it is known as the Labe River.

One of the Goulds: The sons of Jay Gould, New York railroad   135.3–4
executive and financier, were notorious for their matrimonial mis-
adventures. Their quarrels and flamboyant divorce proceedings
filled the columns of the country's newspapers.

138.5   wild larkspur: Prairie larkspur (*Delphinium virescens*) blooms in June with pale blue flowers on a single erect stalk.

138.6   hoarhound: Also spelled horehound, this member of the mint family (*Lycopus americanus*) flourishes in damp places and bears spikes of tiny white flowers. The North American native has no scent and is distinct from the cultivated European horehound (*Marrubium vulgare*), which is aromatic and is used in the manufacture of cough remedies and candy.

138.7   wild cotton: Cather may here be referring to the milkweeds (*Asclepiadaceae*), whose seed pods contain silky floss, but she may also be referring to the rose mallow (*Hibiscus moscheutos*), whose creamy-white hollyhock-shaped flowers resemble those of the true cotton (*Gossypium hirsutum*).

138.7   foxtail: Foxtail is the common name for weedy grasses in the genera *Alopecurus* and *Setaria;* they are perennial weeds and their cylindrical, brush-like flower clusters are said to resemble foxes' tails. The yellow foxtail (*Setaria lutescens*) and green foxtail (*Setaria viridis*) are common in cultivated areas.

138.7   wild wheat: Cather may be referring either to a native grass that is wheat-like in appearance or to self-seeded cultivated wheat.

138.21–23   "The Bohemians . . . missionaries came.": The Bohemians were Christianized in the ninth century when St. Cyril and St. Methodius were sent as missionaries from Byzantium in 863 at the request of Prince Rostislav. Before that time, tree worship was practiced by the Bohemians.

139.3   lindens: Linden is the common name for deciduous trees of the genus *Tilia*, native to the North Temperate Zone but widely cultivated for their shade and ornament. The linden was a sacred tree to

Indo-European peoples, especially those of eastern Europe, and was held to have certain medicinal properties. A tea is made from the infusion of linden (also known as lime) flowers.

the French country: The community Cather names Sainte-Agnès is   144.2–3
based on a settlement of French Canadians in the vicinity of Campbell, Nebraska, in the late 1870s. Their small frame church was called St. Ann's and was built in the country, but when Campbell was established in 1886 they moved the church into town. Campbell is located in Franklin County, Nebraska, on the western boundary of Webster County.

battery: the pitcher and catcher of a baseball team.   145.1

alfalfa . . . corn: Corn was the first crop planted in Nebraska because   154.3–11
it yielded well and because there were no satisfactory alternative crops, the soil and climate being unsuited to spring wheat. But by the end of the century, winter wheat, particularly Turkey Red, had been introduced and proved successful because it ripens early, thus escaping the dangers of dry weather, insects, and diseases. Alfalfa (*Medicago sativa*), also known as lucerne, is a clover-like legume grown as forage for cattle. Alexandra calls it "the salvation of this country" because it is drought-resistant (it has a long tap root), gives the heaviest yield per acre of any hay, and produces large quantities of nitrogen, thereby enriching the soil.

City of Mexico: Mexico City. Cather is evoking the rhythm of the   158.17
Spanish, *Cuidad de Mexico*.

Reform Church: Calvinist churches of the Protestant Reformation   170.8
are referred to as Reform or Reformed churches. There is no record, however, of a Reform church in the area of Bladen or Red Cloud.

343

171.13–14   Gottland: Cather may mean Gotaland, the southern portion of Sweden that is drained by the Gota River or, less likely, Gotland, a Swedish island in the Baltic Sea.

173.20   Dawson: Dawson City, in the western Yukon territory of Canada, developed after the gold strike at nearby Bonanza Creek in 1896.

179.20–21   Porfirio Díaz: Soldier and president of Mexico, Díaz (1830–1915) governed his country from 1886 to 1911.

181.24   California Jack: Two-handed version of the card game high-low-jack. A form of pitch.

196.24–197.2   "Mais oui, . . . clairvoyante!": This paragraph translates "'Of course,' . . . 'It's my mother's house on L'Isle-Adam. You are very wise, my daughter.' . . . 'Come here, my boys! We are in the presence of a real fortune-teller!'" L'Isle-Adam is a town in the Val D'Oise region of France, north of Paris.

212.18–19   that Swedish song . . . about the ship boy: "Den Lille Botsmannen" (The Little Sailor) is a popular Swedish folk song.

215.12   header: A grain-harvesting machine that cuts off the heads of grain and loads them into the wagon. The header was pushed by a team of six horses and cut a swath from 10 to 20 feet wide, so that as much as 20 to 40 acres could be harvested in a day.

215.15   steam thresher: A threshing machine separates the grain from the straw or chaff. Threshers run by steam replaced horse-powered ones by the mid-1880s. See Illustration 13.

218.13–14   wheat . . . shatter: If not harvested in time, the head of the wheat will burst and scatter its seeds to reproduce.

344

"Gloria": Probably from the *Petite Masse Solennelle*, by Giaocchino   218.25
Antonio Rossini (1792–1868).

the great confirmation service: Cather likely had in mind the occa-   225.6
sion when Bishop James O'Connor of Omaha came to St. Ann's
parish and administered the sacrament of confirmation to a class of
twenty-five children and adults. This took place on May 16, 1881,
roughly 15 years before the time period depicted in the novel.

the church triumphant: In Catholic theology, the souls of the faith-   226.11
ful in heaven.

first frame church: See note 144.3.   227.8

"Ave Maria": This prayer was set to music by various composers.   228.8
Gounod's, composed in 1852, was one of the most popular settings.

Herod: The story of King Herod's massacre of the Hebrew chil-   229.6
dren is told in Matthew 2:16–17.

Sancta Maria, . . . Ora pro nobis!: Holy Mary, . . . Pray for us.   229.8–10

"The Holy City": A popular religious song with music by Ste-   230.7
phen Adams (Michael Maybrick) and words by Frederick Edward
Weatherly, copyrighted in the U.S. in 1892.

101st Psalm: The first line reads "I will sing of mercy and judgment: 245.3
unto thee, O Lord, will I sing." Two other lines from this psalm are
keyed to the story. Line six begins "Mine eyes *shall be* upon the
faithful of the land," while line eight reads "I will early destroy all
the wicked of the land; that I may cut off all wicked doers from the
city of the Lord."

Lindell Hotel: The Lindell Hotel in Lincoln, at the corner of 13th   255.4
and M streets, was rebuilt in 1886 and was considered the most
elegant in the state. See Illustration 14.

255.13–18   university campus: The iron fence, with gates which were locked at night, was put around the campus in 1892. The armory was the second building erected on the campus. The red brick library (now Architecture Hall) was finished in 1895. See Illustration 15.

257.17–19   Cherry County . . . coyotes can scratch down to water: Located in the Sandhills region of north central Nebraska, Cherry County has good agricultural land because of its abundant underground water supply.

264.20–21   Henceforth the world will only be . . . to me, —: These lines are a variation of lines 322–23 from Lord Byron's "The Prisoner of Chillon": "And the whole earth would henceforth be / A wider prison unto me."

267.1   Klondike: The Klondike River is situated in the western Yukon territory of Canada. It became famous in 1896 with the discovery of gold in Bonanza Creek and other small tributaries, with nearly 30,000 prospectors swarming into the area.

272.22   county clerk's plat: map or land chart, showing the names of the landowners.

Textual Apparatus

Textual Commentary

THIS first volume of the Willa Cather Scholarly Edition presents a critical text of Willa Cather's second novel, *O Pioneers!*, which is as close to Cather's intention for it at the time of its original publication as current scholarship can establish. With the exception of an early typescript of the prefatory poem, "Prairie Spring," no manuscript, typescript, or proofs have survived. For the text of the novel proper, two editions are relevant: the 1913 first edition and the 1937 Autograph Edition, both published by Houghton Mifflin. In accord with principles established by textual scholar W. W. Greg,[1] copy-text for *O Pioneers!* is the first printing of the 1913 edition, the extant text closest to Cather's own hand and so most likely to preserve her use of accidentals. Cather's explicit instructions concerning accuracy in the use of foreign words and in the transcription of dialects account for most of the emendations in this critical text. This text also corrects typographical errors and inconsistencies. The textual apparatus lists all substantive variants under "Emendations" and "Rejected Substantives"; a full historical collation

349

of variants, including accidentals, is on file in the Editorial Resources Center, Department of English, University of Nebraska–Lincoln.

Composition and Publishing History

Although no manuscript, typescript, or proof survives, we can reconstruct the composition and Cather's involvement in the publishing history of *O Pioneers!* from letters, interviews, essays, and publication records. We know from her letters and interviews that Cather characteristically wrote a draft in longhand, then revised as she typed a second and third copy; she sent her revised typescript to a typist, who prepared a clean typescript; and she made further changes and corrections on this typescript before sending it to the publisher (Bohlke 41, 76). There is no reason to doubt that she followed essentially this process while writing *O Pioneers!*

In letters she wrote while creating *O Pioneers!*, Cather described her efforts to give to her subjects — the people and places she felt so keenly about — the tone and distinction that would lift them above the commonplace (wc to Mrs. Frances Cather, 23 February 1913). In the final stages of creating *O Pioneers!*, Cather wrote in her letters of its appearance as she envisioned it. As if her text, like the country she wrote of, were stretching,[2] Cather began referring to her story in terms of its size (which she described in a letter to her friend Zoë Akins [21 October 1912] as three times as long as "The Bohemian Girl," and in a letter to her Aunt Franc, Mrs. Frances Cather [23 February 1913], as two times as long as *Alexander's Bridge*). To announce her subject, she published "Prairie Spring" in the December *McClure's Magazine* as a little verse about the country that was the hero of her book. She decided to name her story after Walt Whitman's "Pioneers! O Pioneers!"; by referring to his poem as "O Pioneers!" she made the title her own (WC to Sergeant, undated [early 1913]).

Cather admitted frankly to Elizabeth Sergeant that she was nervous over the book, for this was the story she had long wanted to write and she would hate to fail on it (undated letter [early 1913]). When proofs began to arrive, she at first avoided looking at them, though they were piled on her desk. But once she got to work, her attention to fine detail was intense. She sent the story to Sergeant, asking her particularly to correct the French. She had tried to transcribe the strange "dialect," with all its inconsistencies, that she had heard people speak when she visited Nebraska the previous summer. But she felt she had been unsuccessful, and therefore would prefer to have it simply correct (letter of 22 April 1913). It was a concern she repeated in later correspondence with R. L. Scaife, production manager at Houghton Mifflin, to whom she complained that the copyreader for *O Pioneers!* had not followed her preference for printing foreign words in italics; she requested that italics be used in *The Song of the Lark* and asked that a proofreader correct her errors. Again she had transcribed language, this time German and Spanish, and she asked that her phrases be checked with severity (12 May [1915]). Cather's commitment to *O Pioneers!* intensified in the fall and winter following publication, when she received letters from its admirers. Many of the letters were from people who had known Nebraska in the early days, and Cather was pleased that her representations seemed true to them.

Her concern for "tone" and "distinction" extended to an exceptional concern for the format of her books; indeed, she had a remarkably clear sense of what she wanted. Two years after the publication of *O Pioneers!*, Cather wrote to her editor at Houghton Mifflin, Ferris Greenslet, that he had never given her a cover she had liked, and she referred approvingly to the binding of the English "edition" (actually issue) of *O Pioneers!*[3] Calling its color and composition delightful, she asked if he might copy it for *The Song of the Lark* (30 June [1915]). In subsequent letters she continued to use the American *O Pioneers!* typographical design as a touchstone, asking Houghton Mifflin to repeat its type and paper (rough and cream-colored) for *My Ántonia* in order to give the text the same look as her first pioneer novel (18 November 1917; 1 December 1917). When *My Ántonia* appeared, she wished only that its paper were slightly more "yellowish" (which she wrote over the canceled word "cream"), like that used for *O Pioneers!* (30 September [1918]).

The following year Cather wrote to Greenslet, asking yet again that the color of the cloth be changed when new copies of *O Pioneers!* were bound: she described the clay-mud brown as too ugly, and she requested a sober brown like that in a sample she enclosed (18 October [1919]). Later she again wrote to Greenslet on the subject, complaining that the *O Pioneers!* mustard-plaster binding was beginning to get on her nerves. She inquired how many copies remained bound in that ugly cloth, and she asked that Houghton Mifflin provide a new binding in the cloth she had sent to Greenslet some time before. She liked the typography (see Illustrations 2–4), and she approved of the good paper that Houghton Mifflin had printed it on; she asked them to provide a decent binding (28 December 1919).

Casing changes on a later book resulted in an additional change to *O Pioneers!* Upon seeing the dummy for *My Ántonia*, Cather asked that her middle initial be dropped from the cover and the spine, explaining that the "S" made her name too businesslike in contrast to the personal title above it (wc to Bishop, undated [early March 1918]). Whether by her own request or at the publisher's initiative, this request was carried out in reprintings of *O Pioneers!*, and after 1918 Cather's middle initial does not appear on the front cover or the spine.

Cather's wishes were not always respected, though. She considered the colored frontispiece by Clarence Underwood to be incongruous and asked that it be dropped (wc to Greenslet 28 December 1919). Despite Greenslet's assurance that the frontispiece would be dropped in the next printing (letter of 30 December 1919), it was retained in a black-and-white version (see Illustration 1) for some time. Page ii of the book, however, continued to advertise *O Pioneers!* "with colored frontispiece."

353

Finally, seven years after *O Pioneers!* was first published, Cather wrote that she was delighted with the new binding (11 January [1920]). However, her dissatisfactions with advertising exacerbated those with production, and in January 1921, she left Houghton Mifflin for Alfred A. Knopf, with whom she was to remain for the rest of her life. "Next to writing her novels, Willa Cather's choice of Alfred Knopf as a publisher influenced her career . . . more than any action she ever took," recalled her companion, Edith Lewis, for Knopf provided the working conditions she needed: financial security, protection from intrusions so that she could write, and "absolute liberty to write exactly as she chose" (Lewis, 115–16). Yet in 1921 Cather wrote to Greenslet that her break was only from Houghton Mifflin's publicity people, not from him, and unless he requested otherwise, she would refuse to say she had left him (12 January 1921). The terms of parting were prescient, for fifteen years later Cather was to work once again with Greenslet and Houghton Mifflin on her Autograph Edition.

In the meantime, cheap issues from Houghton Mifflin made questions about paper stock and binding moot. Even during the period Cather was expressing concern over Houghton Mifflin's production of her book, she cooperated in making it readily available during World War I (as she did later in World War II). In 1917 Cather agreed to receive reduced royalties for copies of *O Pioneers!* that were sold in the Soldier's Libraries series, a gesture she was to repeat for the Armed Services Editions series during the Second World

War. More troubling for her, in 1928 Greenslet wrote that Houghton Mifflin was considering allowing *My Ántonia* to be published in a cheap issue as one of the new Book League of America's monthly bonuses (3 November 1928). Alarmed, Cather offered *O Pioneers!* to save *My Ántonia*, agreeing to have *O Pioneers!* appear in the Riverside Library Star Books series at a reduced cost of $1.00 and for which royalties were "a uniform rate of five cents a copy" (Greenslet to WC, 17 May 1932). Though sales from this cheaper issue contributed to her relatively generous royalties in 1929 ($402.50 as compared to $204.68 in 1927), by 1932 Cather objected when she learned of the regular issue's diminishing sales (clothbound at $2.50, for which she was receiving a twenty percent royalty). Indeed, she saw in her last report that the regular issue had no sales at all, and she asked for an increase of her royalties on the cheap issue of *O Pioneers!* (2 May 1932). In reply, Greenslet listed royalties the book earned each year, argued that broad sales at a reduced price were better for an author than fewer sales at a higher price, even though royalties remained constant, and said that though they couldn't increase the book's royalty in the cheap issue, they could, "of course, drop it and return to the regular one" (17 May 1932).

In response, Cather appealed to their friendship: sell what was in stock of the Riverside issue, but please print no more of it, and please restore the regular one, she asked, adding that she felt confident it would have a steady if not a large sale (31 May 1932). Greenslet, always gracious in his correspondence with her, tried to make the best of her wishes: he knew allowing the cheap issue to go out of print would be a blow to "the more impecunious section of the public, which [was] rapidly increasing in proportions," but he obliged, and offered to "refreshen slightly the format of the book and give it a fresh whirl of advertising" (2 June 1932). Perhaps there was advertising; changes in format were minor (e.g., the list of Cather's books on the advertising page was updated, the box around it was dropped, and the frontispiece was omitted). In any case, collations have established that the plates set for the first edition were used for all reprintings until 1987.

The final chapter in the history of *O Pioneers!* was its revision for the subscription (Autograph) edition of her books planned for 1937. Curiously, it was Maxwell Perkins who, representing Charles Scribner's Sons, first proposed a collected edition, writing Alfred Knopf in 1932 that "certainly, . . . if there is any distinction in this form of publication, she of all Americans is entitled to it" (quoted in Lewis, 180–81). The plan was to be "not more than a thousand sets of ten or twelve volumes, the first volume of each set to be signed by her," Alfred Knopf later recalled ("Miss Cather," 215). Rather than releasing the rights that they held to the first four of Cather's novels, Houghton Mifflin proposed publishing the collected edition themselves (Knopf did not publish such editions). The matter was left there for some time, until in a 1936 letter to Greenslet, Cather asked if Houghton Mifflin still wished to publish her complete works, and he responded affirmatively (8 March 1936).

Cather wanted to review the books to make corrections, and Greenslet suggested she do so during the summer of 1936, with new text due in the fall. She "gave a great deal of time and conscientious effort" to the new edition (Lewis 181). Though holograph revisions of *O Pioneers!* for the new edition have not survived, we can reconstruct Cather's procedures from correspondence: she made corrections in the margins of pages, with a list of all her corrections pasted on the front free endpaper of each volume (wc to Greenslet, 8 September [1936]). The Autograph Edition "as corrected and revised by the Author" first appeared in 1937. Cather's relationship with her early publisher had come full circle, for the Autograph Edition was described as a "collaboration" between Willa Cather and Bruce Rogers (the designer and typographer), and was printed at the esteemed Riverside Press. Attention to production quality extended to every detail, and the prospectus even included a full description of paper (natural rag with deckle edge) and type (Janson, with long descenders, "notable for their clarity and brilliance, features which are so characteristic of Miss Cather's writing") (Rogers 3, 7, 8–9).

Printing History

The printing history of *O Pioneers!* is quite straightforward, as described by Joan Crane in *Willa Cather: A Bibliography* and confirmed by our independent research. The first edition was published by Houghton Mifflin in June of 1913; American galleys were used to obtain the English copyright, and American sheets were sent to William Heinemann for the English issue. The plates made for the first edition, and the photo-offset plates employed after the original plates began to deteriorate seriously, have been used for nearly all subsequent printings of the novel (more than 42 printings to date), including the paperback 1978 Sentry "edition" (used in the collation for the critical edition).

The second edition of *O Pioneers!* is the first, and only signed, volume of the thirteen-volume Houghton Mifflin Autograph Edition, published in 1937 and 1938 and limited to 970 copies. For this second edition, Cather made substantive revisions in the text of the novel; these revisions are listed in the textual apparatus under "Rejected Substantives" and "Emendations." Cather's attention to *O Pioneers!* seems concentrated upon the text; there is no record that she objected to the deterioration of the type of the first edition, as she did when she revised *My Ántonia*, and apparently no one recommended patching the early plates. In 1940 Houghton Mifflin used the Autograph Edition plates for a second issue, the less expensive Library "edition" (actually an impression; letter from FG to WC, 8 October 1940). In 1973, a facsimile of the Autograph Edition (with facsimile signature), limited to 200 copies, was published in Kyoto, Japan.

A third, Armed Services edition was published in 1945. Its only substantive difference from the first edition is its omission of the epigraph poem "Prairie Spring." The compositors who reset type for the Armed Services edition made single-word contractions and corrected one typographical error, but otherwise faithfully reproduced the 1913 first-edition text. *O Pioneers!* has been published in large-type and Braille editions, produced on disc in the Talking Book series, and recorded on tape. It has been translated into Bengali, German, Gujarati, Hindi, Chinese, Italian, Japanese, Polish, Portuguese, Spanish, and Swedish.

* * *

Unlike the rest of *O Pioneers!*, the epigraph poem "Prairie Spring" exists in prepublication form: a typescript with corrections in Cather's handwriting that she enclosed with her 5 July 1912 letter to Elizabeth Sergeant. The poem was first published in *McClure's Magazine* in December 1912, then in the 1913 first edition of *O Pioneers!*; the *Sunday Nebraska State Journal* of 10 June 1917; the 1923 (first and second) editions of *April Twilights and Other Poems*; and the Autograph editions of *O Pioneers!* and *April Twilights* (with *Alexander's Bridge*). Because the typescript that Cather prepared for setting *O Pioneers!* has been lost, the Cather Edition has adopted as copy-text for "Prairie Spring" the first edition, being the version closest to Cather's hand. A collation of the typescript with the first edition reveals the following substantive changes: whereas the typescript is untitled, the first-edition poem is introduced with the title "PRAIRIE SPRING." The refining of line 8, "The sullen fires of sunset dying," began on the typescript, with "fading" written in Cather's hand above the hand-canceled "dying," and this refining apparently continued in the fugitive prepublication form with the deletion of "The" in the same line. Accidental changes are minor: the typescript "somber" becomes in the first edition "sombre" (line 2); a comma following "men" is replaced by a semicolon (line 6); a comma following "long" is removed (line 7); a comma following "sunset" is added (line 8); and a semicolon following "desire" is replaced by a comma (line 16).

Collation of Texts and Analysis of Variants

Relevant texts for the Cather Edition of *O Pioneers!* are the first edition and the Autograph Edition, plus the early type-script of "Prairie Spring" and *McClure's Magazine's* publication of that poem. The editors conducted two solo sight collations and three team collations of the first edition, first impression, against the Autograph Edition; they also conducted one machine collation each of the first edition, first impression, against the 1962 Sentry paperback and against a post-1977 printing of the Sentry paperback, as well as spot collations of the first edition, first impression, against three post-1918 printings. These machine collations confirmed that the plates set for the first edition were used through all reprintings of that edition until 1987; type could be identified and traced as it deteriorated (see also Crane). Machine collations of three copies of *O Pioneers!* in the Autograph Edition provided a check against the possibility that plates were revised during that printing. To confirm its relationship to the first edition, the editors conducted spot collations of the Armed Services edition (i.e., a full collation of the first part, "The Wild Land," then spot collations of passages in which previous collations had revealed typographical errors, corrections, and substantive variants). Finally, the editors conducted solo and team collations of all versions of "Prairie Spring" published in Cather's lifetime.[4]

A study of substantive changes for the Autograph Edition of 1937 reveals a general movement toward restraint. Some corrections reflect a concern for accuracy (e.g., the misspelled "zenias" is corrected to "zinnias" [50.20]). Other changes make meaning more specific (e.g., the general reference to "the meal" becomes the more precise "dinner" [86.11]), and in three instances, replacement of a neuter pronoun with a gender-specific one intensifies the role of an animal in a scene (14.18; 122.13; 190.12).

Additions made for the Autograph Edition characteristically contribute to the logic of a scene: by adding the clause "Old Jensen will take my wagon home," Cather absolved Carl of negligence (see "Rejected Substantives," 16.24), and by specifying that the Berquists' cow jumped through "the thatch" of a dugout roof ("Rejected Substantives," 37.15), she made the comic action more realistic. Sometimes revisions signal an apparent change in intention. In the 1913 edition, Alexandra and Frank used the name "Maria," a form of intimate address, for Marie Shabata (178.22; 239.9; 239.10). Perhaps feeling that the echo of Gounod's "Ave Maria" was too obvious, Cather changed all instances to "Marie" in the Autograph Edition.

Other revisions contribute to a general softening effect: Marie's "lusty admirers" (19.17) becomes her "uncle's cronies" in the 1937 edition; "the farm people" (19.21) becomes "the country people"; and the dying Marie Shabata, who is "mutilated" in the 1913 version (237.19), is more decorously "wounded" in 1937. In the first edition, a drummer, seeing Alexandra, "actually let his cigar fall to the sidewalk" (15.13); for the Autograph Edition Cather subdued the action by replacing "actually" with "almost." Similarly, she refined colloquial phrases into more formal speech: the 1913 phrase "been up looking" (78.25) is replaced by "been visiting—looking"; "Anybody here feels" (129.23) with "They feel"; and "out among" (226.14) with "among."

Finally, in the Autograph Edition Cather deleted explanatory matter: a part of the description of Marie Tovesky's eyes (18.7–9)[5] and a definition of "the old things" that the dead may feel (250.14–15). Most dramatically, she dropped three extended descriptions when she revised: the fortune Marie Shabata told to Father Duchesne, following which he declared her "une veritable clairvoyante!" (196.15–197.3); an extended description of the dead Marie and Emil, their story told by Emil's bloodstained hand and by two white butterflies fluttering above the lovers' bodies (241.15–242.1); and the final description of Alexandra Bergson and Carl Linstrum, a conventionally sentimental passage in which Carl kisses Alexandra softly while she leans "heavily on his shoulder," murmuring that she is tired and has been lonely (273.20–274.1).

As revisions of substantives reveal a shift toward restraint, so do the revisions of accidentals. Corrections on the few surviving typescripts of later novels show that Cather paid close attention to matters of spelling, paragraphing, punctuation, and hyphenation and other compound-word formations. The changes made for the Autograph Edition of *O Pioneers!* are consistent with Cather's later practices, and may be presumed to be authorial.

Cather began to adopt British spelling conventions as early as *A Lost Lady* (1923), and kept to them for the rest of her career. She brought *O Pioneers!* into conformity with her other work by making 56 spelling changes in her revision. The most frequent variant is in words terminating in *-or*, which are consistently changed to the British form, *-our*. For example, there are 30 instances of "neighbor(s)" being spelled "neighbour(s)," and 14 instances of "color(ed)" spelled "colour(ed)." Many other of these variants appear less frequently, e.g., "clamored" to "clamoured," "armory" to "armoury," "humor" to "humour," "parlor" to "parlour," etc.

Other spelling changes for the Autograph Edition are less pervasive but are also consistent with British conventions and with Cather's later work. "Gray" becomes "grey," "plow" becomes "plough," "drouth" becomes "drought," "checkers" becomes "chequers," "mustache" becomes "moustache," "self-defence" becomes "self-defense," "skeptical" becomes "sceptical." Another consistent class of changes doubles the final "l" in present- and past-participial forms of verbs: e.g., "traveling" to "travelling," "quarreled" to "quarrelled." The numeral "101st" in the first edition is spelled out "one hundred and first" in the Autograph Edition; "most" when used as a dialect variation of "almost"

in the first edition is formalized with an apostrophe—
" 'most"—in the Autograph Edition.

Changes in capitalization also seem to reflect a return to
stricter conventions. In the 1913 edition, Cather often capitalized only one word of compound proper names: e.g., she
refers to "the Elbe valley," to "the Catholic church" (when
referring to a specific building), and to "uncle Otto" and
"uncle Xavier." In the Autograph Edition these names become "the Elbe Valley," "the Catholic Church," "Uncle
Otto," and "Uncle Xavier." This principle of a return to
stricter conventions may account for other changes in capitalization involving names: "Hanover station" becomes
"Hanover Station," and "a mass of Rossini" becomes "a Mass
of Rossini." On the other hand, Cather had capitalized the
word "university" in the first edition even when it did not
refer specifically to the name of a school; sometimes the
capitalized word was even used as an adjective, as in "the
University band" or "the University dances." These and
other general references to the university were regularized to
lower case in the Autograph Edition.

Two changes in capitalization verge on being substantive
changes. When Carl says "before we start north" in the 1913
edition, north is simply a direction. In the Autograph Edition
he says, "before we start North"; in the context of the discussion of the Yukon goldfields, the capitalized word suggests a
place name—the North, evoking images of snow, ice, and
the midnight sun. Similarly, when Cather says in 1913 that
Ivar lived in his dugout "without defiling the face of na-

ture," "nature" refers generally to the landscape. When she changed her description in the Autograph Edition to "without defiling the face of Nature," the capitalization personifies nature and the face becomes almost human.

A few capitalization changes are closely related to punctuation. Again the shift is toward more conventional forms. In the 1913 edition, words following question marks and exclamation marks are sometimes seen as part of the same sentence. One lowercase "the" following a question mark is changed to upper case in the Autograph Edition, as is a lowercase "fortunes" following an exclamation point.

The Autograph Edition introduces commas that are regular in their use following introductory phrases, enclosing parenthetic expressions, and separating items in a series. In other cases first-edition commas are replaced by semicolons, colons, or dashes in the Autograph Edition. Combined commas and dashes, which occur frequently in the first edition, are replaced by the dash alone in the Autograph Edition: e.g., "pond, — " to "pond — ." Combined colons and dashes in the first edition are replaced with colons alone. Semicolons in the first edition are also sometimes replaced by colons to direct attention to an appositive at the end of a sentence and to separate main clauses when the second amplifies the first.

Cather's treatment of speech in the first edition, with some of her characters' speeches being contained within paragraphs of the text, is also looser than her later practice. Most of the variations in paragraphing between the two editions consist of these direct quotations being placed in new paragraphs. The first edition also routinely uses double quotation marks for speech, while the Autograph Edition uses single quotation marks, another British usage.

An additional feature of Cather's early practice was the preservation of a space between the elements of many contractions: e.g., "did n't," "could n't," "does n't," "is n't," "must n't," "need n't," "should n't," "was n't," "were n't," and "would n't." These contractions are more conventionally printed as single words in the Autograph Edition. The contractions "don't" and "won't" appear as one word in both editions.

Numerous variants exist in compound-word formation and hyphenation within lines of text (excluding end-of-line ambiguities). Corrected typescripts of some of her later works show that Cather tended to use hyphenated words freely and that she continued to add hyphens as she revised. The general effect is one of tightening, of joining words more closely together. This effect is achieved by linking two or three separate words by hyphens (16 instances and 2 instances, respectively), and by combining hyphenated words into one word, "frost-bitten" into "frostbitten" (13 instances). Fewer changes in compound words went in the other direction, opening up words into phrases. In 8 cases, a hyphenated form is changed to two words: e.g., "good-night" to "good night." In 5 other cases a hyphen was added to break one word into its components: "nightgown" to "night-gown."

Emendations in the Cather Edition

The present edition is based on the 1913 Houghton Mifflin first edition as copy-text, emended to reflect Cather's intention as she prepared *O Pioneers!* for its first publication. Therefore, our general editorial policy has been to correct printer's errors and to incorporate Cather's corrections of factual error as emendations; we have not accepted her stylistic revisions as emendations. Following Cather's explicit request that her foreign words be checked, corrected when necessary, and italicized (wc to Scaife, 12 May [1915]), we have incorporated seven corrections of the spelling of foreign names, and rendered French, Spanish, and German words and phrases in italic type. Cather's corrections of inconsistencies of dialect have been adopted also. We have also made those revisions of accidentals that are necessary for the sense of the text. We have corrected two inconsistencies in the spacing of contractions, bringing them into conformity with the practice of the 1913 edition, and we have resolved inconsistencies in the formation of compound words.[6] All of these changes are reported in "Emendations."

We have reproduced the 1913 Houghton Mifflin first-edition text, therefore, except for authorial substantive revisions for accuracy, necessary changes in accidentals, adjustments in the spacing of some contractions, and the matters of design and styling that were called for in the creation of this new edition. The editors have collaborated with the designer to create an edition that reflects Cather's wishes for the presentation of *O Pioneers!*

Notes

1. By providing a rationale for the selection and emendation of a copy-text (or the text basic to establishing a critical text), W. W. Greg's "The Rationale of Copy-Text" has been called "the most influential document in modern editorial theory" (Tanselle 167). Greg gave the preference to the text "closest to the author's hand" for the copy-text, and he based his preference on the argument that in revising, authors tend to emphasize "substantives" (words) rather than "accidentals" (spelling and punctuation), while typists, copyeditors, and compositors are more likely to change accidentals. By this reasoning, each transcription or resetting is likely to introduce additional unauthorized changes. Greg's conclusion was that in the absence of evidence to the contrary, the text closest to the author's hand is likely to be closest to his or her intention and should be selected as copy-text.

2. In describing the creation of her novel, Cather wrote of letting the country be the hero, an idea she incorporated in the novel itself. Alexandra explains that she and the other homesteaders hadn't "much to do" with their success, for the land "worked itself. It woke up out of its sleep and stretched itself, and it was so big, so rich, that we suddenly found we were rich, just from sitting still" (108.6–11).

3. Cather was referring to the first English issue of the first American edition (using American sheets). See Crane, 35–36.

4. The editors made use of a copy of the first printing of the first edition of *O Pioneers!* from the Bernice Slote Collection in the Archives of Love Library, University of Nebraska–Lincoln: SPEC/SLOTE/PS/3505/A8702/1913; identification number

368

R02102 80557. Later printings of the first edition examined were from the Special Collections of Love Library, University of Nebraska–Lincoln: SPEC/PS/3505/A8702/1913; acquisition number 176087 (inscribed 1925); and from the general collection of Love Library, University of Nebraska–Lincoln: PS/3505/A8702/1913; identification numbers R02008 17221 and R02008 41123. Copies of the Autograph Edition of *O Pioneers!* used are from (1) the Archives of Love Library, University of Nebraska–Lincoln: SPEC/PS/3505/A87A15/1937x v. 1; identification number R02028 71475, copy 294, signed; (2) the Willa Cather Historical Center, a Branch Museum of the Nebraska State Historical Society, Red Cloud, Nebraska: 808.8/ C28na; number 502; and (3) the Auld Public Library, Red Cloud, Nebraska: number 538. The 1940 Library Edition is in the general collection of Love Library, University of Nebraska–Lincoln: PS/3505/A87A15/1937bx; identification number R02008 98120. For the 1962 Sentry edition, the editors used a copy in the Editing Resources Room, 314 Andrews Hall, University of Nebraska–Lincoln: uncatalogued. The editors also made use of a copy of the post-1977 printing of the Sentry edition from the Willa Cather Pioneer Memorial, Red Cloud, Nebraska.

For "Prairie Spring," the editors made use of the following:

"Prairie Spring" typescript with corrections in Cather's hand, enclosed with letter to Elizabeth Sergeant dated 5 July 1912; original at the Pierpont Morgan Library, New York; photocopy in Rosowski office, University of Nebraska–Lincoln.

"Prairie Spring" in *McClure's Magazine* 40 (December 1912): 226; bound copy in Love Library, University of Nebraska–

Lincoln: 051/M13/v.40/1912–13; identification number R02122 39188.

"Prairie Spring" in *Sunday Nebraska State Journal* (Lincoln), under "Nebraska has been the Inspiration of Many Poets" (10 June 1917): 3-C; photocopy made from microfilm located at Nebraska State Historical Society, Lincoln.

"Prairie Spring" in *April Twilights and Other Poems*, Knopf, 1st edition (limited), 1st printing, copy 203, signed, 1923, in the Special Collections of Love Library, University of Nebraska–Lincoln: SPEC/SLOTE/PS/3505/A87A8/1923bx; identification number R02102 80515.

"Prairie Spring" in *April Twilights and Other Poems*, Knopf, 2nd edition (trade), 6th printing, 1961, in the Special Collections of Love Library, University of Nebraska–Lincoln: SPEC/FAULK-NER/PS/3505/A87A8/1923; identification number R02065 77667.

"Prairie Spring" in *Alexander's Bridge and April Twilights*, Houghton Mifflin, Autograph Edition, vol. 3, 1st printing, copy 141, signed, 1937, in the Special Collections of Love Library, University of Nebraska–Lincoln: SPEC/SLOTE/PS/3505/A87A15/1937x/v.3; identification number R02106 00804.

5. In 1913 Cather had described Marie Tovesky's eyes as looking like gold-stone, "or, in softer lights, like that Colorado mineral called tiger-eye" (18.7–9). However, in 1935, only two years before the new edition of *O Pioneers!*, she had described Lucy Gayheart's eyes as being "like that Colorado stone we call the tiger-eye" (*Lucy Gayheart*, p. 2). Possibly she sought to avoid the repetition.

6. To resolve end-of-line hyphenation, the following criteria were

applied in descending order: (1) if one or more instances of the same form occurs elsewhere in the first edition, the Cather Edition resolves on the principle of majority rule; (2) if one or more examples of similar words occur elsewhere in the first edition, the Cather Edition resolves by analogy; (3) if one or more examples of the same word or of similar words occurs in the first edition of Cather's works chronologically close to *O Pioneers!*, the Cather Edition resolves by example or analogy; (4) in the absence of these criteria, the following common-sense guidelines are used to resolve a questioned form: (a) possible or likely morphemic forms, (b) one or more examples of the same word or similar words in the Autograph Edition, (c) *Webster's New International Dictionary* of 1909, and (e) hyphenation of two-word compounds when used as adjectives.

Works Cited

Bohlke, L. Brent, ed. *Willa Cather in Person: Interviews, Speeches, and Letters*. Lincoln: U of Nebraska P, 1986.

Cather, Willa. Letter to Zoë Akins. 21 Oct. 1912. Ms. Collection. University of Virginia Library, Charlottesville.

———. Letter to Helen Bishop. Undated [Mar. 1918]. Ms. Collection. Houghton Library, Harvard University, Cambridge.

———. Letter to Frances Cather. 23 Feb. 1913. Private Collection.

———. Letters to Ferris Greenslet. Ms. Collection. Houghton Library, Harvard University, Cambridge.

———. Letter to R. L. Scaife. 12 May 1915. Ms. Collection. Houghton Library, Harvard University, Cambridge.

———. Letters to Elizabeth Sergeant. Ms. Collection. Pierpont Morgan Library, New York.

———. *Lucy Gayheart*. Boston: Houghton Mifflin, 1935.

———. *O Pioneers!* Boston: Houghton Mifflin, 1913.

Crane, Joan. *Willa Cather: A Bibliography.* Lincoln: U of Nebraska P, 1982.

Greenslet, Ferris. Letters to Willa Cather. Ms. Collection. Houghton Library, Harvard University, Cambridge. Used by permission of Houghton Mifflin Company and by permission of The Houghton Library.

Greg, W. W. "The Rationale of Copy-Text." *Studies in Bibliography* 3 (1950–51): 19–36. Rpt. with minor revisions in *The Collected Papers of Sir Walter Greg.* Ed. J. C. Maxwell. Oxford: Clarendon P, 1966. 374–91.

Knopf, Alfred A. "Miss Cather." *The Art of Willa Cather.* Ed. Bernice Slote and Virginia Faulkner. Lincoln: U of Nebraska P, 1974. 205–24.

Lewis, Edith. *Willa Cather Living: A Personal Record.* New York: Knopf, 1953.

Rogers, Bruce. "The Autograph Edition of the Novels and Stories of Willa Cather." Prospectus. Boston: Houghton Mifflin, 1937.

Tanselle, G. Thomas. "The Editorial Problem of Final Authorial Intention." *Studies in Bibliography.* Ed. Fredson Bowers. Vol. 29. Charlottesville: UP of Virginia, 1976. 167–211.

Emendations

THE following list records all changes introduced into the copy-text, the 1913 Houghton Mifflin first edition. The location of the reading by page and line in the present edition is given in the outside column. The reading of the present edition appears to the left of the bracket in the inside column; the source of that reading appears to the right of the bracket, followed by a semicolon and the copy-text reading. The abbreviation AE identifies the 1937 Houghton Mifflin Autograph Edition as the source of emendation, while CE (Cather Edition) indicates changes initiated in the present edition. The emendations in this list correct lexical inconsistencies and typographical and spelling errors. An asterisk indicates that the reading is discussed in "Notes on Emendations."

37.11–12	Berquists'] AE; Berquist's
50.20	zinnias] AE; zenias
*53.14	farmwork] CE; farm work
58.13	would n't] CE; wouldn't

*60.2	chinch-bugs] AE; chince-bugs
*60.3	*sauerkraut*] CE; sauerkraut
73.3	wheatfields] AE; wheat-fields
*76.19–20	shade-hat] CE; shade hat
86.20	speak.] AE; speak .
*110.7–8	'*Wo bist du, wo bist du, mein geliebtest Land?*'] CE; 'Wo bist du, wo bist du, mein geliebtest Land?'
113.14	could n't] CE; couldn't
114.21	besides] AE; beside
*136.8	plow] CE; plough
*136.9	Sainte-Agnès] AE; Sainte-Agnes
136.10	Moïse] CE; Moses
144.17	Sainte-Agnès] AE; Sainte-Agnes
*145.14	Séverine] CE; Sévérine
*145.15	Alphonsine] CE; Alphosen
172.13	sateen] AE; satine
*179.21	Díaz] CE; Diaz
189.2	Sainte-Agnès] AE; Sainte-Agnes
189.5	Sainte-Agnès] AE; Sainte-Agnes
*195.17	*mantillas*] CE; mantillas
195.20	Sainte-Agnès] AE; Sainte-Agnes

*196.24–197.2   *"Mais, oui,". . . . "C'est L'Isle-Adam, chez ma mère. Vous êtes très savante, ma fille." . . . "Venez donc, mes garçons! Il y a ici une véritable clairvoyante!"*] CE; "Mais, oui,". . . . "C'est L'Isle-Adam, chez ma mère. Vous êtes très savante, ma fille." . . . "Venez donc, mes garçons! Il y a ici une véritable clairvoyante!"

199.19–20   any one] CE; anyone

*206.1   Napoléon] CE; Napoleon

217.25   gotta a green] AE; gotta green

218.22–23   Sainte-Agnès] AE; Sainte-Agnes

*220.2   Moïse] AE; Moses

220.7   Sainte-Agnès] AE; Sainte-Agnes

224.8   Sainte-Agnès] AE; Sainte-Agnes

225.3   Sainte-Agnès] AE; Sainte-Agnes

225.16   Sainte-Agnès] AE; Sainte-Agnes

*226.3   red-brick] AE; red brick

226.21–22   Sainte-Agnès] AE; Sainte-Agnes

228.8–9   Sainte-Agnès] AE; Sainte-Agnes

229.22   Sainte-Agnès] AE; Sainte-Agnes

233.19   .405 Winchester] AE; 405 Winchester

*237.12   one-o'clock] AE; one o'clock

262.19   I not care] AE; I no care

272.24   brothers'] AE; brother's

Notes on Emendations

farmwork] Finding the two forms "farmwork" and "farm work" in both the first and the Autograph editions of *O Pioneers!*, the Cather Edition emends to the one-word form by analogy to the forms "farmhouses" and "overwork" in the first edition. 53.14

chinch-bugs] Based on the Autograph Edition emendation and on information from the Oxford English Dictionary, the critical edition emends the spelling of this form from "chince-bugs": the British spelling "chince-bug" was a seventeenth-century usage, referring to the bedbug, and not to the New World insect destructive to crops. 60.2

sauerkraut] Italic type is used on the basis of Cather's stated preference for printing foreign words. 60.3

shade-hat] Finding both "shade hat" and "shade-hat" in the first and Autograph editions, the Cather Edition emends to the hyphenated form by analogy to the first-edition form "sun-hat." 76.19–20

'*Wo . . . Land?*'] The song title is emended to italics on the basis of Cather's stated preference for printing foreign words. 110.7–8

Sainte-Agnès] The accented spelling of the Autograph Edition is adopted because it is consistent with Cather's wishes for accuracy 136.8

377

in regard to French forms. Other instances where the form is emended to "Sainte-Agnès" include 144.17, 189.2, 189.5, 195.20, 218.23, 220.7, 224.8, 225.3, 225.16, 226.22, 228.9, and 229.22.

136.10   Moïse] This name appears in the first edition twice as "Moses" and twice as "Moïse." The emendation from "Moses" to "Moïse" here and on 220.2 is based on the Autograph Edition reading and on Cather's wishes for accuracy in regard to French forms.

145.14   Séverine] The accenting of this name is emended on the basis of Cather's instructions for accuracy in regard to French forms.

145.15   Alphonsine] This name is emended from Cather's "Alphosen," presumably a phonetic spelling, to the correct feminine form. The editors find historical confirmation in A. J. Gaudreault, *Some Early History of Campbell, Nebraska*, who lists an Alphonsine as one of the daughters of the French-Canadian farmer F. X. Demars, who in 1873 settled in Webster County close to where the Franklin County town of Campbell (the prototype of Sainte-Agnès in *O Pioneers!*) would be founded in 1886.

179.21   Díaz] The accented spelling of this name is used on the basis of Cather's instructions for accuracy in regard to Spanish forms.

195.17   *mantillas*] The Cather Edition emends to italics on the basis of Cather's stated preference for printing foreign words.

196.24–197.2   "*Mais . . . clairvoyante!*"] The passage is emended to italics on the basis of Cather's stated preference for printing foreign words.

206.1   Napoléon] The accented spelling of this name is used on the basis of Cather's instructions for accuracy in regard to French forms.

226.3   red-brick] In the first edition, this compound appears hyphenated once and as two words once; in the Autograph Edition, it is hyphenated twice. Here the emendation to the hyphenated form is made based on analogy to the first-edition form "red-headed," on the Autograph Edition reading, and on the compound's use as an adjective. (The editors find that "drug-store," for example, used as an adjective is hyphenated in the first edition [23.1 "drug-store cellar"]; used as a noun [12.1 "the drug store"], it is not hyphenated.)

one-o'clock] As in the case of "red-brick," the hyphenated form is   237.12
adopted based on the Autograph Edition reading and by analogy to "drug-store" used as an adjective in the first edition.

Rejected Substantives

THE following list records all substantive variants between the 1913 Houghton Mifflin first edition (the copy-text) and the 1937 Houghton Mifflin Autograph Edition that are rejected in the present edition. Substantive variants for *O Pioneers!* include word changes and changes in punctuation and spelling that affect oral readings, excluding preferred British spelling. The reading of the present edition appears to the left of the bracket; the Autograph Edition reading appears to the right. Framing words are included with articles, personal pronouns, idioms, and passages of one or more sentences. End-of-line hyphenation has been resolved silently based on internal evidence in the copy-text.

14.18   its tail] her tail

15.13   actually] almost

15.14   sidewalk and went] sidewalk. He went

15.15   saloon. His] saloon, and his

16.25   place? It's] place? Old Jensen will take my wagon home. It's

18.7–9   gold-stone, or in softer lights, like that Colorado
          mineral called tiger-eye.] gold-stone.

19.17   lusty admirers] uncle's cronies

19.21   farm] country

27.20   Their neighbors] His neighbours

29.6   cannot] could not

29.14   his daughter] his own daughter

30.19   little] a little girl

30.19   took] used to take

37.13   tearing] jumping

37.15   through] through the thatch,

54.10   hear.] hear!

67.6   further] farther

74.23   breath] breadth

76.4   weaves] wove

78.25   been up looking] been visiting — looking

79.7   cranky at] cranky with

84.6   further] farther

84.24   her wrist] the wrist

86.11   the meal] dinner

101.5	interrupted] interrupted her
104.10	that here] that
122.13	itself] himself
125.12	waste,] waste!
125.18	creature,] creature!
125.20	walk?] walk—
126.18–19	selling them twenty-five] selling them at twenty-five
129.24	Anybody here feels] They feel
160.17	They're] They are
174.4	kind of a doll] kind of doll
176.6–7	in the winter] in winter
178.23	Maria] Marie
181.10	though] although
184.19	its pleasure] her pleasure
185.13	persisted] had persisted
190.12	they] he
193.8	child.] child!
196.14–15	Fortunes,] Fortunes!
196.15–197.3	fortunes!" ¶ The young priest, Father Duchesne, went first to have his fortune read. Marie took his long white hand, looked at it, and then began to run

off her cards. "I see a long journey across water for you, Father. You will go to a town all cut up by water; built on islands, it seems to be, with rivers and green fields all about. And you will visit an old lady with a white cap and gold hoops in her ears, and you will be very happy there." ¶ "*Mais, oui,*" said the priest, with a melancholy smile. "*C'est L'Isle-Adam, chez ma mère. Vous êtes très savante, ma fille.*" He patted her yellow turban, calling, "*Venez donc, mes garçons! Il y a ici une véritable clairvoyante!*" ¶ Marie] Fortunes!' ¶ Marie

197.24–25	would not] did not
207.7	kind of a girl] kind of girl
212.12	kind of a musical] kind of musical
212.20	like] liked
213.6–7	would n't] would not
213.16	was n't] was not
213.16	was n't] was not
214.11	cheek] check
219.3	homewards] homeward
226.14	out among] among
231.20	that] which
237.19	mutilated] wounded

239.9   Maria] Marie

239.10   Maria] Marie

241.16–242.1 slumber. After she lay down there, she seemed not
             to have moved an eyelash. The hand she held was
             covered with dark stains, where she had kissed it.
             ¶ But the stained, slippery grass, the darkened
             mulberries, told only half the story. Above Marie
             and Emil, two white butterflies from Frank's alfalfa-
             field were fluttering in and out among the
             interlacing shadows; diving and soaring, now close
             together, now far apart; and in the long grass by the
             fence the last wild roses of the year opened their
             pink hearts to die. ¶ When] slumber. ¶ When

250.14–15   born, that comfort people like the feeling of their
             own bed does when they are little."] born."

252.25   noticed that it improved] thought she noticed an
             improvement in

255.3   Burlington depot] Burlington Station

266.12   uncomfortable] unhappy

268.20   you] anybody

268.21–22   you know] now

268.24   house now] house

271.12   said Alexandra] she said

271.23   though] although

385

271.25   like] as

273.15   Carl.] Carl!

273.20–274.1   sigh. ¶ They had reached the gate. Before Carl opened it, he drew Alexandra to him and kissed her softly, on her lips and on her eyes. ¶ She leaned heavily on his shoulder. "I am tired," she murmured. "I have been very lonely, Carl." ¶ They went] sigh. ¶ They went

Word Division

L IST A records compounds or possible compounds hyphenated at the ends of lines in the 1913 edition and
which are resolved as hyphenated or as one word as listed
below. See note 6 to the "Textual Commentary" (p. 370) for
a discussion of the criteria used for resolving these forms.
List B contains the endline hyphenations that are to be retained in quotations from the present edition.

LIST A

4.13–14	countrymen
8.21–22	smoking-cars
9.5–6	china-painting
14.8–9	wagon-box
15.5–6	windmill
20.22–23	prairie-dog
21.15–16	half-section

22.10–11	cigarmakers
22.14–15	sitting-room
34.19–20	horse-doctoring
36.3–4	snow-on-the-mountain
41.24–25	cupboard
53.14–15	low-spirited
61.10–11	rocking-chair
61.13–14	upland
70.5–6	threshing-machine
76.15–16	wheat-cutting
78.4–5	headstone
78.21–22	twenty-one
85.8–9	coffee-cups
85.15–16	sisters-in-law
86.21–22	barefoot
97.21–22	punchbowls
100.22–23	property-owner
109.2–3	gold-fields
115.17–18	overworked
127.3–4	snow-on-the-mountain
134.23–24	bluegrass

136.25–137.1	pale-yellow
144.2–3	breast-pocket
151.11–12	rain-drops
159.12–13	ball-grounds
163.7–8	doorway
195.3–4	forehandedness
196.8–9	clothes-closet
199.17–18	flower-markets
200.5–6	bootblack
200.9–10	twenty-three
201.14–15	postman
206.13–14	cornfields
211.5–6	Sainte-Agnès
216.10–11	broom-straw
216.11–12	sweeping-broom
271.18–19	bull-fights
223.4–5	sweetheart
223.10–11	card-table
229.13–14	overtook
229.24–25	shallow-hearted
234.2–3	sitting-room

246.8–9	Sainte-Agnès
247.19–20	ashes-of-rose
247.23–24	windmill
250.22–23	Saint-Agnès
257.21–22	to-day
261.23–24	footpath
268.18–19	dew-drenched
283.14–15	courtroom
285.24–25	kinsmen
286.7–8	note-paper
287.7–8	self-possession
291.16–17	street-car
300.12–13	traveling-suit

LIST B

16.3–4	china-painting
18.8–9	tiger-eye
21.12–20	to-day
27.7–8	half-section
33.2–3	fair-skinned
39.11–12	snow-on-the-mountain
76.19–20	shade-hat

80.17–18	over-furnished
83.4–5	dinner-table
86.16–17	sitting-room
90.13–14	water-troughs
107.9–10	thirty-five
129.5–6	good-bye
133.17–18	love-lorn
148.7–8	seed-corn
159.25–160.1	far-fetched
163.17–18	to-morrow
172.24–25	yust-a
194.12–13	half-hearted
203.3–4	good-night
204.20–21	high-strung
218.22–23	Sainte-Agnès
226.21–22	Sainte-Agnès
228.8–9	Sainte-Agnès
257.22–23	cheerful-looking
271.6–7	straw-stacks

This book was typeset in Linotype Janson Text on a Linotron 202 by Keystone Typesetting, Inc. The type size used for the novel text is 11.5 on 17 pt. Printed by Edwards Brothers, Inc. The paper is Glatfelter 55lb. natural, supplied by the printer. The book was designed by Richard Eckersley.